THE WOMEN'S PRESS BOOK
OF NEW MYTH AND MAGIC

THE WOMEN'S PRESS BOOK OF
New Myth and Magic

EDITED BY HELEN WINDRATH

First published by The Women's Press Ltd, 1993
A member of the Namara Group
34 Great Sutton Street, London EC1V 0DX

British Library Cataloguing-in-Publication Data
A catalogue record for this book is available
from the British Library

ISBN 0 7043 4347 9

Phototypeset in 10½ on 12pt Garamond by
Intype, London
Printed and bound in Great Britain by
BPCC Paperbacks Ltd
Member of BPCC Ltd

Acknowledgements

The Women's Press would like to thank the following:

'A Hot Time' is from *Grandmothers of the Light* by Paula Gunn Allen. Copyright © 1991 by Paula Gunn Allen. Reprinted by permission of Beacon Press.

'Floating' from *One Dark Body* Copyright © 1993 by Charlotte Watson Sherman is published by arrangement with HarperCollins Publishers, Inc New York, New York, USA. 'Floating' appeared as a short story in *Killing Color* published by Calyx Books in 1992.

The Naiad Press Inc for permission to reprint 'Mother Was an Alien', first published in *Dreams and Swords* (1987) by Katherine V Forrest.

Contents

Words of Power

JANE YOLEN

Late Blossoming Flower, the only child of her mother's old age, stared sulkily into the fire. A homely child, with a nose that threatened to turn into a beak and a mouth that seldom smiled, she was none the less cherished by her mother and the clan. Her loneness, the striking rise of her nose, the five strands of white hair that streaked through her shiny black hair, were all seen as the early signs of great power, the power her mother had given up when she had chosen to bear a child.

'I would never have made such a choice,' Late Blossoming Flower told her mother. 'I would never give up *my* power.'

Her mother, who had the same fierce nose, the white streak of hair, and the bitter smile but was a striking beauty, replied gently, 'You do not have that power yet. And if I had not given up mine, you would not be here now to make such a statement and to chide me for my choice.' She shook her head. 'Nor would you now be scolded for forgetting to do those things which are yours by duty.'

Late Blossoming Flower bit back the reply that was no reply but merely angry words. She rose from the fireside and went out of the cliff house to feed the milk beast. As she climbed down the withy ladder to the valley below, she rehearsed that conversation with her mother as she had done so often before. Always her mother remained calm, her voice never rising into anger. It infuriated Flower, and she nursed that sore like all the others, counting them up as carefully as if she were toting them on a notch stick. The tally by now was long indeed.

But soon, she reminded herself, soon she would herself be a woman of power, though she was late coming to it. All the signs but one were on her. Under the chamois shirt her breasts had finally begun to bud. There was hair curling in the secret places of her body. Her waist and hips were changing to create a place for the Herb Belt to sit comfortably, instead of chafing her as it did now. And when at last the moon called to her and her first blood flowed, cleansing her body of man's sin, she would be allowed at last to go on her search for her own word of power and be free of her hated, ordinary chores. Boys could not go on such a search, for they were never able to rid themselves of the dirty blood-sin. But she took no great comfort in that, for not all girls who sought found. Still, Late Blossoming Flower knew she was the daughter of a woman of power, a woman so blessed that even though she had had a child and lost the use of the Shaping Hands she still retained the Word That Changes. Late Blossoming Flower never doubted that when she went on her journey she would find what it was she sought.

The unfed milk beast lowed longingly as her feet touched the ground. She bent and gathered up bits of earth, cupped the fragments in her hand, said the few phrases of the *Ke-waha*, the prayer to the land, then stood.

'I'm not *that* late,' she said sharply to the agitated beast, and went to the wooden manger for maize.

It was the first day after the rising of the second moon, and the florets of the night-blooming panomom tree were open wide. The sickly sweet smell of the tiny clustered blossoms filled the valley, and all the women of the valley dreamed dreams.

The women of power dreamed in levels. Late Blossoming Flower's mother passed from one level to another with the ease of long practice, but her daughter's dream quester had difficulty going through. She wandered too long on the dreamscape paths, searching for a ladder or a rope or some other familiar token of passage.

When Late Blossoming Flower had awakened, her mother scolded her for her restless sleep.

'If you are to be a true woman of power, you must force yourself to lie down in the dream and fall asleep. Sleep within sleep, dream within dream. Only then will you wake at the next level.' Her head had nodded gently every few words and she spoke softly, braiding her hair with quick and supple hands. 'You must be like a gardener forcing an early bud to bring out the precious juices.'

'Words. Just words,' said Late Blossoming Flower. 'And none of *those* words has power.' She had risen from her pallet, shaking her own hair free of the loose night braiding, brushing it fiercely before plaiting it up again. She could not bear to listen to her mother's advice any longer and had let her thoughts drift instead to the reed hut on the edge of the valley, where old Sand Walker lived. A renegade healer, he lived apart from the others and, as a man, was little thought of. But Late Blossoming Flower liked to go and sit with him and listen to his stories of the time before time, when power had been so active in the world it could be plucked out of the air as easily as fruit from a tree. He said that dreams eventually explained themselves and that to discipline the dream figure was to bind its power. To Late Blossoming Flower that made more sense than all her mother's constant harping on the Forcing Way.

So intent was she on visiting the old man that day, she had raced through her chores, scanting the milk beast and the birds who squatted on hidden nests. She had collected only a few eggs and left them in the basket at the bottom of the cliff. Then, without a backward glance at the withy ladders spanning the levels or the people moving busily against the cliff face, she raced down the path towards Sand Walker's home.

As a girl child she had that freedom, given leave for part of each day to walk the many trails through the valley. On these walks she was supposed to learn the ways of the growing flowers, to watch the gentler creatures at their play, to come to a careful understanding of the way of predator and prey. It was time for her to know the outer landscape of her world as thoroughly as she would, one day, know the inner dream trails. But Late Blossoming Flower was a hurrying child. As if to make up for her late birth and the crushing burden of early power laid on her, she refused to take the time.

'My daughter,' her mother often cautioned her, 'a woman of true power must be in love with silence. You must learn all the outward sounds in order to approach the silence that lies within.'

But Flower wanted no inner silence. She delighted in tuneless singing and loud sounds: the sharp hoarse cry of the night herons sailing across the marsh; the crisp howl of the jackals calling under the moon; even the scream of the rabbit in the teeth of the wolf. She sought to imitate *those* sounds, make them louder, sing them again in her own mouth. What was silence compared to sound?

And when she was with old Sand Walker in his hut, he sang with her. And told stories, joking stories, about the old women and their silences.

'Soon enough,' Sand Walker said, 'soon enough it will be silent and dark. In the grave. Those old *bawenahs*' – he used the word that meant the unclean female vulture – 'those old *bawenahs* would make us rehearse for our coming deaths with their binding dreams. Laugh *now*, child. Sing out. Silence is for the dead ones, though they call themselves alive and walk the trails. But you and I, ho,' – he poked her in the stomach lightly with his stick –

'we know the value of noise. It blocks out thinking, and thinking means pain. Cry out for me, child. Loud. Louder.'

And as if a trained dog, Late Blossoming Flower always dropped to her knees at this request and howled, scratching at the dirt and wagging her bottom. Then she would fall over on her back with laughter and the old man laughed with her

All this was in her mind as she ran along the path toward Sand Walker's hut.

A rabbit darted into her way, then zagged back to escape her pounding feet. A few branches, emboldened by the coming summer, strayed across her path and whipped her arm, leaving red scratches. Impatient with the marks, she ignored them.

At the final turning the old man's hut loomed up. He was sitting, as always, in the doorway, humming and eating a piece of yellowed fruit, the juices running down his chin. At the noise of her coming he looked up and grinned.

'Hai!' he said, more sound than greeting.

Flower skidded to a stop and squatted in the dirt beside him.

'You look tired,' he said. 'Did you dream?'

'I tried. But dreaming is so slow,' Flower admitted.

'Dreaming is not living. You and I – we live. Have a bite?' He offered her what was left of the fruit, mostly core.

She took it so as not to offend him, holding the core near her mouth but not eating. The smell of the overripe, sickly sweet fruit made her close her eyes, and she was startled into a dream.

The fruit was in her mouth and she could feel its sliding passage down her throat. It followed the twists of her inner pathways, dropping seeds as it went, until it landed heavily in her belly. There it began to burn, a small but significant fire in her gut.

Bending over to ease the cramping, Flower turned her back on the old man's hut and crept along the trail towards the village. The trees along the trail and the muddle of grey-green wildflowers blurred into an indistinct mass as she went, as if she were seeing them through tears, though her cheeks were dry and her eyes clear.

When she reached the cliffside she saw, to her surprise, that the withy ladders went down into a great hole in the earth instead of up towards the dwellings on the cliff face.

It was deathly silent all around her. The usual chatter of children at their chores, the chant of women, the hum-buzz of men in the furrowed fields were gone. The cliff was as blank and as smooth as the shells of the eggs she had gathered that morning.

And then she heard a low sound, compounded of moans and a strange hollow whistling, like an old man's laughter breathed out across a reed. Turning around, she followed the sound. It led her to the hole. She bent over it, and as she did, the sound resolved itself into a single word: *bawenah*. She saw a pale, shining face looking up at her from the hole, its mouth a smear of fruit. When the mouth opened, it was as round and as black as the hole. There were no teeth. There was no tongue. Yet still the mouth spoke: *bawenah*.

Flower awoke and stared at the old man. Pulpy fruit stained his scraggly beard. His eyes were filmy. Slowly his tongue emerged and licked his lips.

She turned and without another word to him walked home. Her hands cupped her stomach, pressing and releasing, all the way back, as if pressure alone could drive away the cramps.

*

Her mother was waiting for her at the top of the ladder, hands folded on her own belly. 'So,' she said, 'it is your woman time.'

Flower did not ask how she knew. Her mother was a woman of great power still and such knowledge was well within her grasp, though it annoyed Flower that it should be so.

'Yes,' Flower answered, letting a small whine creep into her voice. 'But you did not tell me it would hurt so.'

'With some,' her mother said, smiling and smoothing back the white stripe of hair with her hand, 'with some, womanhood comes easy. With some it comes harder.' Then, as they walked into their rooms, she added with a bitterness uncharacteristic of her, 'Could your *healer* not do something for you?'

Flower was startled at her mother's tone. She knew that her association with the old man had annoyed her mother. But Flower had never realised it would hurt her so much. She began to answer her mother, then bit back her first angry reply. Instead, mastering her voice, she said. 'I did not think to ask him for help. He is but a man. *I* am a woman.'

'You are a woman today, truly,' her mother said. She went over to the great chest she had carved before Flower's birth, a chest made of the wood of a lightning-struck panomom tree. The chest's sides were covered with carved signs of power: the florets of the tree with their three-foil flowers, the mouse and hare who were her mother's personal signs, the trailing arbet vine which was her father's, and the signs for the four moons: quarter, half, full, and closed faces.

When she opened the chest, it made a small creaking protest. Flower went over to look in. There, below her first cradle dress and leggings, nestled beside a tress of her first, fine baby hair, was the Herb Belt she had helped her mother make. It had fifteen pockets, one for each year she had been a girl.

They went outside, and her mother raised her voice in that wild ululation that could call all the women of power to her. It echoed around the clearing and across the fields to the gathering streams beyond, a high, fierce yodelling. And then she called out again, this time in a gentler voice that would bring the women who had borne and their girl children with them.

Flower knew it would be at least an hour before they all gathered; in the meantime she and her mother had much to do.

They went back into the rooms and turned around all the objects they owned, as a sign that Flower's life would now be turned around as well. Bowls, cups, pitchers were turned. Baskets of food and the drying racks were turned. Even the heavy chest was turned around. They left the bed pallets to the very last, and then, each holding an end, they walked the beds around until the ritual was complete.

Flower stripped in front of her mother, something she had not done completely in years. She resisted the impulse to cover her breasts. On her leggings were the blood sign. Carefully her mother packed those leggings into the pano-mom chest. Flower would not wear them again.

At the bottom of the chest, wrapped in a sweet-smelling woven-grass covering, was a white chamois dress and leggings. Flower's mother took them out and spread them on the bedding, her hand smoothing the nap. Then, with a pitcher of water freshened with violet flowers, she began to wash her daughter's body with a scrub made of the leaves of the sandarac tree. The nubby sandarac and the soothing rinse of the violet water were to remind Flower of the fierce and gentle sides of womanhood. All the while she scrubbed, Flower's mother chanted the songs of Woman: the seven-fold chant of Rising, the Way of Power, and the Praise to Earth and Moon.

The songs reminded Flower of something, and she tried to think of what it was as her mother's hands cleansed her of the sins of youth. It was while her mother was braiding her hair, plaiting in it reed ribbons that ended in a dangle of shells, that Flower remembered. The chants were like the cradle songs her mother had sung her when she was a child, with the same rise and fall, the same liquid sounds. She suddenly wanted to cry for the loss of those times and the pain she had given her mother, and she wondered why she felt so like weeping when anger was her usual way.

The white dress and leggings slipped on easily, indeed fit her perfectly, though she had never tried them on before, and that, too, was a sign of her mother's power.

And what of her own coming power, Flower wondered as she stood in the doorway watching the women assemble at the foot of the ladder. The women of power stood in the front, then the birth women, last of all the girls. She could name them all, her friends in the tribe, who only lately had avoided her because of her association with the old man. She tried to smile at them, but her mouth would not obey her. In fact, her lower lip trembled and she willed it to stop, finally clamping it with her teeth.

'She is a woman,' Flower's mother called down to them. The ritual words. They had known, even without her statement, had known from the first wild cry, what had happened. 'Today she has come into her power, putting it on as a woman dons her white dress, but she does not yet know her own way. She goes now, as we all go at our time, to the far hills and beyond to seek the Word That Changes. She may find it or not, but she will tell of that when she has returned.

The women below began to sway and chant the words of the Searching Song, words which Flower had sung with them for fifteen years without really understanding their meaning. Fifteen years – far longer than any of the other girls – standing at the ladder's foot and watching another

Girl-Become-Woman go off on her search. And that was why – she saw it now – she had fallen under Sand Walker's spell.

But now, standing above the singers, waiting for the Belt and the Blessing, she felt for the first time how strongly the power called to her. This was *her* moment, *her* time, and there would be no other. She pictured the old man in his hut and realised that if she did not find her word she would be bound to him forever.

'Mother,' she began, wondering if it was too late to say all the things she should have said before, but her mother was coming towards her with the Belt and suddenly it was too late. Once the Belt was around her waist, she could not speak again until the Word formed in her mouth, with or without its accompanying power. Tears started in her eyes.

Her mother saw the tears, and perhaps she mistook them for something else. Tenderly she placed the Belt around Flower's waist, setting it on the hips, and tying it firmly behind her. Then she turned her daughter around, the way every object in the house had been turned, till she faced the valley again where all the assembled women could read the fear on her face.

> Into the valley, in the fear we all face,
> Into the morning of your womanhood,
> Go with our blessing to guide you,
> Go with our blessing to guard you,
> Go with our blessing and bring back your
> word.

The chant finished, Flower's mother pushed her towards the ladder and went back into the room and sat on the chest to do her own weeping.

Flower opened her eyes, surprised, for she had not realised that she had closed them. All the women had disappeared, back into the fields, into the woods; she did not know where, nor was she to wonder about them. Her journey had to be made alone. Talking to anyone on the road this day would spell doom to them both, to her quest for her power, to the questioner's very life.

As she walked out of the village, Flower noticed that everything along the way seemed different. Her power had, indeed, begun. The lower bushes had a shadow self, like the moon's halo, standing behind. The trees were filled with eyes, peering out of the knotholes. The chattering of animals in the brush was a series of messages, though Flower knew that she was still unable to decipher them. And the path itself sparkled as if water rushed over it, tumbling the small stones.

She seemed to slip in and out of quick dreams that were familiar pieces of her old dreams stitched together in odd ways. Her childhood was sloughing off behind her with each step, a skin removed.

Further down the path, where the valley met the foot-hills leading to the far mountains, she could see Sand Walker's hut casting a long, dark, toothy shadow across the trail. Flower was not sure if the shadows lengthened because the sun was at the end of its day or because this was yet another dream. She closed her eyes, and when she opened them again, the long shadows were still there, though not nearly as dark or as menacing.

When she neared the hut, the old man was sitting silently out front. His shadow, unlike the hut's black shadow, was a strange shade of green.

She did not dare greet the old man, for fear of ruining her quest and because she did not want to hurt him. One part of her was still here with him, wild, casting green shadows, awake. He had no protection against her power. But surely she might give him one small sign of recognition. Composing her hands in front of her, she was prepared to signal him with a finger, when without warning he leaped up, grinning.

'*Ma-hane*, white girl,' he cried, jumping into her path. 'Do not forget to laugh, you in your white dress and leggings. If you do not laugh, you are one of the dead ones.'

In great fear she reached out a hand towards him to silence him before he could harm them both, and power sprang unbidden from her fingertips. She had forgotten the Shaping Hands. And though they were as yet untrained and untried, still they were a great power. She watched in horror as five separate arrows of flame struck the old man's face, touching his eyes, his nostrils, his mouth, sealing them, melting his features like candle wax. He began to shrink under the fire, growing smaller and smaller, fading into a grey-green splotch that only slowly resolved itself into the form of a *sa-hawa*, a butterfly the colour of leaf mould.

Flower did not dare speak, not even a word of comfort. She reached down and shook out the crumpled shirt, loosing the butterfly. It flapped its wings, tentatively at first, then with more strength, and finally managed to flutter up towards the top of the hut.

Folding the old man's tattered shirt and leggings with gentle hands, Flower laid them on the doorstep of his hut, still watching the fluttering *sa-hawa*. When she stood again, she had to shade her eyes with one hand to see it. It had flown away from the hut and was hovering between patches of wild onion in a small meadow on the flank of the nearest foothill.

Flower bit her lip. How could she follow the butterfly? It was going up the mountainside and her way lay straight down the road. Yet how could she not follow it? Sand Walker's transformation had been her doing. No one else might undo what she had so unwillingly, unthinkingly created.

To get to the meadow was easy. But if the butterfly went further up the mountainside, what could she do? There was only a goat track, and then the sheer cliff wall. As she hesitated, the *sa-hawa* rose into the air again, leaving the deep green spikes of onions to fly up towards the mountain itself.

Flower looked quickly down the trail, but the shadows of oncoming evening had closed that way. Ahead, the Path of Power – her Power – was still brightly lit.

'Oh, Mother,' she thought. 'Oh, my mothers, I need your blessing indeed.' And so thinking, she plunged into the underbrush after the *sa-hawa*, heedless of the thorns tugging at her white leggings or the light on the Path of Power that suddenly and inexplicably went out.

The goat path had not been used for years, not by goats or by humans either. Briars tangled across it. Little rock slides blocked many turnings, and in others the pebbly surface slid away beneath her feet. Time and again she slipped and fell; her knees and palms bruised, and all the power in her Shaping Hands seemed to do no good. She could not call on it. Once when she fell she bit her underlip so hard it bled. And always, like some spirit guide, the little grey-green butterfly fluttered ahead, its wings glowing with five spots as round and marked as fingerprints.

Still Flower followed, unable to call out or cry out because a new woman on her quest for her Power must not speak until she has found her word. She still hoped, a doomed and forlorn hope, that once she had caught the *sa-hawa* she might also catch her Power or at least be allowed to continue her quest. And she would take the butterfly with her and find at least enough of the Shaping Hands to turn him back into his own tattered, laughing, dismal self.

She went on. The only light now came from the five spots on the butterfly's wings and the pale moon rising over the jagged crest of First Mother, the leftmost mountain. The goat track had disappeared entirely. It was then the butterfly began to rise straight up, as if climbing the cliff face.

Out of breath, Flower stopped and listened, first to her own ragged breathing, then to the pounding of her heart. At last she was able to be quiet enough to hear the sounds of the night. The butterfly stopped, too, as if it was listening as well.

From far down the valley she heard the rise and fall of the running dogs, howling at the moon. Little chirrups of frogs, the pick-buzz of insect wings, and then the choughing of a nightbird's wings. She turned her head for a moment, fearful that it might be an eater-of-bugs. When she looked back, the *sa-hawa* was almost gone, edging up the great towering mountain that loomed over her.

Flower almost cried out then, in frustration and anger and fear, but she held her tongue and looked for a place to start the climb. She had to use hands and feet instead of eyes, for the moonlight made this a place of shadows – shadows within shadows – and only her hands and feet could see between the dark and dark.

She felt as if she had been climbing for hours, though the moon above her spoke of a shorter time, when the butterfly suddenly disappeared. Without the lure of its phosphorescent wings, Flower was too exhausted to continue. All the tears she had held back for so long suddenly rose to swamp her eyes. She snuffled loudly and crouched uncertainly on a ledge. Then, huddling against the rockface, she tried to stay awake, to draw warmth and courage from the mountain. But without wanting to, she fell asleep.

In the dream she spiralled up and up and up into the sky without ladder or rope to pull her, and she felt the words of a high scream fall from her lips, a yelping *kya*. She

awoke terrified and shaking in the morning light, sitting
on a thin ledge nearly a hundred feet up the mountainside.
She had no memory of the climb and certainly no way to
get down.

And then she saw the *sa-hawa* next to her and memory
flooded back. She cupped her hand, ready to pounce on
the butterfly, when it fluttered its wings in the sunlight
and moved from its perch. Desperate to catch it, she leaned
out, lost her balance and began to fall.

'Oh, Mother,' she screamed in her mind, and a single
word came back to her. *Aki-la*. Eagle. She screamed it
aloud.

As she fell, the bones of her arms lengthened and flat-
tened, cracking sinew and marrow. Her small, sharp nose
bone arched outward and she watched it slowly form into
a black beak with a dull yellow membrane at the base. Her
body, twisting, seemed to stretch, catching the wind, first
beneath, then above; she could feel the swift air through
her feathers and the high, sweet whistling of it rushing
past her head. Spiralling up, she pumped her powerful
wings once. Then, holding them flat, she soared.

Aki-la. Golden eagle, she thought. It was her Word of
Power, the Word That Changes, hers and no one else's.
And then all words left her and she knew only wind and
sky and the land spread out far below.

How long she coursed the sky in her flat-winged glide
she did not know. For her there was no time, no ticking
off of moment after moment, only the long sweet soaring.
But at last her stomach marked the time for her and,
without realising it, she was scanning the ground for prey.
It was as if she had two sights now, one the sweeping
farsight that showed her the land as a series of patterns
and the other that closed up the space whenever she saw
movement or heat in the grass that meant some small
creature was moving below.

At the base of the mountain she spied a large mouse and

her wings knew even before her mind, even before her stomach. They cleaved to her side and she dived down in one long, perilous swoop towards the brown creature that was suddenly still in the short grass.

The wind rushed by her as she dived, and a high singing filled her head, wordless visions of meat and blood.

Kya, she called, and followed it with a whistle. *Kya*, her hunting song.

Right before reaching the mouse, she threw out her wings and back-winged, extending her great claws as brakes. But her final sight of the mouse, larger than she had guessed, standing upright in the grass as if it had expected her, its black eyes meeting her own and the white strip across its head gleaming in the early sun, stayed her. Some memory, some old human thought teased at her. Instead of striking the mouse, she landed gracefully by its side, her great claws gripping the earth, remembering ground, surrendering to it.

Aki-la. She thought the word again, opened her mouth, and spoke it to the quiet air. She could feel the change begin again. Marrow and sinew and muscle and bone responded, reversing themselves, growing and shrinking, moulding and forming. It hurt, yet it did not hurt; the pain was delicious.

And still the mouse sat, its bright little eyes watching her until the transformation was complete. Then it squeaked a word, shook itself all over, as if trying to slough off its own skin and bones, and grew, filling earth and sky, resolving itself into a familiar figure with the fierce stare of an eagle and the soft voice of the mouse.

'Late Blossoming Flower,' her mother said, and opened welcoming arms to her.

'I have found my word,' Flower said as she ran into them. Then, unaccountably, she put her head on her mother's breast and began to sob.

'You have found much more,' said her mother. 'For see

– I have tested you, tempted you to let your animal nature overcome your human nature. And see – you stopped before the hunger for meat, the thirst for blood, mastered you and left you forever in your eagle form.'

'But I might have killed you,' Flower gasped. 'I might have eaten you. I was an eagle and you were my natural prey.'

'But you did not,' her mother said firmly. 'Now I must go home.'

'Wait,' Flower said. 'There is something . . . something I have to tell you.'

Her mother turned and looked at Flower over her shoulder. 'About the old man?'

Flower looked down.

'I know it already. There he is.' She pointed to a grey-green butterfly hovering over a blossom. 'He is the same undisciplined creature he always was.'

'I must change him back. I must learn how, quickly, before he leaves.'

'He will not leave,' said her mother. 'Not that one. Or he would have left our village long ago. No, he will wait until you learn your other powers and change him back so that he might sit on the edge of power and laugh at it as he has always done, as he did to me so long ago. And now, my little one who is my little one no longer, use your eagle wings to fly. I will be waiting at our home for your return.'

Flower nodded, and then she moved away from her mother and held out her arms. She stretched them as far apart as she could. Even so – even farther – would her wings stretch. She looked up into the sky, now blue and cloudless and beckoning.

'*Aki-la!*' she cried, but her mouth was not as stern as her mother's or as any of the other women of power, for she knew how to laugh. She opened her laughing mouth again. '*Aki-la*'.

She felt the change come on her, more easily this time, and she threw herself into the air. The morning sun caught the wash of gold at her beak, like a necklace of power. *Kya*, she screamed into the waiting wind, *kya*, and, for the moment, forgot mother and butterfly and all the land below.

'Words of Power' is from *Visions*, edited by Donald R Gallo, published by Delacorte.

Conditions of Employment

MARGARET ELPHINSTONE

The young woman in the duffle coat lay face down on the slope above the waterfall, sobbing her heart out. The ground was soaking wet and last year's sodden leaves clung to her clothes and hair. Her cheek was smeared with mud but she ignored it. There was no comfort in the wet wood in January, but she didn't want comfort. All she needed was the noise of the falls, to give her permission to cry as loud as she liked. The burn roared on, imposing no time limits. She wept passionately, until her throat hurt so much she could sob no more and her whole body was shaken so she had to gasp for breath. The waterfall was as loud as ever, mocking her weakness. Suddenly she stood up, glaring at it, wiping her wet cheeks with grubby hands. A smear of mud trailed across her nose.

'Shut up!' she screamed. The waterfall ignored her.

She was scrabbling at the bank now, squatting at the edge of the moss that marked the reach of the spray. There were boulders there, and small rocks. She prised a rock free and levered it up. It was slimy, and as heavy as she could hold in two hands. Somehow she picked it right up, shoulder-high, then hurled it with all her strength into the white water.

'Shut up! Shut up! Shut up!'

The water absorbed it without a sound, without seeming to yield an inch.

She was pulling out another rock, round and moss-covered. She stood up, right at the edge of the slippery bit. She was scarlet in the face now, regarding the burn with pure hatred. She was about to raise the stone, and then she paused.

She was speaking now, slowly and deliberately, loud enough for the burn to hear, over its own noise.

'Either...' she said, the stone clammy between her hands, 'either I have something... just one thing. Either I get a job, or, if not a job, a lover... Either that, or something will happen. Something that hurts. Like this!' She raised the stone and flung it.

This time it wasn't taken in at once. It hit a rock halfway down the fall, and bounced up again. It descended into the burn in a couple of heavy thuds and landed in the pool below, with a great splash that was just audible.

She stared after it. 'Preferably both,' she said. 'You hear that? It has to be one or the other, but I want both. Otherwise...' She grappled with the third rock. It was bigger than the other two and it left a larger scar, bare mud with a trickle of wet sand at the bottom. She could hardly lift it but, panting, she got it clear of the edge and threw as hard as she was able. It landed heavily in the pool, leaving a momentary ripple, even over the turbulence from the falls.

'If I don't,' she threatened, looking down at the pool, 'someone will get hurt.' She wiped her eyes again, her flush subsiding. It seemed a silly, pointless thing to have done.

'Presumably me.'

The Job Centre was just the same as it was every Friday. She saw at a glance that almost every card on the rack was familiar. They still wanted a school leaver to stack shelves in the supermarket for £1.20 an hour. They were still looking for a qualified night care assistant in the home for the elderly at £1.50 an hour, pay for your own uniform. The fashion company was still wanting machinists to work at home, supply your own sewing machine, £3 for every finished garment. They still wanted a forestry manager with at least five years' experience. The job in the solicitor's office had gone. She wondered vaguely from where an experienced legal secretary had landed who wanted £3 an hour that badly. It couldn't be anyone who was up on the local gossip.

She stuck her hands in the pockets of her ancient duffle coat, and looked along the racks in the same order as every week, aware of the indifferent eyes of the two assistants following her. They never seemed to have much to do. They were probably looking at the mudstains on her coat, and the new patch on her jeans. She had ripped them the other day, throwing stones.

There was a new card at the end of the rack.

Experienced steeplejacks, no doubt. She glanced at it cautiously, with a feeling she was being watched from the desk behind her.

'Well guardian,' it said. 'No experience necessary. Excellent pay. Interviews by arrangement. Residential . . .' and so on.

She stared at the card for a minute or two. The wording did not change. Then she braced herself, and turned to face the secretary, who quickly shoved her magazine into a drawer and looked up enquiringly.

'What is a well guardian?' she asked diffidently.

'Name please,' said the secretary, turning to the files.

'Miranda Duthie. What is a well guardian?'

There was a pause while the secretary looked through a file. 'Yes,' she said. 'That only came in a day or two ago. Do you want me to fix an interview?'

'What is a well guardian?'

'It doesn't seem to say. I can arrange an interview if you like.'

It seemed a very odd arrangement for a job interview.

21

Miranda stood at the crossroads at the place where the spruce plantation ended and the land opened out into a moor. It was a clear blue day, like a mirage of spring, only the wind off the hills had the bite of frost in it, and the peaks themselves were sprinkled white, glinting cruelly in the sun.

Three roads met at the top of a little plateau, so that the whole moor was spread out in view, open and frozen. The night wind had burned the roadside frost into beautiful intricate patterns. Miranda walked on them absent-mindedly, her feet inside her boots numb with cold, despite three pairs of socks. Below the plateau there was an old packhorse bridge, just wide enough for a car to pass on the thinly tarmacked road which led south. The burn chattered over the stones beneath it, shrunken with cold, and a row of icicles adorned the arch of the bridge. Miranda wandered down to the bridge and stared at the water. She glanced at her watch. Nearly ten. It was the strangest place for an interview. If it turned out to be a joke, she'd be furious. If she complained to the Job Centre they'd probably take no notice. She could write to her MP. The last time she'd done that he'd replied very gently, as if she were a shorn lamb led astray by Bolsheviks.

Ten o'clock. She began to retrace her steps to the crossroads.

'Miranda Duthie?'

She swung round. She knew the road was deserted. She'd seen that it was.

It wasn't. A woman stood on the bridge, smiling politely.

'Oddny,' she said.

'I beg your pardon?'

'My name is Oddny. You must be Miranda?'

'Yes.' Miranda tried hard to pull herself together. 'I've come to be interviewed.'

'Of course.'

There was a short pause while the two women looked

each other over. Miranda was not impressed. She knew she was shabbily dressed herself but there was some excuse for that, as she'd never had a job in her life, and not for want of trying. However, she didn't go for the ethnic homespun look at all, and this woman seemed to carry it to extremes. She was dressed in a heavy undyed woollen skirt, with a plaid draped around her like the old prints of Highland dress that adorned the lounge bar in the local pub. Her boots were all too obviously homemade, being clumsily cut and sewn together with big stitches of leather thongs. Her hair was dark, very long and thick, with two strands woven into plaits and fastened at the back of her head.

I bet she smells of garlic and woodsmoke, thought Miranda resentfully. I don't think I fancy this.

'Will you come and see the well?' suggested Oddny gently.

'The well? Oh yes, of course. The well.'

'It's just along here.'

It gradually became clear that Oddny had country notions of distance. They walked for half an hour in silence. After a mile or so they left the road and skirted the moor. Presently the country became wilder; the hillocks that edged the mountains became rougher, scarred by small precipices and sweeps of scree. The two women picked their way carefully across. The high peaks themselves were drawing nearer and, as they did so, the wind grew keener, bringing with it the smell of snow. It was a desolate place, caught between mountains and the silent ranks of spruce below. At this time of year the grass was yellow and sodden, interspersed with withered clumps of heather which scratched at their boots as they passed.

They scrambled round the foot of a precipice, and found themselves on the flank of a corrie. The ground fell away steeply from the hills that surrounded it on three sides, so steeply that in places the slope turned to outcrops of rock. It might have been a dismal place, only the corrie faced south, looking out over the tops of older trees, birch and rowan and hawthorn, over a wide expanse of lowland broken by hillocks, mostly blanketed in trees. There was a loch down there, gleaming grey in the winter sun, and the smoke of a village beyond, lying like a pall under the weight of the still air.

As they climbed cautiously down they heard water. A burn flowed southwards, to the trees and the blue distance where the sea lay. The spring must be in the corrie itself, for no water streaked the steep sides. Miranda couldn't see until they came close, because the source of the water was hidden by a smooth grass-covered mound and a scatter of boulders. She could hear the burn sounding quite loud. The spring must be in the shelter of the rocks. She could see a little grove of trees, mostly rowan, shielding what must be a pool. Then she glanced up, and her heart gave a painful thump.

There was smoke rising from beyond the boulders, apparently from the grassy mound itself.

'Is that a fire?'

'Oh yes, I kept the fire in. Come down to the well first. It's actually the spring; you can see that.'

It was a deep pool, overhung by rowan, surrounded by moss-covered rock. The brightness of the moss struck a chord in Miranda's mind, and with a slight shock she realised that this must be the same burn as the waterfall by which she had lain . . . was it only last week? She stared down at the pool, vaguely aware of some connection, but it made no sense. The water was brown and deep, bubbling under the rocks where the spring must surface. Her thoughts were all confusion.

'I don't quite see what the job is,' she said.

'No? But this is all,' answered Oddny, with a sweeping gesture that somehow included the pool and the rowans.

'Just to look after the well. I can't tell you more. It's unpredictable, really.'

It made no sense, but Miranda made herself recollect some of the questions she had prepared on the bus, before the long walk from the crossroads had begun to disorientate her. 'You said it was residential?'

'Of course. Come and see.'

Oddny led her along a narrow treacherous path above the pool, round to the back of the green mound. There was a doorway. Oddny ducked and entered. Miranda hesitated. She was not particularly superstitious but there was something about that configuration of rock, one horizontal slab balanced upon two vertical, with the dark rectangle of the threshold between, that stirred some atavistic memory and made her shudder.

'Please come in.' From inside, Oddny's voice sounded thin and hollow. Some instinct made Miranda cross her fingers. She stepped inside.

There was very little light but it was quite comfortable. The fire had sunk into a mass of glowing embers. Oddny was busy raking them together and laying on fresh peat. The place smelt of garlic and smoke. Bunches of unidentifiable dried plants hung upside down from the ceiling. There was a spinning wheel in one corner, with a stool beside it. A carved chest stood on one side of the fire and a sleeping platform on the other, piled high with woven blankets. There were pots of varying sizes ranged by the door. That was all.

'You could bring anything of your own that you wanted. It goes with the job, so it's all yours.

'Thank you.' Miranda knew that she was soon going to have to explain that this was hardly what she was thinking of, but curiosity prevented her for the moment. That, and desperation. She had been unemployed for too long to have retained any rigid expectations. She decided to test the situation by asking another of her questions.

'What about pay?'

The young man in the antique shop turned back from the window and put down his magnifying glass. He regarded Miranda across the clutter on his desk, in some bewilderment.

'There's no doubt about it,' he was saying, almost reluctantly, 'they are genuine, first-century Roman coins. In fact they must be some of the earliest Romano-British coins minted.' He looked down again at the coin in his hand, as if it might be spirited away at any moment. 'Quite genuine,' he repeated. 'I only hesitated because of their condition. They must have lain in a hoard for God knows how long. You'd think they'd never seen the light of day.'

He laid the money out on a sheet of writing paper. 'Quite remarkable.'

Miranda waited for a moment for him to take his eyes off her pay packet, then she coughed politely.

'A thousand?' he said suddenly.

Miranda gaped. Pence? she nearly said, but stopped herself just in time, and changed it to, 'What?'

'A thousand pounds,' he said, and grinned, a little crookedly. 'It's a good thing you came to a reputable dealer, you know.'

'Why?' she asked suspiciously.

'You're supposed to cultivate a mask-like expression. A thousand. I daresay you can use it.'

Miranda decided not to resent that and looked him over. He seemed quite pleasant, though rather faded-looking, presumably as a result of spending his days in this place. Brown hair, brown jacket, brown corduroy trousers, much too baggy, and scuffed brown shoes. He even had brown frames to his glasses.

'A thousand it is,' said Miranda.

He left her and disappeared into the back of the shop. Presumably he had a safe there. This shop didn't seem too hot on security but perhaps he thought she had an honest face. The doorbell was loud enough to warn of an intruder. He came back with a cheque book and stopped to wipe his glasses. 'Can I ask who sent you here?'

His eyes were not brown, but quite startlingly blue. She realised for the first time that he was worth a second glance. 'The shop on the High Street. They said you specialised in coins.'

'Ah.' He sounded gratified. 'It just shows. Water on a stone: how powerful it can be. If you persist long enough, you get there in the end.'

'Where? Fame?'

'Anything you want. Here, you'd better check this.'

Miranda read through the cheque carefully. Then she pocketed the advance on her first month's salary. She saw his hand held out and, slightly taken aback, shook it.

'You'll come here if you get any more like that?'

'I expect I shall,' said Miranda.

It was a week or two before there was any work to do at all, and then for quite a time it was only routine matters. Her first visitor was a girl of about ten, who had a large wart on her thumb.

'Goodness, I don't know,' said Miranda, startled by the simple request. 'Why did you come here, anyway?'

The girl was a plain freckled child in a polyester anorak and tight jeans. She gave Miranda a look as brown and unfathomable as the depths of the pool at twilight and explained patiently, 'We've always come here.'

'Oh,' said Miranda, and thought fast. 'Well, go down to the pool and dip the thumb in three times. Then turn in a circle moonwise and go straight home without saying a word to anybody. Show the thumb to the full moon when it rises next Thursday and that should do the trick.'

The child left, apparently satisfied, and Miranda returned to her green mound to eat prawns and avocado, and read

The White Goddess. It was the first new hardback she had ever bought.

The following day brought a boy with acne. She advised him to bathe his face in burnwater every moonlit night and to give up fried foods and chocolate. Then came a girl of twelve who was worried because she didn't have a boyfriend. Miranda taught her how to read tea leaves, and gave her a reading list of romantic novels. After the girl had gone, she worried that perhaps that wasn't right but it was too late and she was presently interrupted by an old man whose cow was sick. Miranda told him a charm to St Bride, made up on the spur of the moment, and suggested that he ring the vet.

That night she sat down to chicken in aspic and a half bottle of vin rosé, thinking she had earned it.

The next day brought a girl of sixteen, pale and agitated, who bore a marked resemblance to her first visitor. She gave Miranda a box of After Eights. 'From Jenny. The wart went. The morning after the full moon it was gone, just like that.'

'Of course,' said Miranda. 'And can I help you?'

The girl explained.

Oh dear, thought Miranda, this is getting controversial. Well, I can only do what I'm paid to do. 'How many weeks late?' she said aloud.

'Two.'

Miranda breathed a sigh of relief, and reached up to cut a little bunch of pennyroyal which she handed to the girl. She explained how to make a tea. 'Drink it tonight,' she said. 'Bow three times to the waning moon, and call upon every goddess you can remember the name of. Look them up in an encyclopaedia if you don't know any. If nothing happens with that, try this phone number.' she scribbled a name and number. 'But don't put it off. It must all be done before the moon has waned.'

The girl thanked her profusely and left. Miranda went

back to her brand new copy of *Folklore of the British Isles* and sat by the fire, munching After Eights. It was a long time before she turned a page. She was not used to responsibility and she found it weighed an uncomfortable amount.

'Norse,' said the brown young man. 'Danish coins. Tenth century, I should judge.' He closed the book he had been consulting, and peered at Miranda through his glasses. 'Of course, this area was Norse at that time but, even so, we can safely say that this is a unique find in south-west Scotland.' He cleared his throat. 'May I offer you a cup of coffee?'

'Thank you,' said Miranda, and hesitated. 'Can you give me a price?'

He looked uncomfortable. 'I can, of course. Wait while I put the kettle on ...' Miranda followed him to the back of the shop and watched him rinse two mugs, then measure out coffee. 'It's a difficult question, value. There is a monetary value – of course there is – and I'm sure it's all fair and square. But ...'

Miranda didn't help him. They sat down, one on each side of the large desk.

'I'm quite interested in archaeology myself,' he said. She noticed that his normally pale skin was somewhat flushed. 'The historical value of these things is in its context, I'm sure you know that. Can I ask you ...?' He paused, then the words came out with a rush. 'Where are you finding these coins?'

'I'm being paid. Monthly. Every new moon. I was told to find them in a hollow rock above a well, when the new moon has risen. And I do.'

There was a long silence.

'Could you tell me a little more, perhaps? If you don't object, that is?'

She thought it over, and realised somewhat to her surprise that she didn't object. In a way it would be a relief to check her own sanity against some external standard. He could have cheated her before. Maybe he had, of course, but she doubted it.

'It's all fair and square,' said Miranda. 'If I tell you what I'm doing, will you promise not to interfere in any way, whatever your view of the matter may be?'

He shook his head slowly. 'No, I don't think I can.'

'Why not?'

'Not if I thought it was doing harm. I couldn't promise.'

She frowned. 'And if it isn't?'

'If it isn't, then I promise.

Miranda stirred her coffee, and looked down into the swirling liquid. 'Very well, then. Listen.'

Three days later, she had another case to deal with.

She had been out shopping again. Dusk was falling by the time she had walked the five miles from the village where the bus stopped. It had taken her a long time to climb the hill, because she had so much to carry. She was no longer wearing her old duffle coat, but a smart new jacket with a new red jumper underneath. On her feet she had new boots that didn't leak. Her bag was full of books and groceries: in the still evening air she could pick up the faint scent of freshly ground coffee from the parcel jammed in her left pocket.

The sight of a horse quietly cropping the brown turf above the pool stopped her in her tracks. It was a very large horse, and its white coat glimmered in the twilight. It was saddled and bridled, and it struck Miranda there was something ornate, even outlandish, about its tack. She thought back to her days of hanging about the local riding school. None of the horses had been dressed up like that. She approached cautiously, for horses made her slightly nervous at the best of times.

The man was sitting in her favourite spot on the dry

rock above the pool, out of reach of the encroaching moss. He was gazing south into the darkening valley, apparently deep in thought. She had half expected that he would be wearing armour, but he wasn't. He was dressed in a plain woven tunic and leggings but he wore a large sword strapped to his belt. His hair was dark and fell to his shoulders. For one brought up on Malory he seemed disappointingly scruffy.

'Hello,' said Miranda, trying not to sound irritated, although she had been looking forward to a quiet evening, and he was sitting in the seat she regarded as her own.

'Good evening, mistress.' He stood up and bowed deeply, just as she had expected him to do.

'Can I help you?' asked Miranda cautiously, putting down her shopping bag.

'I hope so.'

'Well, wait a minute then. I must just put all this away.'

She wondered if she should invite him in, but it was a mild evening with no breeze and she wasn't sure if he'd want to come. When she had made up the fire and put her things away, she went outside again.

It seemed to have got much darker in a few minutes, but she could make him out quite clearly, still sitting on the rock above the pool.

'I'm here now.'

'Yes.' It was a relief that he didn't speak in Pictish, or ancient Gaelic. 'I came for a prophecy,' he said.

Well, tough luck, she thought. 'Oh, yes?' encouraged Miranda politely.

'I'm sorry to keep disturbing you,' he said, apparently misreading her tone. 'We have no other way of knowing what has changed.'

'Not at all. You haven't disturbed before, anyway.'

'It is most civil of you to say so. I know that last time you told me to have patience for at least five generations, but I think that time has now passed, and I hope you won't be angry if I trouble you again.'

Miranda could think of nothing intelligent to say, so she didn't speak.

'We hear nothing,' he went on, 'and we see nothing. But there are undercurrents which reach even under the earth. The air grows foul, even where we breathe it. There are sounds in the hills where there were no sounds before. Many have departed, bird and beast and spirit. The hills are bruised and empty, and there is rumour of ugly things further off. I find myself beginning to wonder if it is time.'

'Time for what?'

'When the Sleepers shall be awakened, and this long vigil of mine shall be fulfilled.'

'Oh my God,' said Miranda, beginning to understand. 'You don't mean it? Where are the Sleepers?'

She could sense his surprised gaze upon her. 'The Guardian of the Well knows the Sleepers,' he said. 'They are under Cairnsmore, as they have always been.'

'Oh yes, of course. It must have slipped my memory.'

'But what say you, mistress? Is it time?'

'God knows.'

She saw him bow his head. 'Indeed that is true. The gods know, and therefore I have come to ask you for a prophecy.'

'Well, it's very hard to say. You want to know if the final peril is upon us, so that the hour comes when you must awake to rise again and save this land?' Not a bad speech, thought Miranda to herself. Maybe I could squeeze out a prophecy if I put my mind to it.

'Even so. How do you judge matters? How is this world? I perceive that there is peril, and my senses tell me that it may be mortal. Is this my country's hour of need, think you, when I should waken the king?'

Miranda replied, 'Well, it's an hour of need all right. I'm not sure how much help the king would be, though. I mean, it's very reassuring to know he's there – at least, I've always found it so, but it's going to take an awful lot of explaining.

'How so?'

'Well, just to put you all in the picture. And what can he do about it all? He can't stop radioactive pollution, or the war, or change the economy, and would he even want to save the National Health Service, or put money back into education? What would he do about the unemployed? You know, I'm not at all sure that it's a practical proposition.'

'Is this the prophecy?'

'No. I'll have to think that over. This is merely a preliminary discussion.'

'You are very wise.' His tone was humble, she realised.

'I wish I were. I don't read the papers. And not having any radio up here – well, anything could have happened. It probably has. I'll tell you one thing, though. You're quite right about the mortal peril. Let me think ... Why don't you come back in three days – that'll be Friday, and I'll let you know whether it's time?'

He bowed. 'I will do your will, mistress. On the day of the goddess I will come, as you say.'

'I said Friday. Oh I see.'

'Farewell, Guardian of the Well.'

'Farewell, Watcher of the Sleepers.'

There was some information about the Sleepers in the library but nothing local They seemed to be reposing under a good many hills of varying sizes across the country. They were rare north of the Border, in spite of the relative importance of Lothian and Orkney in *The Matter of Britain*. There was no mention of Galloway at all. Miranda sighed, and piled up the volumes from the Royal Commission on Ancient Monuments. Not that the cave was likely to be a monument. She'd tried everywhere she could think of.

She hadn't thought of asking the man in the post office but, later that day, when she called for her post on the way home, they got into conversation. When she mentioned the cave on Cairnsmore, he didn't seem particularly surprised. He knew at once which Cairnsmore she meant.

'Do you know exactly where it is?' she asked him.

He looked at her sideways. 'If you've a map, I could show you. There's only the mound, and a pile of rocks. Nothing much to take photos of, or anything like that.'

'I haven't got a camera. Here, it's an old map, but nothing will have changed up there, will it?'

'Only the hydroelectric, and that's far enough from where you want. Now look here . . .'

There was nothing to see at all. Certainly there was a mound, roughly where he'd put a cross on her map, and also a pile of stones, if one could call half a mile of scree and boulder a pile of stones. Miranda sat down on the edge of the mound and considered.

It was difficult to think because of the wind. It had been a wild day down in her corrie, the bare rowans bending to the gale, then tossing up to their full height again between every gust, with a sound like a distant sea. Up here it was a full gale. There was nothing to move before it; only the grass lay even flatter in patches, as if a herd of mammoths had been lying across the slopes like cows in a meadow. Higher up there were grubby patches of snow, glistening in the sun as they melted reluctantly into the hill. Miranda moved round to the leeward side of the mound, into the shelter of a large rock. The little pocket of stillness caught the weak sun and held it, extracting a faint warmth in spite of the draughts that eddied round the rock.

In the prosaic light of a March morning it was difficult to justify her search. She had to believe all that happened, because there was her job, her home, and her pay, all there to prove it. She had wanted something to happen for years; indeed, recently she had become quite desperate about it. She was beginning to wish now that events would locate themselves more solidly in a world she recognised. It would be easier, thought Miranda, if I were doing something I could write home about. It was impossible even to try to explain. Her mother had asked if she had a nice boss and her father had asked if there was a Union and, if so, whether she was paid up.

What could she say? 'I wish I had something I could explain,' said Miranda aloud. 'I wish this cave would produce some evidence. Just so I know where I am.'

There was a slithering sound above her and a couple of stones skimmed past her, bouncing down the slope. She looked up.

'Goddammit!'

Miranda jumped to her feet. It didn't sound like a Sleeper, but there'd been no one else in sight all day over the entire mountain.

'Hello?' she called nervously across the wind. No answer. She began to scramble upward. 'Hello?' she called again.

A shout came back from above. She couldn't hear the words. She tackled the rocks on hands and knees, and clambered back on to the mound.

It wasn't a Sleeper. It was a plump middle-aged woman in a scarlet anorak, arrayed in what looked like the very latest hiking equipment. She seemed to be clutching part of a camera. The camera appeared to be in trouble. A fallen tripod lay pathetically across the rocks, and the rest of the camera had rolled further down. The woman had presumably been scrambling after it but now she seemed to be stuck.

'Can I help you?'

She could indeed. She could help the woman to her feet,

and retrieve the camera. Miranda did all this and more. She got the camera fixed back on the tripod, made sure everything was steady in spite of the wind, then together they tested the camera with a couple of shots.

'Well, it sounds all right. I won't know the worst till I get back to town.' The woman looked up. 'Say, I'm grateful to you, I truly am. My name's Helen Louise Caldecott, and I'm truly pleased to meet you.'

Miranda muttered her name, so that the wind whipped it away instantly, and shook hands.

'Sorry, I didn't catch that. Miranda, did you say? Well, that's wonderful. It's a wild place for a hike, isn't it? Do you hike in these mountains a lot? There don't seem to be many trails.'

'That's because not many people do any trailing. If they do, they go straight to the summits. This is a bit out of the way.'

'So what brought you here, Miranda?'

Miranda hesitated. But what harm was there? Americans were supposed to like antiquities. 'I was looking for a legend, I mean a cave. There's supposed to be a cave round here, with a king sleeping in it. And a load of knights. Just under here, somewhere.' It was easier to sound flippant, a bit stupid, even, in case she was about to be mocked.

'You don't say!' But the woman wasn't looking at the mound. She was looking at Miranda. 'Now where did you hear about that?'

'In the post office.'

'You're not telling me it's a matter of international security?'

Miranda looked sulky, in case the joke was at her expense.

'No, wait a minute. I'd like to hear about this. I'm quite serious,' the woman replied.

Miranda looked up. 'I have an interest in this matter myself. Can we sit down out of the wind somewhere?'

Miranda led her back to her sheltered spot. She felt a little overpowered, but the woman was quite friendly and even seemed to know what she was talking about. Miranda hurriedly revised her impressions of Americans on tour, and began to listen. She was offered a share in a flask of coffee and some smoked salmon sandwiches, after which she even began to talk a little herself. The woman seemed impressed.

'So you've been studying Iron Age burial sites yourself?'

'Not exactly. I mean, I don't know anything about it. It was just what I read in the library.'

'You seem to have done a lot of reading.'

Miranda finished her sandwich. 'Well, it's because of my job. I mean, I don't have to but it seems to be relevant.'

'So you've been reading it up on your own initiative?' This with a nod of satisfaction. 'Well, this is interesting. Like I say, I'm doing a book about Arthurian sites, with a chapter on the legends of the sleeping knights, or whatever you choose to call them . . .'

'It won't be Arthur here. This is Galloway.'

'I'm not bothered what they call him in one place or another. He's still the king.'

'But there's quite a few of him.'

'It's going to be a big book. And I didn't know anyone had got on to this site except me. There was a manuscript in the Museum of Antiquities but nothing ever published. And your source was local anecdote? That is very very interesting. Are you a historian?' The question came suddenly, making Miranda jump.

'What, me? No, no. But I did History at school.'

'Liked it?'

'I liked History and English. And Art. I wanted to do Art but they said I lacked imagination, so I sort of gave up.'

'So what did you do?'

The sulky look was back, making Miranda look very

much younger. 'Secretarial,' she muttered, almost inaudibly.

'How was that?'

'Well . . . if I hadn't hated it, and loads of other things hadn't been happening at the same time, I suppose I'd have done all right.'

'So this job is different?'

'Oh, it's not that sort of job. I applied for thirty-seven jobs, and then I sort of gave up for a bit. And now I've got this.'

'Like it?'

Miranda's face changed as if the wind had forced the clouds back off the sun. 'Oh yes, I like it.'

'Permanent, is it?'

Miranda shrugged.

'I only ask, because I was thinking about hiring an assistant. A keen young person who'd be willing to lug that goddam camera about, and help me with my search. Lots of travelling, and a fair salary. Expenses paid, of course. I'd do the driving. You wouldn't be interested?'

Miranda stared at her for a minute. 'I don't know,' she said slowly.

'I have thought,' announced Miranda dramatically.

She was quite pleased with the whole scene. A crescent moon pierced the cold sky behind her, and Venus shone like a beacon over the silent rowan trees. The land was silent, gripped by frost, but the burn was loud, filling the corrie with sound, as the last light faded nightwards. The Watcher of the Sleepers stood before her, head bowed, like a suppliant at the feet of the oracle. She felt a little drunk. She was wearing new clothes too, black from head to foot. In the shop she had felt sophisticated in them; here, she felt invincible.

'I await your doom, Mistress of the Sacred Well.'

Entirely as it should be. 'I have thought,' repeated Miranda, 'and the inspiration has come to me. Do you have a front door key?'

He only hesitated for one moment. 'But assuredly, Mistress, the great oak door lies ten feet inside the tunnel: a double door six inches thick, bound with fearsome spells and hoops of iron, so that no evil thing may enter and none untimely. And I, the Guardian of the Sleeping King, and the Sleeping Flower of Knighthood, I hold the key.'

'Excellent. I want a copy.'

'What?' That shocked him.

'You hear me. The day of peril is at hand. Evil stalks this land, and cannot be appeased by human power. Death threatens the earth on every side, and though the people are afraid they do not act. The day of awakening may be close. You need one who is vigilant, who is aware and who walks the hills, who buys a daily paper and who listens to the *News at Ten*. I am that one, and I will come to your cave and bring you word, when the hour strikes for you to rise.'

'I hear your word, Mistress, but I am troubled.'

'Prophecies are always troubling.'

'I was charged to hold the key, and deliver it to none until the world is ending.'

'Fair enough. You can do that. Did anyone say you weren't to get a copy?'

'No.'

'Then you know what you must do.'

'I suppose so.'

'Repeat it.'

'I must go to the smith of the gods who forged the key, and wove the spells surrounding it, and ask him to make a copy, which I will deliver to you at this well.'

'Very good. Next Friday.'

'As you say, Mistress.' He straightened up, and seemed to relax a little. 'Then our business is concluded?'

'It seems so.'

39

'Well, that's good,' he said, coming towards her. 'And here are my gifts. You forgot to ask for them before.'

'I didn't forget,' lied Miranda. 'It was a test.'

'I hope I pass? There is wine here, and apricots, spices from the East, and honey from the Western Isles. There is cloth woven from the finest wool, and amulets of ivory.'

'Goodness me, the horse must be worn out.'

'No doubt,' he said, obviously without considering the matter. He appeared to be thinking about something else, for presently he said, 'And if you have the key, how will you know the door?'

'Well, I think it must be in that place where there's a peculiar pinnacle of rock on the slope up from the mound. Those arched slabs below it could be a doorway, if one could squeeze past the rock at the entrance.'

'You found that?' His voice was suddenly sharp. 'When?'

'The other day. And soon I'll have photos, if the camera was working. Is there a spell to move that rock? We couldn't budge it.

'Mistress, you see further than I reckoned. When I give you the key, I will give you the word of opening, for I know that I must trust the Guardian of the Well.'

'That's very good of you. And thank you for all these gifts. I'm much obliged.'

Suddenly he was very near her. 'It is my greatest pleasure, lady, to do anything for you.'

Miranda looked round at him, startled. She recognised his manner but in this context it took her completely by surprise. She couldn't think how to react, until she felt his arm slide round her waist. Well, she knew how to deal with that; whatever kind of a resurrected knight he might be, this was not on.

'Hey, stop that,' she said, wriggling away from him. She confronted him over her pile of presents. 'Now look here,

Mister Watcher Knight. This is harassment. I'm at work and I don't like it.

'No, no, you don't understand. I love you.'

'Really?'

'From the moment I first laid eyes on you. You, I mean, Not you, as you were all the other times.'

'Oh.' Her head was spinning, it seemed so inappropriate. She managed to say coldly, 'Are you sure you're not married?'

'Not for fifteen hundred years.'

'Oh?'

'We brought no women into the cave,' he said simply. 'My past is quite a long way behind. I'm sure we can disregard it.'

'And what did the women reckon to that?'

'To what? Well, we didn't really consider it. That is, we didn't ask them. Perhaps we made a mistake.'

'I shouldn't worry about it. No doubt we organised our own methods of survival.'

'I'm very sorry.' It was the humble tone back again, and it annoyed her.

'Now you must go, before the moon rises high enough to touch the water. Stay longer at your peril!'

He retreated at once, and mounted the white horse in one swift graceful movement. At a few yards distant, under the moonlight, he looked quite courtly after all.

'Lady, I go. Until seven nights from now, I go.'

'So she wants me to visit the sites with her, helping with the photos and taking notes. There's a lot of routine work I can do in local libraries. If I get on well, she might need me to go back to the States with her. She could get me a visa as a research assistant, because I'm a local expert. She can do that because of what she is at her university. I'd be working at the university too, you see. I think I'd fancy that.'

The brown man surveyed the line of coins laid out on a white sheet of paper. He didn't seem to be finding much pleasure in them today. It took him a while to answer. 'I'll miss you,' he said at last. 'I thought you'd be around for a while.'

'I didn't say I was going. I can't,' explained Miranda. 'I'd have to give notice, and that would mean leaving a note at the hollow in the rock. It won't be new moon for three weeks, and then she'd have to find a replacement, I suppose.'

'But that's not your problem.' He seemed to speak reluctantly. 'This sounds like a real opportunity. I think you should take it.'

'It is my problem, though. I can't just leave the well.'

'Why not?'

'I'm the well guardian.'

He raised his eyebrows, as if there were a question about it.

'Now look,' said Miranda. 'I've done a responsible job for God knows how many centuries. I've got an important project, which I've been working on for fifteen hundred years, and it's just reaching a crucial stage. It's my job. Do you think I'm going to walk out and leave it?'

'Have you really?' He was looking at her rather anxiously, and again she read his thoughts.

'Not I, Miranda, silly. I, the well guardian. Don't you know the difference?'

'It's a little beyond my ken,' he said apologetically. He was about to say something else, but apparently changed his mind, for he began studying the coins again. 'Though the pay would be incentive enough for some. The two Welsh ones now . . .' He turned back to the reference book. 'Absolutely unique in this area, I should say. And the others . . . if they really are Pictish, then you've created an archaelogical earthquake and they'll find the ripples right through to California, so you'll be feeling them in this new appointment of yours for years to come. You do trust me to take them to Edinburgh for you?'

'Of course I do.'

He looked at her gravely. 'You honour me.'

'Oh?'

'I'll do my best for you, Miranda. I don't know ... I was hoping ...'

'Hoping what?' she prompted him, puzzled.

'I thought there'd be plenty of time, with your coming in every month like this. I look forward to it, you see. The thing is ...' He took off his glasses, and began to polish them thoroughly. 'I was planning to go on holiday soon. I know somewhere I can get a cheap flight. I thought of Greece, Delphi, you know. Olympia, Epidauros, Mykonos and Delos. That sort of thing. I was going to ask you if you'd like to come.'

Miranda's jaw dropped. She sat and goggled at him.

'I speak Greek,' he said. 'I know my way around a bit. I don't know if you've been to Greece at all?'

'I've never been abroad in my life,' said Miranda slowly.

'Well ...' His blue eyes were large and beautiful. 'I don't know if you'd feel like coming with me, but it would make me very happy if you did.'

Dear Oddny,

I know it's not a new moon, so I'm not sure if this will reach you. The job is going well. I just have to finalise a major project this evening, which I hope will meet with your approval. Routine matters are going well. The spring has been a bit low lately because of the snow on the hills. I am sure it will pick up again, and I expect the burn to be in spate as soon as the thaw begins. There are buds on the rowans, and the nettles are growing nicely by the front door.

If convenient, I would like to give in my notice as soon as possible. Not having a written contract, I'm not

sure what the terms are. The fact is that I have been
offered a good job and I would like to start next month.
I would also like to take a couple of weeks' holiday
before that. If a fortnight's notice (or less) is convenient
to you, perhaps you would let me know.

Yours by moonshine,
Miranda Duthie

Saturday morning ushered in the spring. The southerly
breeze was soft and balmy, and there was a new smell of
growing grass. The first leaves were unfurling on the
rowans, and the pool sparkled in the sun. The thaw had
come and the snow had retreated to the highest peaks.
Only the burn was white now, the pool overflowing with
meltwater from the hills. Miranda stood at the entrance to
the mound, her hair tousled and her eyes still full of sleep.
She stepped down to the well to wash her face, and found
Oddny waiting like a statue under the rowans. Dewdrops
shone like beads in the folds of her plaid and her skirt was
dark with spray. Her cheeks were pink with morning cold.
Miranda wondered if she had been standing there all night,
waiting for her to wake.

'Hello.'

'Hello, Miranda.' Oddny smiled at her. She seemed
pleased about something. 'Thank you for your letter.'

'Oh. That's all right.'

'Did you get what you wanted last night?'

Miranda pulled at a silver chain which hung around
her neck and extricated something from the folds of her
dressing-gown. It was a large iron key. She held it out to
Oddny, who took it gingerly, frowning a little.

'It's the key of the door to the cave,' explained Miranda.
'I also have the words to open the rock. The agreement
now is that the guardian of the well will warn them when
the time has come, and they will arise at her bidding, and
be ready to receive her advice.'

Oddny looked at her in wonder. 'He gave you such a promise? The Watcher? He said that?'

'Yes.'

'That surly youth!' exclaimed Oddny. 'I've never got so much as a smile out of him in a thousand years, let alone a concession. You have done a greater thing than I ever imagined, Miranda. Do you want me to write you a reference?'

'I thought he said too much, if anything. Yes please, I think that would be very useful.'

Oddny pulled a roll of parchment from one drooping sleeve. She sighed. 'I suppose you'll want it in modern English? You may have to help me with the spelling.'

'That's all right,' Miranda watched her take a quill and an inkpot from the depths of the plaid. She cleared her throat, and asked tentatively, 'What about my notice? Is that all right?'

'To tell the truth, I was delighted,' said Oddny, a little absently, scratching away with the quill across the parchment. 'It was good to have a holiday – I haven't had one for centuries, but I was beginning to miss the place. I'll be glad to be home again.'

'Home? Oh I see. I didn't realise . . .'

'But it was the right thing to do. You have achieved something which I now see was most urgent and necessary. I thought you rather demanding at the time and, really, I can do my job quite well without having rocks hurled at me. But we are here to help, and no supplicants can ever be ignored once they take the trouble to ask. I should have remembered then that there are two sides to everything. If you hadn't been needed, you wouldn't have come. And you are satisfied?'

'I have everything I want now, thank you.'

'For the moment.'

'Yes.' Miranda watched Oddny writing. She did it slowly and beautifully, but Miranda had a feeling that her script would prove quite illegible to any normal employer. Luckily her next employer wasn't too conventional. 'So you feel all right about the key? I mean it felt like a responsibility. I've started reading the paper, you know. I never bothered before. And I got a little radio. I can leave it with you, if you like.'

Oddny raised her head. 'Whatever for?'

'Well, you know . . . I thought if I was holding the fate of the country in my hands I ought to take it seriously. I mean, I'm quite willing to save the world if necessary, but there's loads of other things I don't want to miss. There's a lot of things I want to do, but . . . you don't mind being left with the key?'

'The key belongs with the well guardian. The well guardian takes it into her hands, and the well guardian will use it when the time comes. Here's your reference. Do you want to read it? And check the spelling, if you would. The alphabet changes so fast it's hard to keep track of it. You do right to go, Miranda. See the world, and respect water. Water is much more powerful than you think.'

'Conditions of Employment' is from Margaret Elphinstone's collection of stories *An Apple from a Tree*, published by The Women's Press.

Mother Was an Alien

KATHERINE V FORREST

The idea to smuggle Mother off Verna III came to Father when Jed Peterman fell down a hill of keteraw and proceeded to smother in a pile of mutherac, managing to do this in spite of all his training and thorough briefings on the planet's topography. Father, his crew chief, found him, and in disgust kicked him further down the hill, starting an avalanche which buried poor Peterman forever.

Why would Father risk years of severe punishment to bring an alien to Earth? Mother looked like one of the Sirens of Earth legend. Glossy dark silken hair reached to her voluptuous hips and covered cantaloupe-sized breasts. As if that wasn't enough to capture a young Earthman there were her extraordinarily beautiful eyes – the colour of pure emerald. And Mother, an inexperienced Vernan child of only forty-five, was enthralled with Father's virility and willing to go with him anywhere.

Father cut Mother's hair to collar length and concealed her remarkable eyes in grey infra-protect lenses. Judicial application of plastisculpt coarsened her nose and chin and ears. The barest touch of a surgiscope knife added temporary lines around her eyes and mouth. Still, his plan would never have worked except for the flappy tents the space crews wear which hid Mother's cantaloupes.

Exercising his authority as crew chief, Father accused 'Peterman' of violating Earthcode MCLVII – sexually harassing a female alien, a misdemeanour – and imposed a

47

sentence of solitary confinement for the duration of the return trip to Earth. Of course, only Mother's days were solitary.

Upon arrival on Earth, poor 'Peterman' vanished, AWOL from the Service. And Father took Mother to the pleasure capital of Vega where he married her. So long as she did not have to be fingerprinted or have her blood tested she could easily pass as an Earth female, albeit spectacularly endowed; and given her extreme youth it was unlikely that she would face exposure through medical discovery for many years. Perhaps by then, Father reasoned, the laws would have changed. And so Mother and Father set up housekeeping in Calivada.

Mother did have her idiosyncrasies. She made noises at night – sometimes like the klaxon warning of a fluorocarbon alert, sometimes reminiscent of nineteenth century war-whooping Indians. She was by now pregnant and since Vernan babies become conscious in the womb after the first month, the first words I heard were from Father, grumbling during one of her spectacular effusions: 'Great Calvin Coolidge, can't you hold that down a little? Everyone in the neighbourhood knows what we're doing.'

'A Payrungasmad curse on the neighbours. Can you do that again, dear?'

Father was furious when he learned of her pregnancy. 'Great James Garfield, how could you let that happen!' he bellowed. 'We've been married only six weeks! You said you'd take ovavoid!'

'No I didn't, you just gave me the pills,' Mother informed him coolly. 'I did what all Vernan females do when their males leave it up to them. Each time before we made love I concentrated hard and thought negative thoughts.' She shrugged. 'Sometimes it works, sometimes it doesn't.'

For a while Father screamed incoherently, then asked in

a hoarse voice, 'Why didn't you take the pills? Why why why?'

'Those things have never been perfected in 300 years. Imagine what they'd do to a Vernan. At least we don't have to worry about birth control for a while, dear,' she said seductively. 'Isn't that good?'

Father, who was accustomed to adjusting swiftly to emergencies in space, had calmed down somewhat. But he said plaintively, 'What do we do now? I'll have to find someone, pay a huge bribe. Then worry about blackmail. Maybe I can think of a way to smuggle you back to Verna-Three.'

'Don't worry,' Mother said. 'I'll manage.'

Meanwhile, reports of Mother's foibles had spread throughout the district, especially after she daily emptied tea leaves from the vacuum tubes and explained to a curious neighbour that she always sprinkled tea leaves on her floors, tannic acid being wonderful for the disposition. And when another astonished neighbour watched Mother pluck choice leafy titbits from the front hedge and eat them for her lunch, Father realised that even in Calivada Mother was a bit too *outrée*. So he hustled her off to an isolated but fully mechanised farmhouse near the border. She did not mind in the least; pregnant Vernan women crave solitude. She spent much of her time telescanning Earth's history and culture and learning agronomy and hydroponics, which she realised we would soon need.

Vernans do not require an interminable nine months for gestation; mother and baby work together to make things much more efficient. And so five months later, Mother gave birth. It took about an hour for us to be born, one by one.

'Great Ulysses Grant!' Father screamed, tearing at his hair. 'It's a goddamn litter!'

'It's all your doing,' Mother retorted, more than a little miffed. 'The male determines the number. That's how it is on Verna. The more sperm, the more chance for more eggs to be fertilised. And Geezerak knows you're a regular sperm factory.'

'Great Woodrow Wilson, how could I know that,' Father said shakily as Vesta and I were born, the last two, bringing the grand total to nine, all of us girls.

'One Y chromosome,' Mother grumbled at him. 'You couldn't spare even one Y chromosome.'

'Never again!' hollered Father. 'No ovavoid pills, no more you know what!'

'Suit yourself. You could take them yourself, you know. I'll be sore for a day or two, anyway. And lower your voice,' Mother said as we all began to wail, 'you're disturbing the girls.'

In a voice shaking with horror Father said, 'Clothes! Great Herbert Hoover, clothes for nine girls!'

'I'll manage,' Mother said.

'How will you ever take care of them?'

'I'll manage,' Mother said.

'Even choosing names for nine girls!'

Mother said distractedly, fastening liquiblots to each of us, 'The girls and I settled all that before they were born.'

'What!' Father shrieked.

Frightened by him, I began to cry. 'There there, Minerva,' Mother cooed, picking me up. 'Dear,' she said to Father, 'it's a . . . strong communication. It's gone, now that they're born. I can't really explain. Anyway, males never understand how it is between mothers and babies.'

'What have I wrought,' Father whispered, tiptoeing away.

Little did he know.

Isis was the first of us to indicate special gifts. When she was eight, Mother discovered that she had full comprehension of a teleclass in spatial calculus. I had already chosen my specialty – history – and was able to explain to my family that mathematical genius usually manifests itself quite early. It was then that Mother warned us all to be careful, that our family could not afford the bright light of publicity. Isis, soon bored with calculus, entertained herself by plotting stock market curves.

Thanks to Mother's agronomy and hydroponics expertise, the farm had become virtually self-sufficient, and Father and Mother managed to conceal our existence for quite a while. After that, although the nine of us drew attention we had grown at very different rates and were physically dissimilar. To our chagrin, we had inherited more of Father's build than Mother's; but fortunately, we had also acquired fingerprints.

Father spent more and more time away, volunteering for missions of six months and longer duration, coming home for a few weeks of loving attention from Mother, then blasting off again. It was hard to blame him. During his time home nine squealing little girls climbed all over him, but he was frustrated in his attempts to enjoy us; he was unable to win so much as a game of gin rummy or any other game of skill by the time we were six. Hera knew more about the space ships he flew than he did by the time she was eleven. He was less and less able to participate, even in dinner table discussions of any kind.

As we turned sixteen, Father had been gone for more than a year. A beribboned representative from the Service visited, gazed at us in astonishment, then broke the news that Father had been last seen pursuing a fellow crewman in a shuttle craft and had vanished near a black hole.

'He was a hero,' said the representative.

Hera, by now an expert in astrophysics, said through her tears, 'If he'd just known to set the coordinates for – '

Mother sobbed loudly and stamped on Hera's foot.

The representative went on to explain Mother's survivor benefits. 'Rough going, supporting such a big family,' he said sympathetically. 'Even with generous benefits.'

Mother dried her tears. 'I'll manage.'

The stock prognostications of Isis were now invaluable. Mother's investments financed travel and advanced educations for us all.

Once we completed our home-based education and ventured out into the world we thought it would be more difficult to hide our gifts, especially when we all performed spectacularly well scholastically, and later, professionally. But we had one overwhelming advantage: We were women. Scant significance was attached to any of our accomplishments.

It was Diana, now a geneticist, and Demeter, a meditech, who made the first great contribution to our future. They discovered through experimentation that most Vernan genes were dominant and consequently mutation-resistant.

'It's why you had girls,' Diana explained to Mother. 'You couldn't have had a male no matter what.'

Venus, our biologist, joined in further research. Additional experiments showed that our life expectancy was thirty years longer than an Earth male's; that unlike Mother who was pure Vernan, we were more likely to bear only two or three babies at most at one time, all girls; and that they would inherit the intellectual capacity of their mothers.

Selene the poet and Olympia the philosopher made the final valuable contributions, documenting and forecasting the continuing irrationality of Earth beliefs, customs and mores, and clearly demonstrating the need for concern – and change.

We have just completed a week-long meeting of extra-ordinary scope, and have made our plans.

We will all marry. We will all have as many births as our individual situations allow. And pass the word on to our daughters.

Isis has shown that if we have multiple births, and succeeding generations continue at that rate, exponentially there will soon be a female population explosion.

And we are perfectly concealed. Men will continue to notice us only for their sexual and nesting needs – which is what we want them to do. And by the time they observe that there has been an astonishing number of births of baby girls, it will be much too late.

I am Minerva the historian, and this the first chapter of our saga . . .

'Mother Was an Alien' is an extract from Katherine V Forrest's novel *Daughters of a Coral Dawn*, published by The Women's Press.

Playing With Fire

ELLEN KUSHNER

Nobody went into the Old City without protection. That was only common sense. The place was full of cut-throats and crazies; swordsmen and flimflammers and thieves on the run, as well as certain other types that the young university scholars giggled about in the boldness of their purity. But Aelwin's university career had not been marked by common sense: and now that she was leaving, it was even less so. Besides, there were some things she wanted to find out.

Her black scholar's robe, which she neglected to remove, protected her for a few streets. Then she stepped over a line in the dust drawn by knives she hadn't even noticed – in her black robe at university, she was used to being invisible, anonymous. Things were different here. She was about to lose her life, though not her dignity, when someone took an interest.

'Who's the scholar?' asked a bystander with a sword. The action stopped. She was a young woman, tall and dark and pleasant-faced.

'Scholar!' exclaimed a fighter. 'We thought she was a crazy, or a daredevil – walked right into a knife fight!'

Aelwin pressed her lips together. She knew she was doing it, but she couldn't seem to help herself. 'You weren't actually fighting,' she told them primly, just like one of her professors correcting an inadequate thesis.

One of them brandished a knife under her nose. 'Yeah,

well we weren't actually playing cards, either! What do you think this is for?'

'Skinning cats,' she answered pertly. 'Look, you can't expect people to just make way for you if you want to start a fight in the middle of the street. Don't you have – '

The young woman with the sword grabbed her arm and pulled her nearly off balance.

'You can explain it later. To the survivor.' The swordswoman surveyed Aelwin from dirty hair to scuffed sandals, not missing the trembling hands clutching the black robe between them. 'You are a very strange person. Come have lunch with me.'

'So are you. I don't have any money,' Aelwin said stiffly.

'I'll take care of it.'

'I'm not for sale,' the girl said loudly, to anyone who was still listening. 'I'm on an important research project. I – '

'You don't know what you're doing. Come and eat; I expect you're hungry. You'll think more clearly when you've had some food. There's a pie shop round the corner.'

Aelwin was indeed hungry. She proved to be what the swordswoman's mother had called 'a good eater'. Not that it showed. She was tall, but she was bony, with knobby wrists. Every joint formed right angles, as if her frame were only meant to hang clothes on rather than to be decorated by them.

'Who are you, anyway?' The scholar spoke around her mouthful of half-chewed pie. 'The queen or something? How did you stop those knife people?'

'My name's Isobel Crowe.' She took a long pull of cider. 'I'm just a swordsman. But that counts for something, around here.'

If she expected the scholar to act impressed, Crowe was disappointed.

'Oh, really? Whom do you kill?'

'Whoever they pay me to. When I can get a job. I don't do knifework,' Crowe frowned severely. 'No stabs in the dark; just duelling. Out in the open.'

'Do you have principles?'

'Patrons.' Crowe didn't know why Aelwin laughed. 'But I'm picky. I like a challenge.'

'Killing people's not a challenge?'

'Only in a proper duel, with a good opponent. Otherwise, it's just butchery. You don't fight?'

'Of course not. Putting anything sharp in my hands would be homicide. I don't even sew.'

'So you really are a scholar. What do you study?'

'Fish entrails. Menus.'

'No, I mean at university.'

'I'm not *at* university now, am I?' Aelwin demanded huffily, one hand twisting the sleeve of her scholar's robe. 'My name is Aelwin and if you have any other questions you can direct them to the public scandal sheets.'

Crowe grinned. 'Are you a scandal, Aelwin? Are you a celebrity? I don't read.'

'You mean you *can't*?' For a moment, the scholar lost her studied nonchalance.

'Haven't learned; haven't bothered. Plenty of time to learn when I'm old. I'll stop fighting at twenty-five or so.'

'Twenty-five's not exactly a crone.'

'No, but your edge goes, or your luck, by then. You ever see – ' quickly, Crowe amended the question – 'I bet you never saw a swordfight.'

'How much?'

'How much what?'

'How much do you bet?'

'Well, it was . . . I just . . .'

'Ha,' said Aelwin. 'You're afraid to lose.'

'Actually,' Isobel Crowe said slowly, covering her mounting mirth, 'I'm afraid to win. You said you didn't have any money.'

'I'll owe you,' the scholar said doggedly.

'Aelwin...' asked Crowe, 'have you ever heard of a tavern called the Green Tree?'

'No. I must say, it's not a very original name. There's one on every corner.'

'I think you'll like it there,' Crowe said, and led the way.

Even in full daylight the Green Tree was dark and smoky. Like birdsong in a murky dawn, the calls of gamblers cut through the cloudy air. You could follow the right sounds to tables where people were challenging each other to a game of dice, or seven-up, or screw-your-partner... a game for every temperament, all involving the exchange of money for the illusion of fortune.

Aelwin drew in a long breath, her pleasure unmarred by the coughing it brought on. 'This,' she said hoarsely, 'is something *like*!' Eyes watering, she stared avidly at the scene of debauchery before her.

'What's your game?' asked Isobel.

The terror of the Boar's Head Tavern Ladies' Gambling and Debating Society licked her lips, remembering past triumphs. 'Seven-up. But I haven't got any –'

'I'll stake you.'

The swordswoman began to flip her coin, but, remembering Aelwin's vaunted athletic prowess, leaned over and handed it to her instead. 'You can pay me back when you've won. I'll be at that table there. If you get into any trouble, call me.'

Aelwin peered through the murk. 'There's nothing *at* that table there. Just drinking. Are you a drunk, or did you promise your dying mother not to touch the cards, or what?'

'No. I just don't enjoy gambling. There's no skill in it. No challenge.'

Aelwin shrugged, and shambled off to her destiny.

With the scholar safely pointed at the seven-up table, Isobel Crowe sat herself down for drink and gossip. The Green Tree was a place where jobs turned up, and the truth was, she was getting hungry for one. It had been too long since her last public duel: a nobleman's mistress had hired her in some stupid argument about a rival's false eyelashes. That was the kind of job she got, when she got any. She couldn't turn them down, she needed to eat; but if that was all that anyone ever saw her do, she'd never get the fights she craved. The good ones. With the fighters who counted.

Without being asked, the pot-boy brought her her usual ginger beer, hot enough to burn the mouth but not the judgement. Emma Golightly slid down the bench to Crowe's side, and under cover of a welcoming hug muttered, 'Szifre's back. Sitting by the fire. Dirty toad.'

He was a sailor, a foreigner with a wicked blade. In his own country, he was said to be in trouble with the law. Whenever Szifre was in town, he made straight for the Green Tree. He'd cut Isobel out of a job once, and was likely to do it again. She'd better keep an eye on him.

Isobel had buried her nose in her tankard when a hand landed heavily on her shoulder. She snorted beer out across the table and spun around.

'Holy *Lucy*!' Aelwin shouted. 'What are you trying to do, *kill* me with that thing?'

Crowe palmed the stiletto and slid it back into her sleeve. 'Well, yes. If you'd been someone else. You really shouldn't sneak up on me like that.'

'So I see,' said the scholar drily. 'All right. I won't. I just came to tell you, I need some more money. So I can pay you back. Those – *people* – ' she jerked her chin at the seven-up table, 'they don't exactly play for walnuts. Of course, the bigger the stakes the bigger the win, right? As soon as my luck comes again.'

In fact, the pride of the Boar's Head Tavern Ladies'

Gambling and Debating Society was in way over her head. But there was no point in backing out now.

Crowe dug out a couple of coins. 'Why don't you change games?'

'No, no,' Aelwin said distractedly, her eyes already back on the table, glittering with the vision of quick profit. 'I'm just getting the hang of this one.'

Crowe watched the scrawny black figure weave its way back across the floor, picking between stretched-out legs and clumps of onlookers. Suddenly she saw the unkempt head go down, and then Aelwin rose to her feet, brushing off her sleeves. She seemed to have fallen over the feet of a large man in brightly striped trousers, with heavy black ringlets who was enthroned on a bench by the fire. It was Szifre, of course, trying to look innocent. Isobel shifted her weight forward.

'Excuse me,' Aelwin said loudly to Szifre. 'I hope I didn't hurt your feet.'

'My feets is fine, sweetie,' Szifre answered.

'If you moved them,' Aelwin said sternly, 'they wouldn't be in people's way.'

'I no moof them. You find you way.'

Aelwin just stood there, glaring in fury as though her eyes could set fire to his beard. Szifre tossed a purple scarf over her head. With great care she pulled it off, blew her nose in it and handed it back. Automatically, he almost took it, before swatting her hand aside in disgust and demanding, 'What you want, anyhow?'

'I want you to move those things at the end of your legs that the rest of us in common courtesy have agreed to call feet. Do you understand me, or would you like me to repeat it with shorter words?'

Crowe let out her breath in admiration. The girl was in a kind of verbal berserker rage. Aelwin was very stiff and pale, projecting her words with great clarity. In the tavern, the gaming slid to a halt; the bets now were on the contest that was taking place.

'What you want?' Szifre rumbled. 'You want fight?'

'Not particularly,' Aelwin rapped out. 'I'd like to tear out your liver and roast it over slow coals. And eat it.'

'Fight,' he concluded. 'You got you sword?'

'I don't need one. I'll be happy to strangle you with your own snot-rag – '

'Yes,' Isobel Crowe said. 'She has a sword.'

Szifre rose, smiling stickily. 'Crowe, my sweetie! Beautiful Crowe. How is it with you?'

Isobel's hand was on her sword. 'You want a fight. I'm claiming this one.'

'Why you do this thing, beautiful Crowe?'

She shrugged. 'You asked for it. Don't back out on me, Szifre.'

'Hah!' he roared. 'I back out? I roast you coals, you rotten dog-girl, and then I roast you girlfriend's, too!'

Isobel shrugged again, and stepped out into the ring the taverners had cleared for them. Aelwin had scrambled up on to Szifre's bench, and was standing there watching with her back to the wall. Isobel wondered whether she'd had the sense to bet money on the fight.

The crowd grew even quieter when Szifre stepped into the ring. He drew a heavy, wide-bladed sword with a cutting edge – something from Elmat, maybe. She'd heard about them. Her rapier was better for distance, but she'd have to watch the point of impact blade-on-blade, or he might snap her in two. If he had any sense he'd be trying to close on her, to come within her range without letting her under his guard. He had the advantage of height, but she thought she was smarter.

Already it was clear that Szifre was a talker. 'Ha-AAH!' he growled, glaring at his opponent. No wonder people hired him; he was as good as a play. Isobel stared back impassively. Let him make the first move. He was bound to: he had the showman's instinct, and would want to establish first control of the bout. But control, she thought, easily deflecting a downward cut with a corkscrew twist that nearly swept open his front, lay not in who made the moves, but who could make the most of them. So she let Szifre show off all his favourite strokes in the first exchange – and all he knew of her so far was that a feint to the left wouldn't fool her, and that she had a trick of disengage that fooled him every time. By the time he'd learned how to react to it, she'd have it changed. Already he was favouring defence on the right side, because he was so sure she would attack there ...

It was, after all, Aelwin's first duel. The swordswoman couldn't resist showing off for her. Crowe paced Szifre back and forth across the floor, making him fight high, fight low; she even did a little spin. The new sword stretched her in unaccustomed ways. It was like a new dance partner. She went in closer than she should have, just to see what he would do, and nearly had her leg sliced. She spun away, and blocked his upward cut at the last second. That was enough experimenting. The blade darted in her hand now, refusing to let him rest and rethink his attack. His defence was stronger than she'd expected.

Isobel backed off. Now they circled one another, faking starts to entice the other into rashness. All this virtuosity was tiring them both out. Crowe tried the right-hand feint again, but this time Szifre didn't fall for it. She did a little trick with her sword, a tantalising weave of the tip of total ineffectualness and great aesthetic beauty that maddened slashers like Szifre.

He spat on the floor. 'Come on, Crowe,' he growled. 'Come and kiss it.'

To kiss someone else's blade meant you had been killed by it. Alive, you only kissed your own.

She crouched low, where her speed gave her advantage. He aped her posture; they looked like a pair of crabs.

'Get his feet!' someone shouted, amid cackles of laughter.

'SHUT UP, YOU FOOLS!' It was Aelwin's voice, slicing through the tavern air. Szifre's head jerked in the scholar's direction, just for a moment, long enough for him to see Aelwin cast her hand in a throwing motion, long enough for Crowe to see her advantage and take it. She reached through his guard at last, snicked his forearm. Szifre roared in pain and surprise, and came at her, the flat sword spinning like a windmill. She parried the blow, but her wrist stung with the impact. Again his arm rose, streaming now with blood; again she lifted hers, and as the blades struck one another, the whole tavern burst into flame.

Isobel thought, *I'm dead*! and then, as the coiling, heavy smoke entered her lungs, she thought, *No, I'm not*.

'Let's go!' There was a cold hand in hers. It reminded her of her mother's when she had fever. It pulled her along. She had her eyes shut against the smoke, and not to see the flames she knew she must be running through.

'That's better.'

Isobel collapsed on the ground, clean air tearing into her lungs, her mouth watering convulsively.

'Just cough, it will clear your lungs out,' Aelwin said solicitously. 'You must be all worn out. That was a very good fight. At least, I think it was. It looked good, anyhow.'

She was perched on the edge of a rain barrel. They were in a side alley, not too far from the Green Tree. Aelwin's face was streaky with soot.

'The fire!' Crowe gasped, stumbling to her feet. 'Let's go – whole quarter – easy tinder – '

'Fire? No fire; it was just a lot of smoke. Probably the chimney backed up.' As if to belie her words, a trail of smoke wafted down the alleyway. But there were no people, no screaming; no signs of fire in the Old City. 'If you're feeling better, I can take you home. You have gotten pretty grimy.'

'I'm going to throw up,' Isobel said grimly.

'Oh, dear. Here's – have you got a handkerchief?'

Aelwin wet it and put it on the swordswoman's neck. It helped.

Naturally, Isobel thought; *she's the kind of person who never has her own handkerchief.* I'll be lending her mine for the rest of my life.

'I think you'd better go home, now,' Aelwin insisted; 'if you'll show me where it is.'

Isobel Crowe's rooms were not on the ground floor of her lodging house. She preferred to be less accessible. She pulled open her big double doors, and enjoyed Aelwin's gasp of awe.

The house had been someone's mansion, back when the Old City was the only city. Now it was broken up into rented apartments. Isobel lived in the grand ballroom.

She awoke the next morning to the unmistakable, enticing smell of pancakes. Crowe rolled out of the camp bed she slept in in the little chamber off to the side, where ladies had once retired to repair themselves. She had last seen Aelwin winding her way up to the minstrels' gallery.

'I'm a rook,' the scholar had said last night over the bottle of wine they'd shared, as she spread the wings of her long black sleeves; 'I want my rookery.'

'But I'm Crowe!' Isobel objected.

'Don't fence puns with me. You are a knight. I am a rook. Everyone else, of course, is a pawn.'

Aelwin had made a small morning fire in the enormous ballroom chimney. Carved cherubs and wyverns looked on with interest as she dropped batter on to an old iron skillet. 'My friends and I,' she explained, '*survived* on these at school!'

She might not have a handkerchief, Isobel reflected with

the philosophical contentment of the well-fed, but she certainly could cook.

They were both still grubby from yesterday's smoke. Carrying water up two flights of stairs was not how Isobel wanted to spend her day. She proposed a trip to the baths.

'That fire,' Crowe said as they walked, 'there *was* a fire, Aelwin, not just smoke; I saw it when I struck his blade!'

'Hmm,' said Aelwin.

'You're awfully calm about it,' Crowe accused her. 'You were calm yesterday, as well.'

'It's my philosophical background,' Aelwin explained. 'If you read enough, you find there's nothing in the world that hasn't happened before. However strange. "Freaks of Nature", they're called. In the year of the Norlan Conquest, when Aelmarl the Gormless finally lost his already shaky throne, there were seen portents of an astonishing nature. Two-headed calves were born, and lightning struck the same house three times.'

'What about fire that doesn't burn?'

'Perhaps summer lightning came down the chimney. Perhaps it was a miracle. To save you.'

'Save me? From what?'

'From that pig. With the sword.'

'Aelwin.' Crowe stopped in the middle of the street. 'I did not need saving.'

'Yes, you did. You'd gotten him bloody, and he was really mad. Also, he was much bigger than you – not to mention his sword.'

A sudden wave of sorrow washed over Isobel Crowe. Maybe her friend was right; maybe this was indeed the fight she would have lost, the one that was always coming someday. Without the peculiar smoke, she'd now be laid out flat on a bier, with the shadows and the candles and the chanting . . . she shook her head. It was a bright spring day. The fight had not been determined; she'd had as good a chance at Szifre as he had at her; and she had pinked him first. As for candles and chanting – that was for old dead kings, for someone in a romance.

'Come on.' Isobel led the way to the baths. 'You really *don't* know anything about fighting, do you?'

First they dipped, and then they went into the steam room. Through the wreaths of mist Isobel saw Emma Golightly, turning gently coral.

'Hello!' said Emma, in the languid way of the truly warm and wet. 'It's the hero. Congratulations.'

'Is Szifre dead, then?' Isobel eased herself on to a bench.

'No, but he's gone. Shipped out on the *Coriander* first thing this morning, I hear. Can't say I'm sorry.'

Isobel waited for her to say something about the fire, but she was disappointed. Finally, she had to ask: 'Sweating out the last of the smoke, Emma? What about that fire, then?'

'Ah,' Emma said. 'That's the real reason he had to go. They're calling it witchcraft. You should have seen yourself, Is! All lined with blue flame – I thought you'd caught on fire, until the smoke started, and then I didn't know what to think!'

'Blue flame?' Isobel looked at Aelwin, who was sitting all hunched up, despite the heat. 'You didn't say anything about blue flame.'

Aelwin shrugged, ducking her head even deeper between her shoulders. 'I must not have been looking.'

Isobel shrugged in her turn. Aelwin had been looking, all right. But either Emma was exaggerating, or Aelwin really didn't like thinking about anything she couldn't study in a book.

Crowe lay back, feeling her skin begin to prickle with sweat. She watched dreamily as the steam swirled in the air above her. It was making shapes like summer clouds, right over her head. A flower became a tree became a dragon, growing like a blossom, wings unfurling like rose petals until it filled her eyes, and yet she could see everything on it perfectly, every golden scale rimmed with black, reflecting back at her her own reflection, tiny and pink, her sword upraised –

'*Watch it!*' Emma's voice rang sharply in the tiled steam room.

With effort, Isobel turned her heat-logged head to look at her. Emma said, 'You made me jump, poking at me like that. What are you doing, practising in here?'

Isobel realised that her arm was upraised, extended as if to strike at the ceiling over her head. 'Sorry,' she said; 'I must have been dreaming.'

'Melting, more like.' Aelwin's skin was as red as a beet. 'I'm thirsty. I've been poached. Let's go for another dip.'

They ran into Emma again when they were all getting dressed. 'I thought you were never coming out of there,' Emma said. 'Look what I got!'

She pulled a thin book out of her pocket. 'More magic: *The Pathways of Love, being a Simple Volume, Easy to Con, wherein Anyone may find the Secrets of True Happiness with Simple Tests of the Lover's Faith and Heart, as whispered at the Death-bed of Rupert Magus to his Only Loyal Apprentice, Levinson, Doctor of Sorcery, University of Palindrome.*'

It took her a long time to get through the title: Emma's line of work did not call for too much reading. 'Sounds pretty good, huh? It's a bunch of magic spells you can do yourself. I tried the first one, "To Find if Your Lover be True to You," but it took me so long to get through all the words. I think I got some of it wrong. Anyway, nothing happened.'

'Oh, Emma,' Crowe said. 'You don't believe all that stuff, do you?'

Emma shrugged. 'Who cares? It's fun.'

'Let Aelwin read it for you. She goes really fast. Here, Aelwin, find us a good one – '

But the scholar was staring down at the proffered book as though it were a dead rat. 'The printer ought to have his licence revoked. Making money off idiots with this garbage. If people can't manage their own lives by using their brains, they should just kill themselves and spare us the trouble of feeling sorry for them.'

Fortunately, Emma was of an easygoing temperament. With anyone else, that speech would have netted Crow another duel. 'Oh, come on, Aelwin.' Emma pushed the book into the girl's hands. 'It's just a bit of fun.'

The snap of Aelwin's wrist sent the book sailing across the room. 'Don't give me that! I'm in enough trouble as it is!' Then she noticed the two women staring at her, more shocked than angry. It seemed to occur to her for the first time that she was behaving badly. 'Isobel,' she said graciously, 'Miss Golightly, may I take you out for a drink?'

And that was all the apology they got. She made up for it by being absolutely charming at the tavern they went to, telling them funny stories about a deaf university scholar who'd bought a sailor's talking parrot. For the first time, Isobel noticed the long 'aa's in the scholar's speech; or maybe they were coming out because she was being funny and forgetting to act clever. Her accent, like her name, belonged to the old landed class who had held on to their property after the Norlan Invasion – or later landowners who liked to pretend they had. Aelwin's quirky, innocent arrogance made her seem both older and younger; when she laughed, she looked about eighteen, not much younger than the swordswoman. Crowe was curious; but in the Old City, people respected each other's privacy.

Isobel paid for the drinks, of course. Aelwin was going to pay it all back when she figured out a way to get some money; but Isobel wasn't really keeping count.

The rest of the day was spent in simple pleasures: eating,

drinking and showing Aelwin the vices of the Old City. They went to the market, and bought her a wicked little knife with a bone handle.

Isobel noticed some people staring as she passed, and whispering after. She wished, oh, how she wished that she could even pretend it was about her fighting, that they were saying, 'That's Crowe. Remarkable technique. She'll be going far, and soon.' But she knew they were only checking to see if she still glowed with blue fire, or had begun to sprout horns from the top of her head! Well, she wasn't a fool. But she made a point of swaggering nevertheless: any attention was better than none at all.

The only spot of trouble they ran into was with a blind fortune-teller, brought on not so much by Crowe's reputation as by Aelwin's incomparable rudeness. Old Geata, she was called; everyone knew her, and usually it was quicker and easier to pay her the copper she demanded for telling your 'lucky fortune' than it was to shake her off. Knowing Aelwin's aversion to non-scholarly superstition, Isobel tried to steer clear of the old woman; but she seemed to have her blind sights set on Crowe today, and finally cornered them at a fruit stall.

'Ah, you're a lucky lady, a lucky lady,' Geata began as usual. 'Give me your hand, my darling, let Old Geata tell your lucky fortune.' Her withered fingers, with their surprisingly smooth tips, pored over Isobel's palm. 'You'll travel far . . . farther, maybe, than you've a mind to. And then – oh, then – ' Her blind eyes opened wide: orbs of spilled milk. 'Ah, but to see them dancing! Dancing under the stars!' Her hand clasped Crowe's in an iron grip. 'To be called through wind and water, and not say them nay – you must call them now, my darling, call them for us all before – '

'What is this claptrap?' Aelwin demanded loudly, on a whinier note than usual. 'Doesn't the old bat even know her job? What about your many children, and the tall dark man you're going to marry – not in that order, of course! Honestly, you can't even get a decent fortune for your copper any more.'

Geata turned her sightless gaze on the skinny scholar. 'You may keep your copper, mistress. For I speak with the true power.'

'Oh, come off it.' Aelwin was not to be stared down by witchy old ladies. 'You've no more true power than a lima bean.'

'Do you say so?' The old woman became agitated. 'Geata is my name, and that's a good old name that was here before you Norlaners ever came and laid waste to the Power of the land! You thought you burned the last of us on Widmark Field – but the Power lives in me, it does, and you'd do well not to forget it!'

'Do we have to pay her extra for the speech?' Aelwin drawled.

'Come on, Aelwin,' Crowe muttered, steering her away, 'she's just a poor old lady. Not everyone's had the benefit of your education,' she couldn't resist adding. 'And she calls everyone she doesn't like a Norlaner.'

Talking steadily, she got Aelwin out of there. That night, they got very drunk in Isobel's Grand Ballroom. It may have been a mistake.

Aelwin started off brilliantly, improvising satire on all the Old City characters she'd met, while Isobel rolled helplessly on the floor and begged her to stop. But gradually her talk turned morose.

'People are such fools,' she said. 'They believe anything they want to. That would be all right, if they didn't insist on *doing* something about it!'

'Like what?' asked Isobel, happily rolling an empty bottle from foot to foot across the floor.

'Like killing people – oh.' She looked at the swordswoman. 'I beg your pardon.'

'Quite all right. But why is that stupid? It seems pretty smart, to me.'

'Oh, I didn't mean you. You're an artist, it's not the same. I meant people you don't even *know*, who never did you any harm . . .'

She sounded so mournful Isobel didn't argue. 'It's for money,' she reassured. 'It nearly always is.'

'No it *isn't*!' Aelwin rose from the floor with alarming energy, and began pacing and waving her arms. 'It's sheer bloody-minded cruelty! It's because they're pigs! Look what they do to thieves like poor Lucas. He'll never get that eye back, not if he devotes himself to good works and knitting socks for the rest of his life! Or traitors – they cut their guts open and let them watch – '

'But they know all that ahead of time.' Isobel tried to be the voice of reason. 'Thieves and traitors – they know what might happen.'

'And the massacre of Widmark Field?' Aelwin said bitterly. 'Did they know *that* would happen?'

'You've got Old Geata on the brain. There wasn't any massacre at Widmark – or if there was, it was just part of the war. Why should they round people up and kill them?'

Aelwin brought her face close up to Isobel's. 'Because they were *witches*!' she hissed. 'They rounded them up from all over the land, the teachers and all of their families, and they slaughtered every one and burnt their bodies and their books and everyone saw the smoke for miles – it's true, I found the records! Well, some of them, anyway; the Norlaners may have destroyed the master lists, but they couldn't keep people from writing about the fire they saw, and the people who disappeared. That old lady was right – we *are* all Norlaners, the blood has intermingled in 200 years – we *all* set those fires!' she shouted.

Isobel's blood was racing as though she were facing an enemy. She had never seen Aelwin looking so desperate. 'Here,' she said tentatively, 'have some – ' But the bottle was empty. 'You need some more to drink,' she said. 'I'll go down to the Cock and Hoop and fetch us a bottle.'

'Don't go,' Aelwin said, her face drawn. 'Let me come with you.'

'You're too drunk,' said Crowe cheerfully, strapping on her sword. Being able to take action always made her feel better. 'You'd break your neck on the stairs. Wait here, I won't be long.'

As she shut the door behind her she heard two leathery clunks against the wood: very much the sound Aelwin's sandals would make if she'd thrown them after her.

The night was moonless, but the smoke and dust of the city had cleared enough to uncover a host of stars blazing in the blackness between the rooftops. Whistling tunelessly, Isobel made her way to the Cock and Hoop. She didn't need a light; she knew the streets of the Old City as well as her hand knew the hilt of her sword in the dark.

Just outside the tavern she froze. A shadow by the door had moved slightly. Hand on her hilt, she waited. Then the shadow moved into the light.

It was a child, underfed and ill-clothed like most Old City brats. But when it spoke, its voice was of surprising beauty, liquid and clear. 'Crowe,' it said. 'You are Crowe?'

'I am.' She crouched down and it moved back a step, into the shadows.

'I have a message for Isobel Crowe.'

It was very likely. Messages were one thing children were good for. 'Come inside,' Isobel said, 'and give it to me. I'll buy you something to eat.'

The child shook its head. 'Not in there. Come with me.'

Isobel laughed mirthlessly. She wasn't falling for that one.

'You are bored, Crowe. They know you are bored. They have a job for you. One you will like. It is ... a challenge. This is the night. It will not come again.'

Maybe she was a little drunk, but the words meant something to her.

'Come with me, Crowe. They know you. They will give you what you ask for . . .'

She thought, not of diamonds and money, but of a stern opponent, bright-bladed and dangerous. With witty eyes and a thin-lipped, silent mouth; sleek and fell, who would know her measure, and not know fear.

'I'll come,' she said.

Aelwin waited, but not for very long. She wasn't thinking about the Slaughter of Widmark now. She wasn't thinking about much except for all the reasons she should not have let Crowe go out alone. The thing to do was to hurry and catch up with her. They could meet at the Cock and Hoop, and walk back together. But she couldn't find her sandals.

Finally she discovered them lying against the double doors. She wondered what they were doing there. She pulled them on, and fastened her robe, and clattered down the stairs and out into the night.

Isobel Crowe followed the child out of the Old City. It seemed sure of the way, though it bore no light; and she followed surely in the white gleam of its body. They passed through the artisans' quarter, the echoes of their feet whispering off the bolted shutters. On to broader streets, now, the occasional clip-clop of carriage horses passing by, the drumming hooves of outriders, their torches streaking the road with shadow. Closely packed houses gave way to gates and green lawns (spreading grey now in the starlit dark): the manors of the rich, where Isobel had been before. Still they walked on.

Isobel drew closer to the child. 'Aren't you tired?' she asked. 'Do you want a rest?'

'It isn't far,' the child answered. 'They are waiting.'

And she knew that they were. A special summons, just for her, and the night stretching on in endless walking, past the houses and on into the fields with their windmills and empty shacks. And through the fields alongside a silver stream that flowed backwards into the shadows of trees. And then the shadows engulfed her.

'Where are you?' Isobel said. 'I can't see!'

'Don't stop now,' the liquid voice chimed from between the trees. 'Come!'

And, following the voice, Isobel Crowe pushed her way between branches, pulling her feet free of the tangle of root and thorn. Her hands were scratched, and her face was helpless against things she could not see. Blindly, she pushed on; anything was better than being left alone in the dark.

It was dark on the Old City streets. Aelwin couldn't see her feet. She didn't like it. She cut over to Allen's Way, which was broad enough to let some light in between the buildings, although it was the longer route to the tavern. Even so, she nearly tripped over a body lying huddled in the road. The ragged bundle looked up at her, cursing in a muddy voice: 'Trying to kill us all . . . I warned 'em, trying to kill me, trying to kill you . . .'

She hurried down the street. Don't run, she told herself, they know you're frightened when you run. It would be better when she found Crowe. Behind her the man had risen to his feet and was screaming, 'Kill your feet! Kill your head!' A couple coming from the other way crossed the street to avoid him.

The tavern lights promised warmth and comfort. But as her foot touched the threshold, she stopped. Isobel was not there. Isobel had never gone in at all. She wished she didn't know it quite so strongly; that she could pretend there was a point to going inside where there was light, and people. Shakily, Aelwin turned back into the dark street. Nothing ever came out the way she wanted it.

There was nothing in front of her. In the moment before she opened her eyes, Isobel thought she had fallen off a cliff. But she was in a clearing. There were no trees, no branches; only the flat silver disc of a pool made mirror by starlight. Its reflected glow made it possible to see; but the eerie light did not comfort her.

'Crowe.'

She whirled around swiftly, but there was nothing. 'Show yourself,' she said. The leaves around her rustled. Her ears were straining for a sound she could recognise: a footstep, the sweep of cloth ... The wind made a noise she couldn't hear through.

'No golden bells, no banners ...' said the voice, neither male nor female, resonant as thunder, colourless as the wind. 'You do not know how to hunt me, street-stalker.'

'I was brought here.' Her own voice was pitiful; her words meant nothing.

'Come!' She saw a flash of gold, the sun's gold, the midnight trees. Almost she started after it, but her feet were rooted to the ground – by her will, and not by her will: she was afraid to move. She had never known terror like this; not in a fight, not in the city streets.

'We have found a prize for you, Crowe.' The voice – if it was the same voice – came now from the other side of the clearing.

'A prize worthy of your mettle. We desire to be hunted. Do not fear us. Come after us.'

But they were mocking her. They knew she was afraid. Their voices fed her fear. She didn't want to see them now.

'Oh, Isobel,' the wind sighed, 'oh, Isobel ...'

She put her hands over her ears. 'Who are you?' she shouted.

'We have forgotten our names,' said the voice. 'Hunt us,

hunt us with banners and bells as you once did. Call out to us, that we may remember. We have been longing for you. We woke in a strange place, where your sword was bright with death. We wanted to follow you, but not in that place. Our place is here, at the centre of the moonless night. We came here, and you came after us, my hero.'

On the pond, a darkness stirred. Isobel looked behind her and saw empty glade; but across the mirrory water behind her own reflection a man's head and torso were rising. A man's head, with a goat's horns and ears –

Fear was choking her. But the tiny cold portion of her brain that spoke to her when she was in emergency was saying, *Don't run. If you run now, you'll never be able to stop*.

Seeing him in the water was better than not knowing where he was at all; and if he wasn't really there he couldn't really touch her. Another figure now was staining the pond, whiter than the stars' own image. Rippling over the surface of the water across from her, although the glade shone empty. Again that flash of gold; and fire, white fire in the shape of a horse, a terrible glory on the water –

'Maiden,' said the golden-horned creature, its thundery voice rich with surprise. 'Maiden, let me come to you.'

Its reflection burned its way around the edges of the pool. The ache in Isobel's right hand resolved itself into the metal she was clasping: the hilt of her sword. The feel of it made her want to run just a bit less.

'Stand off,' she said to the thing that was not there, drawing her blade. She pointed it at the reflection of the golden horn, and then felt it twist in her grasp, as though the sword were trying to escape her. *The weight was wrong – the weight was wrong*. Even the tiny cold portion of her brain was suffused with horror. She was wielding a black and twisting snake, moored to the hilt that was all that was left of her sword. She couldn't throw away her sword – the little grain of thought seemed to have gone mad –

Get rid of it! – no, not the hilt, she knew that hilt, it fit her hand, it was being twisted out of her hand by the living, flat-headed blade.

And for the first time she heard the laughter of the goat-eyed man.

Another figure appeared now in the water: a woman, her hair long and dark. A light hung about her that was neither sun nor stars. She lifted one arm, its reflection shining over Isobel's head. And the wind, and the terrible laughter, stopped.

'Let the invisible be made visible.'

Isobel's sword was still. And so she found the courage to look behind her. The goat-eyed man was goat-hoofed as well. He was smaller than she'd expected, but just as monstrous. And across the glade, the white beast dipped its horn in the water and touched its own image.

'Very good,' said the woman sternly. 'Now hear me: I raised you by accident, and I'm sorry. I called on power without knowing its source. You are not wanted here. You must go deep into the heart of the forest, and not come near the city, and leave Crowe alone. Your time will come, but it is not here.'

'Maiden,' the white horse's breath stirred the pond, 'will it be soon?'

'It may be soon. I'll do my best. But now is not the time. Now go, and quickly; for the dawn is coming, and the new moon's rising. And may I add,' she added shyly, 'that you are both very beautiful ...'

The horse turned a tail of white flame, and the goat-man leapt into the trees. As if only they had been holding back the dawn, now a grey light glimmered, and a few birds began to sing.

'Thank you, Aelwin,' Crowe said gruffly.

'I think I had better sit down,' Aelwin muttered. 'I think I might throw up.'

Crowe wet her handkerchief and put it on the back of Aelwin's neck.

'It won't be hard to get back,' Aelwin said when she could talk again, 'just follow the stream to the fields. From there you can see the city.'

Isobel thumped her fist on her thigh in disgust. 'Of course! I should have – '

'No, you shouldn't!' Aelwin snapped back angrily. 'You were facing Powers of the woods at night, on their ground. You were incredibly brave. Nobody else could have done it without panicking – nobody! I don't *ever* want to hear you reproach yourself for *anything* about this night. You were incredible.' She twisted her fingers together. 'Anyway, it was my fault. I tried to save you from that tavern duel when I didn't know the first thing about it. I let something loose in the city and I didn't even try to find out what it was – inadequate research habits,' she muttered. 'I thought it would go away because it didn't belong there. I thought it was pestering you because it couldn't get to me. It didn't occur to me that you were one of *them*.'

'One of *what*?' Isobel demanded, rankled by Aelwin's tone. 'I don't have a horn growing in the middle of my forehead!'

'A hero,' Aelwin said glumly. 'That's why you followed the sending from the tavern to here. It called to you, and you had to come. They never call to *me*.'

'You're too clever for them. They do what you tell them to.'

Aelwin was picking blades of grass and tossing them aside, scowling. 'I'm a nincompoop. An incompetent. *The Pathways of Love*, that's all I'm good for.'

Emma's book! 'Did *you* write that?'

'My friend Beata and I did. We needed the money to stay in school,' she said defensively. 'She was Rupert Magus – I was Levinson. I still get royalties – I'll be able to pay you back soon.'

'Aelwin,' Crowe said with desperate patience, 'let me get this straight. You're some kind of witch – '

'No, no, no!' Aelwin began pacing around the glade. She made a pretty picture with her long strides, her loose hair flying and her exaggerated gestures. 'You *haven't* got it straight at all! There *is* magic in the land. The old lady was right. You have to be born here; and you can't practise it anywhere else. That's why magiae were never a valuable export item. Aelmarl and all the old kings thought themselves unconquerable because of it. But the Norlaners figured out a way to take the country, *and* make the magiae helpless just long enough to round them up like any fallen people and kill them. Men, women and children; teachers and students – they weren't taking any chances. I don't know how it was done: treachery, I suspect. Of course they didn't leave any records. If you'd just wiped out an entire population for the purpose of eliminating their knowledge from the earth, you wouldn't want to leave any traces for people to come upon in later years and get interested in.'

'But some escaped, right? And you're a descendant – '

Aelwin sneered. 'My great-something-grandfather was a Norlan captain. It's a talent that runs in the land, not in particular families. But talent's not enough. There are probably hundreds of potential magiae running around. You have to have training. It's a complicated art. If you'll pardon the obvious parallel: Suppose you'd never seen a sword all your life, or heard of swordplay. It's pretty unlikely you'd just pick up a willow wand and start poking people with it.'

'How did you learn, then?' Isobel breathed.

'The same way I learn everything: from the book. Of course the Norlaners took care to find them all and burn them, too. Oh, it was a great time to be alive. Everyone was scared to death: neighbours were turning each other in for hiding books ... Anyhow, my friend Beata and I were crawling around in a school attic we shouldn't have been in, where students' trunks are stored. We were looking for a box of hers she'd left over the summer. Wedged in between the rafters we found a terribly old trunk, all of wood. It looked as though someone had left it and forgotten it was there. It held what you'd expect: clothes, lamp, toasting fork – and books. First year studies in elementary magic. Also a little hand-written notebook full of love charms, with prolific comments on how well they'd worked. Halmar, his name was; and he never came back for it.'

She was standing quite still, now, her face taut with grief.

'Is that what you made the *Pathways* book out of?' Isobel asked, to keep her from crying.

'Yes. We thought, even if they really turned out to work for one person in three hundred, it would only spread general happiness. It couldn't hurt. We thought. That was before we got called up before the Deans. First it was for compromising our academic principles with such nonsense – the *Pathways* book, I mean. No one knew about the real magic books. Then they discovered an old statute in the University code against witchcraft – dating from guess when? Ha-ha, what superstitious fools even those old scholars were; but there it was in the rules, ladies, now pay up or get out.' For a moment, Aelwin's face brightened. 'The Dean actually tried some of the *Pathways of Love* spells at the trial. Of course they didn't work for her: it's a talent, you know, like being able to sing.'

Isobel nodded, remembering Aelwin's tuneless warblings in the bath.

'Beata paid a fine and stayed. She needs her degree – it would kill her parents if she left. And she wants to become a lecturer. In history. She has a whole theory about looking through archives – it was very useful for researching the massacre.'

'I thought women weren't allowed to lecture in public.'

For the first time, Aelwin smiled. 'I'd like to see them try to stop her.' She pushed her hair back from her face. 'Me, I turned and walked out. I don't need them – and there's nothing I want to study much.'

'Except magic.'

'I learned all those books could teach me. And you saw how well I did with it in that tavern fire! I'm doomed to be a first-year student for the rest of my life.'

'That's not what you said to those . . . powers. You said you would try.' Crowe made an intuitive leap. 'Where are the other books, Aelwin?'

'North,' Aelwin said, her jaw set. 'I think they're upcountry, if there are any at all. Hidden in the wilderness, where even the army couldn't go.'

'Then we'll go there.' She heard herself say it with perfect certainty, and knew as soon as she had that it was right.

Aelwin smiled lazily. 'My dear Isobel, do you know what there is upcountry? Pine trees and bears. Snow and more snow. The food is awful, the entertainment worse. You'd be bored out of your mind.'

'I think,' said Isobel stoutly, trying to match her studied carelessness, 'that I need a little training in woodcraft. The city is so dull these days, so . . . unchallenging.'

'I think,' said Aelwin, 'that it will be enough of a challenge to walk all the way back to your place without falling asleep. Do you have some money? I'd like some breakfast, and then I'm going to bed. In my rookery.'

'All right,' said Crowe. 'What kind of bears?'

A Mystery Story in Two Parts

JENNIFER MCLEAN

Jennifer McLean's story is intended for telling, or at least reading aloud.

The first part is called *Your Own Free Range Egg Supply*. It concerns a woman and some animals of which one is a small ginger cat named Sappho.

The story is set in Dunedin, very much Dunedin as you know it, except that, located within the city boundary, is the Garden of Eden. Eve makes a brief significant appearance, and, as you already know, when Eve is involved, the management is usually upset.

Noeline has a great liking for eggs from free range hens. Accordingly, one day Eve brings her some from the hens that range so freely in the Garden of Eden. Noeline eats most of them but somehow one is left sitting in the bowl on the table in the kitchen which is gently and continuously warmed by a coal range.

One morning Noeline comes into the kitchen to find a heap of fragmented shell in the bottom of the bowl and a small, damp, newly hatched bird drying out in the sun on the window sill.

'Good morning,' says the little bird, inclining politely towards her. 'Your own free range egg supply, and some for Sappho also,' it adds diplomatically, seeing the green and yellow eyes approaching across the floor.

Noeline is not accustomed to talking chickens.

'Are you magic?' she asks.

'No,' says the little bird, 'I am mysterious.'

'Humph,' says Sappho. 'Noeline's a mystery, too. You must be sisters.'

As it turns out, they are all sisters, all three of them, a harmonious household.

The little bird grows, down gives way to ginger feathers.

'I would have preferred red and gold, blue and green,' she says to Noeline, 'but I thought it more tactful –' and she glances towards Sappho's ginger fur. It is a good move. Sappho is besotted with the little bird.

'Did you ever see such beautiful fur?' she says as she grooms the little bird, licking each feather meticulously into place.

Sometimes in fact, Sappho is a confounded nuisance. When the little bird asks, 'How many eggs would you like today, Noeline?' before Noeline can say she wants six because she has visitors coming for lunch, Sappho chips in and says, 'None at all little bird. You just have a rest. You're working too hard.'

Useless animal.

Useless animal? Wait till you hear the rest of the story.

One day there is a knock at the door. Noeline is out so it is Sappho who strolls round the corner to see who wants what.

'Yes?' she says to the man on the doorstep.

'The neighbours are complaining you are keeping domestic poultry in conditions completely opposed to all City Council regulations and bylaws,' says the man. 'You'll have to get rid of it. I'll be back in a fortnight to check up.'

'I'm sure we can arrange something,' says Sappho. 'We do like to keep to the rules, you know.'

'Poultry,' says the man as he goes back to his car. 'Talking cats is what I'd be worried about if I lived round here.'

How right you are, man. Sappho couldn't even talk until the little bird came, now she can read as well and she hasn't wasted any time. She has read every book available on cats, including the story of *Tobermory*, so she knows what a talking cat can accomplish in terms of human discomfiture.

That night, Sappho goes prowling, sliding in doors left momentarily ajar, slipping in and out of open windows, peering through chinks in the curtains of windows closed and obscured.

Next morning, she locates herself on the pavement as the neighbours are going to work.

'Good morning,' she says to the man who is desperately sensitive about his receding hairline. 'I do like your new hairpiece.'

I shall not detail Sappho's comments to the other neighbours. You may keep my secrets and I'll keep yours, and that's the arrangement she comes to with the neighbours.

They ring the Council. 'We are mistaken,' they say. 'Noeline isn't keeping poultry. It's just a canary.'

CANARY

The little bird is very thoughtful when she hears about the canary.

'Noeline,' she says eventually, 'a canary might be rather nice.'

'I think so, too,' says Noeline. 'I like music. I used to sing in the church choir!'

'How many eggs do you need over the next three weeks?' asks the little bird.

So Noeline makes a nourishing mash for the little bird, gives her a handful of wheat and a tin of fresh water as well, and the little bird lays a three weeks' supply of eggs.

Then she arranges herself on the table in the living room, where she can get a good view of the sea, and lays one more egg, which she proceeds to incubate.

Sappho perches beside her, to keep her company and watch over the egg when the little bird leaves it once a day to attend to her affairs elsewhere. But Sappho is puzzled.

'Noeline,' she says, 'come and have a look at this egg, will you?'

'It's got music all over it,' says Noeline. ' "Ode to Joy". I recognise it, we sang it in the choir at Christmas!'

'Anything else?' says Sappho.

'Well,' says Noeline. 'It is a bit big for an egg that's supposed to produce a canary.'

'That's what I think,' says Sappho.

Smart Sappho. When is that cat ever wrong? Inexperienced, that's what the little bird is when it comes to canaries. What she hatches is a Light Sussex Rooster.

A Light Sussex Rooster is a beautiful bird – white, with a blue-black ruff round its neck and blue-black feathers in its wings and curling tail as well, but it's at least half as big again as a Ross Brown. When it crows, you can feel the vibrations a couple of metres away and you can hear it right across the block and beyond.

This time the neighbours are right. You have to admit it. It's all very well for Noeline. She reads and writes until dawn anyway, but what about the rest of us?

The moment comes. The rooster is six months old, he is ready to crow. He opens his beak and into the morning soars a perfect rendition of 'Ode to Joy'!

'No hope,' says Noeline. 'The neighbours hate Beethoven! Especially the neighbours hate Beethoven!'

There is a knock at the door. It is the neighbours.

'Get the axe,' they say. Then they add kindly, 'Don't take it to heart, Noeline. After all, it's nearly Christmas and he's a lovely size for the table.'

Dumb with grief, Noeline goes to get the axe. Sappho droops after her. But look! Look at the little bird. She is not grieved. She is sitting enigmatically, as one supervising. What is going to happen?

Noeline returns, 'I cannot find the axe,' she says.

'I shall get mine,' says a neighbour. He returns. 'I cannot find my axe,' he says.

No neighbour can find any axe. It is a mystery, whenever the neighbours want an axe to chop wood, there the axe is. Whenever they want to kill the rooster, there is no axe.

So the rooster grows unharmed and eventually the neighbours get to like Beethoven, even at sunrise. If you ask me, that's the biggest mystery of all.

'A Mystery Story in Two Parts' first appeared in *Spiral 7*, published by Spiral in association with Daphne Brasell Associates Press, New Zealand.

She Reflects Upon Her Lives

FIONA COOPER

'It's nice of you to visit,' she said, 'I've been lying here thinking and there's so much I want you to know.'

'Tell me,' I said. 'Tell me everything.'

'I was a woman,' she says, 'serving in a Roman house where the master was a writer, a philosopher possibly, and he employed a dozen scribes. It was my job to carry water, to cook, to clean, to look after the master's children, to bathe and dress the mistress.

'I was a slave, I suppose, although when you know nothing different, the word doesn't fill you with those high emotions I feel now. Anger, rage, envy, despair. I remember feeling awe and longing when I passed the high cool room where the scribes worked. Sitting quietly all day and writing, leaving their work to come to meals already prepared, leaving the table and its dirty dishes to return to their mysterious work. Was it envy? I wanted to join them, to work as they did, I didn't want to take it from them.

'Then I was married, I believe. There were children and I loved them. Again, the work of a house and family was my lot, only this time, it was my house, my family, my blood. It's different from taking orders, making your own order. Perhaps I didn't understand children – who ever understands anyone else?

'And then I was a boy. I was a poor boy who was sent to sea, and ever since, my blood has thrilled to the creak of ropes and the proud lines of old ships. I was a cabin boy, a dogsbody, the one they sent up the rigging to see where we were going, the one who hung over the side gawping at the clear waters and strange fish who swam below, gawping up at me. There was a storm, I drowned.

'Since then I have always been able to swim like a fish and there is always youth in my heart. When people have put me down as immature, somewhere, my thirteen year-old boy rubs his bare toe on a scrubbed deck and flushes with rebellion, tosses his head back with defiance and says, yah, I don't care.

'I was a prostitute one time and then one time again. I think I committed suicide the first time and had to learn it all again. My body is my own now. However bad it's been, I've never committed suicide since, although this time, once, in the darkest months, I gathered the instruments of my own death and kept them to hand. Just in case, but hoping against it, because this time I seem to know so much of what I need to learn. This time I've been lucky.

'I have killed and been killed. Even now, I wake up with nightmares about killing.

'So I know the worst. They are suicide, cruelty, murder, meanness, lying.

'The best is like dreams you hate to wake from. To love and be loved all at the same time. Friends. Happiness. Stories. Trees and flowers.

'Trees always. As a small boy on the ship, I knew the mast was a tree and I was safe there. The time, visiting the house of a great man of letters, his staircase had as its heart the trunk of an oak. I walked up with my hand on the smoothed trunk. No words. See the tree outside my window? I knew.

'I've never been wealthy, because I still wonder what it would be like. I think I have the wisdom to see that it's not a goal. I don't want it. Enough contributes to happiness, excess is a ball and chain, a fiscal vampire. Look at the wealthy of the world – it's not a good advertisement. The responsibility!

'What drew us here first, what was so strong that it pulled us into this world of clay and decay?

'It was the adventures and pleasures of the senses.

'Sight and the vari-coloured eyes that own it. The myriad shapes and colours of this planet. We influence and inform it, of course, with that immortal joyous "Why not?" that makes a million different trees and leaves and flowers and fruits, where the function is simply to produce oxygen and cleanse the air for the continuation of life. But clay fights its own needs and chops down trees for chipboard to hold setting concrete on skyscrapers where the air is conditioned. They call it progress. I hope it's circular progress, a true revolution where you return to your starting point with wisdom and knowledge. Ah, sight! Another person walks into a room and our being lights up.

'The five senses seduced us into life.

'*Smell*: the tang of woodsmoke, the scent of a field or a wood and its changing aromas in the rain and the sun. The refinement of winter when so many scents vanish, when the cold numbs our nostrils and only the strongest smell gets through. Clay insists on brick and stone to house it and squeezes plants dry to find scents to freshen the inevitable staleness of closed doors and windows. The sweet smell of another person's hot skin as they sleep with you just woken at their side.

'*Touch*: Wet leaves, rough bark, smooth silk, warm fur, another person's flesh, cotton sheets. Clear a wood and build a house and fill it with things whose texture recalls earth and grass and leaves and branches. Take metal from the heart of the earth and fashion it smooth, carve it to run your fingertips over, to please your eye. To recall the curve of a jug like a smooth stone, the bole of a tree.

'*Taste*: Plunder the world for herbs and spices and fruits and vegetables and meats to please the palate! More than the necessary fuel for the body, make of it an art form. Cordon bleu – the decadent delight of global choice is a phone call away. The taste of your lover's lips, her lovely sweat.

'*Hearing*: Voices, wind in the trees, music at the press of a button. That voice which says I love you and means it, the laughter of love, the teasing, sharing sounds that go beyond words.

Five senses interweaving through every cell of life pulsing on this planet, giving the clay beings experiences of endless pleasure. Other people! What a dazzling web to hold our spirits, reckless about the spider of decay waiting out of sight as she ravels us in.

'We are born torn apart: the clay in fear of its own mortality, the spirit yearning to regain its immortality. The body is in harness to the spirit, the spirit is in chains of skin and bone and time. Life is learning to live in harmony with our divided selves. Knowing yourself so that there is no space between thoughts and actions. Everything has its price and the – foolish – first immortals traded their ethereal foreverness for five senses and a green planet to play on. Nowadays, it seems like a bad bargain, in the global scene, with famines and cruelty and greed and pollution and genocide.

'But when I take a walk,' she said, 'in a wood,' she smiled, 'when I walk with my lover, hold her hand, hear the stream, see the birds, taste the wild grasses, smell the flowers in the sun, it is all worthwhile.

'This time round, I have the nostalgia of one who will be leaving somewhere very dear to my heart. So dear that I know it by heart. I will hold every memory of this living in my spirit, I have learnt so much, I have so much to learn, but I am aware that I will not pass this way again and this time, a door has opened somewhere so that I have been allowed to see that all the time there are choices and it is up to me to choose right.

'Yes,' she said, 'I will be leaving somewhere I love with both body and spirit, and going somewhere I yearn to be. Will you stay with me for a while? Thank you. Bring those roses close to my face and pour me some wine. You are so kind. Sit beside me and hold my hand while I look into your eyes.'

She said, 'There's one last thing I'd like. Would you ... would you sing me an old-fashioned love song?'

I sang until my heart and the dawn were breaking.

Floating

CHARLOTTE WATSON SHERMAN

I

This is a funny place. Maybe cause of the mountain standing up behind our town watching like a big old eye. Or maybe it's that lake stretching way out, reaching black to black, pushing its way cross the earth like it's in a hurry to run away from here. Or maybe it's that twisted-trunk, yellow-leaf tree next to Blue-the-wanga-man's house, with the leaves that shine like gold lamps through the trees, day or night.

But some folks say no, it's not that mountain sitting back watching over us, and it's not that black lake reaching, and it's not that old white-trunked, yellow-tipped tree next to Blue's that Reverend Daniles swears covers a hole leading from this world to the next. The thing that makes Pearl a funny kind of place is all that whispering we hear coming up from the ground.

I first heard it one day when I was walking with Miss Marius from her house to town.

Even though the only place I ever lived was in her house, I never thought of her house as mine. And don't nobody else think no different from me.

My mamma left Pearl soon as I was born, years before the last coal mine closed down and lots of colored folks left town. Folks from Mississippi, Georgia, Louisiana, Alabama. Come all the way to Washington to shake that red dirt off their feet, get those red fingers off their souls. Miss Marius always say, 'You can run to the new South, but you can't hide from the old South, not even way out here.'

But I remember when I was back in my mama's stomach, floating like a pickle in a jar. I remember what was said, the bargains struck.

I could hear them talking while I was floating, sitting in all that water.

A high dark sound, my mama's laughing and crying and a long, sharp tone, smooth as the knife Miss Marius used to cut meat from bone. I remember Miss Marius talking, talking, saying the same words over and over till my mama's cry turned into a stretched-out moan.

And Miss Marius going around in the water with me. Going around in the tart, dark liquid. The low sound of her voice stroking me inside that bag, inside that wineskin where I floated in a dream.

'What did you take, Nola? What did you put up inside yourself, child? Tell me. I'm gonna help you and I'm gonna help this baby, too, but you got to tell me what you put into yourself. I got most of the okra out, but what else? What was it, Nola? Was it something from inside the house, something from the woods?'

And Miss Marius and my mama went around, circling till my mama, exhausted, let the words fall from her lips like some hard, funny shaped stones. 'Blue told me to use cedar berries and camphor,' she said, and that's all I remember from when I was in my mama's stomach. But folks didn't know I even remember that, not even Miss Marius, cause them first years Miss Marius's deep voice and big-knuckled hands was all the mama I thought I'd need.

'Hush that foolishness, child,' Miss Marius always say. 'Everybody needs they mama and you got one just like everybody else. She'll be back when she gets a notion.'

But it scared me when Miss Marius talk like that. I don't know if I like my mama's notions. The very first one she ever took about me left me shriveled up and gasping inside her womb.

That's why I come out looking so old and wrinkled everybody took to calling me Raisin. But I don't think it's the wrinkles that make me look old. I think it's like Miss Marius says, I'm an old old soul.

We live out on the edge of town on the east side, where all the colored people live. Miss Marius's house is the last one you come to fore you hit all them trees and marsh at the edge of the lake, out where old Blue lives.

We live in what used to be an old rooming house. We got a downstairs and a front room and a kitchen with a big black stove.

Upstairs is where we all sleep. Miss Marius and Nathan in the big room at the front of the house with that window letting in all the light from the world.

Miss Marius and Nathan got no children of they own, but Lucille and Lucinda are sisters and they act like they the ones come outta Miss Marius's body, even though Miss Marius say we all her children. Since they been here the longest, longer than my twelve years, they both get to sleep in that room big enough to be a play yard, with all them goop-de-goos they got spread out all around the floor. They both got white-painted beds with flowers all scrolled around they head so when they laying in em, it's like they laying inside a wreath, kind of like a halo around their heads.

I sleep with MC and Wilhelmina and Douglass in the back bedroom, in that big old brown bed that we climb up on to with a stool. It be tight sometimes with all us squeezed up in it, but I'm just glad I don't have to share the bed with Lucille.

Lucille gonna be big, just like Miss Marius. She got a thick-waisted body and short, strong legs. Her neck's thick too, and strong enough for all the yelling she think she gotta do. She like to drop her head back and yell loud as she can.

Her hair ain't black and thick like mine, it's the color of a tree trunk and eyes the color of moonstone.

One time at supper, I made the mistake of trying to tell her how pretty I thought her eyes was, but she raised herself up like a rattler in her chair and hissed, 'Shut your mouth, you old wrinkled-up raisin, fore I put you in a box and sell you to Miss Lomax to eat.'

Everybody at the table laugh when she say that, they scared not to. But Miss Marius and Nathan never crack a smile.

I didn't mind. Whenever they start talking about how wrinkled up and black I am, I just close my eyes and think of a warm soft place like a tub of hot water I can lay my body down in, or a nice dark space like a womb.

Lucille say don't nobody love MC, Wilhelmina, Douglass and me, and that's how come we living with Miss Marius and Nathan. MC ain't nuthin but a baby, so it always make him cry when she say that, but Wilhelmina, Douglass and me all about the same size, so we don't cry, we just look at her.

'Your mamas left you on Miss Marius's porch like a sack of bad-luck pennies. Ain't nobody ever gonna love you,' she liked to say, knowing nobody try to talk about how her own mama left her and Lucinda.

When she say that I think of the time Douglass stuck his hand in a bucket of snakes and pull out three so I won't have to, like Lucille was trying to make me do. And Douglass about as scared of snakes as me.

Douglass's mama took all her children but him back to Memphis a while after the mine closed. She left him with Miss Marius so he'd be in good hands.

'That boy slow, Miss Marius. Look at the way that eye jumps, the way he rocks on his feet. He can't make it on this long trip. Can he stay with you till I get settled? I'll send for him soon as I do.'

Miss Marius say, 'I'll keep him till you ready, Louisa. Y'all go on and make your home.'

Wilhelmina's mama did her about the same as mine did me, cept she use a wire to try to get Wilhelmina out, but it didn't work.

'She a special child, Leona, that's why she here. Leave her with me. I'll take care of her,' Miss Marius say.

Wilhelmina got a mark, look like a blue moon setting on her face. I think about how she sit with MC humming soft as water in his ear the times he sound like there's a hole in him so deep nuthin but water could fill it up.

I think about the way we sleep, four brown spoons with our arms around each other. And I look at Lucille when she say don't nobody love us.

I look at her mean as that goat Miss Marius call Moses on account of his white beard hanging down to the ground. I look at her mean as Moses look at us and I say, 'No, you lying, Lucille. Somebody do love us.'

And I don't even flinch when she grab me by the two plaits Miss Marius wove into my head, I don't even yell when she pull out the weave and swing me by my plaits to the ground.

I only remember the time I was over to Miss Lomax's house when she first got her new TV and out of the blue glowing in the screen I saw a cowboy jump out of a box and dig his heels into a horse's sides. The man jumped off the horse and grabbed a cow by the horns and tried to drag the cow down to the ground.

And when Lucille swung me down by my plaits into the dirt, just like that cowboy roped that cow, I jumped up with a wild look still in my eyes and say, 'You're still lying.' But my legs were turning like wheels on the road.

II

This my secret place. My green, green holy place, inside this circle of red cedar trees, next to that big-leaf maple with moss that clings to it like smooth green skin.

Even the ground is green and covered with leaves, leaves my teacher Miss Dubois say is called oxalis. I put one of the leaves in my mouth and taste its juicy sour, then rub the green softness into my wrinkled skin.

'One day these wrinkles be gone and my skin be smooth and soft as these leaves. One day it will,' I sing into the ears of licorice ferns and salmonberry. Then I lay down to dream on a wild ginger blanket, my smooth, soft second green skin.

A woman comes down the road toward me, a small black bag in one hand. Her eyes are knives and she is not smiling. Behind her is a bright gray cloud. It is raining white balls, but she is not wet. The woman's arms reach for me, brown and unwrinkled. She opens her mouth, but no sound comes out. I turn from her and run toward the black lake. The woman is behind me, running. She is fast, almost faster than me. I run to the edge of the lake, look back at her reaching hands, her mouth opened like an O. I jump.

The water's coolness soothes me, then starts to burn. I call for help, but she is the only one there, standing, waiting at the edge. My head slips below the surface. I scream as I go down.

'Wake up, girl. What's wrong with you?'

I open my eyes and see Sin-Sin standing over me. he's the color of that stone Miss Dubois got on her desk, Brazilian agate. His skin so bright it shines.

'What are you doing in my secret place, Sin-Sin?'

'This ain't your secret place,' Sin-Sin say. 'It ain't

nobody's secret place cause it ain't even no secret. I walk around back here all the time. So does Blue.'

'I never saw neither one of you down here before and I always come down here.'

'Well, so do we. What are you doing falling asleep out in the woods, girl? Don't you know all kinds of things be out here waiting on somebody like you?'

Sin-Sin ain't but fourteen, so I know he don't have to talk like I ain't got good sense.

'Ain't nuthin out here waiting on me no more that it waiting on you. How come you walking around down here?' I ask.

'To get away from my mama,' he say.

'What you want to get away from Miss Dubois for? She nice.'

'That's cause she ain't you mama. She was, you'd be running down here hiding, too.'

'I wish my mama was a schoolteacher,' I say.

'That's cause you ain't never lived with a schoolteacher mama before, that's all. Once you get a taste of all the books she make you read, you be glad you got the mama you got.'

'Miss Marius my mama.'

'That's right? I thought she Lucille and Lucinda's mama.'

'She is, sort of. She our mama, too: me and Wilhelmina and MC and Douglass, she our mama, too.'

'Your mamas left all of you for Miss Marius to keep?' he ask.

'Uh huh,' I say back.

'You're lucky. Mamas are hard on you, making you work all the time around the house, and read all the time and study figures and wash your hands fore you come in the kitchen and always wanting you to clean your ears. And they don't want you to talk like you want to talk. I wish mine would leave me with Miss Marius.'

'Miss Marius all right. I can't stand Lucille. Always act like a razor in her mouth,' I say.

'She's big. Don't nobody mess with Lucille.'

'I told her she a lie, right to her face,' I say.

'You did?'

'Yep.'

'That must be why you hiding in the woods. Lucille gonna get you good for saying that.'

'She ain't gonna get me cause I ain't going back there. I'm gonna stay here and live in these woods,' I tell him.

'How you gonna eat and get clean clothes?'

'I'm gonna eat salmonberries and mushrooms. And I'll make some dresses and pants out of leaves.'

'What about school? My mama's gonna want you to do your homework. She don't care where you live.'

'You could bring my books to me out here. And I could give you my schoolwork for Miss Dubois,' I say.

'My mama don't want me mixed up in no trouble. She say plenty trouble waiting in the world for me later on.'

'I ain't talking about getting in no trouble. Miss Marius say never trouble trouble till trouble troubles you, but she usually be talking about white folks,' I say. I look in Sin-Sin's face, see the sticks and dirt clotted in his hair, the long red scratch reaching cross one cheek like a streak of lightning, the dry white mud on his blue pants.

'You going around looking like that and you worried about getting in trouble for taking my schoolwork to your mama?' I ask. He duck his head.

'I ain't never known you to be scared of no trouble before, Sin-Sin.'

'You don't know nuthin about me, girl,' he say.

Sin-Sin wrong. I know some things. Heard Miss Marius grumbling, 'Ain't nuthin worse than a mind sitting still. Ain't nuthin left for a empty mind to do but worry about other folks' business. Miss Dubois a fine woman. Just what this town needs, and some folks still want to worry over how she got that baby.'

Once I hear Miss Lomax say Sin-Sin was the devil's baby. When I ask what she mean, she say on account of his color, that orange-burning red.

'It ain't natural,' she say. 'What colored folks you know walk around glowing like that?'

I look in Sin-Sin's face now and touch it one time. That soft burning skin. He don't like folks to make much of it, though.

I tell him, 'You're used to living inside all that shine. All I got is these old wrinkles.'

'They don't look no worse than nuthin else to me. Besides, I like old folks,' he say, walking backwards from my secret place, into the fading dark, into the trees.

I go back to Miss Marius's that night. Walk straight up to Lucille and wait. Close my eyes though. I'm too scairt to look death straight in the face.

'Where you been, honey? We already ate, but there's a plate on the stove you can warm,' Miss Marius call out from the front room where she sit with her eyes closed, letting the day settle in her bones.

I open one of my eyes and look at Lucille. She look at me so long I open my other eye.

'You ain't got no sense,' was all she say before walking into the front room to sit with Miss Marius.

Then it seem like every time I go to my secret place, Sin-Sin there. We run through the trees and play explore, picking up leaves and bugs and mushrooms.

We pull some big sticks and leaves together into something looking like a shack, but Sin-Sin say it gonna be a tree house like he read about in a book his mama give him.

'We can't call it that, cause I ain't climbing up in them trees,' I tell him so he can hurry and get that thought out of his head. These trees around here big and tall, go back a long, long way, clear back to what Miss Dubois call Lewis and Clark. He poke out his lips a bit, but we still don't put that house up in them trees.

We find two big rocks for chairs and a piece of log for a table. Most times we just sit inside and tell stories.

'I asked Miss Marius where the Night People come from and she say they always been here. She say one time she saw the Night People down here,' I say.

'What she say they look like?' Sin-Sin ask.

'Just like everybody say, tall as some of these trees, snake-haired and yellow-eyed,' I say. 'That's how she saw one cause its eyes was glowing in the dark and she thought it was a cat way up in the branches, but when she heard it whistle, she knew it wasn't no kind of cat.'

'What was Miss Marius doing out in the woods at night? You can't see no Night People unless you out here at night,' Sin-Sin say. 'She out in the woods looking for Blue? My mama said Miss Marius and Blue was friends when they was young.'

'No. She wasn't looking for no wanga-man. She out here looking for Miss Buchanan.'

'That lady walk around all the time talking to herself and stay out by the dump?'

'Miss Marius say that how she got like she got. When they was girls they was friends and Miss Buchanan was all right then.

'But one day she got it in her head to run off to the woods cause her mama had died and her daddy wouldn't stop acting like he was crying all the time, even after her mama had been dead for a long time, and Miss Buchanan couldn't take it no more cause she thought her daddy would've liked it better if she was the one to go, which wasn't true, Miss Marius say, but the girl wasn't thinking right by then, so she took off.

'Miss Marius thought she knew about where Miss Buchanan had hid herself, so she set off to go get her. Well, after she walked way up in here, she thought she'd gotten lost, which was funny for her cause she thought she knew these woods like the back of her hand, even in the dark.

'It was about then she looked up and seen them two shining yellow eyes in a tree. She thought it was a cat, but then she saw it shake its head side to side real slow and she saw them snakey ropes swing around. She couldn't make out no arms or legs, so she thought it must be sitting up in the tree.

'Then it turned them yellow eyes on a spot back of Miss Marius and start whistling. She say it don't sound like nuthin from this world. She still don't move a muscle, cause she think it might suck her up in them trees or something. So she stay still while she look in them eyes.

'She say it seem like something was being passed on to her while she was looking in them eyes, seem like she feel a humming in her body.

'Then she heard a moan coming from somewhere behind her. She turn her head to try to see exactly where the moan was coming from and then she hear a whirring sound and turn her head back to them eyes, but they was gone.

'She move over to the moaning and find Miss Buchanan laying on some moss. She didn't never say nuthin that made sense no more.'

'I bet they put a spell on her. That's what they supposed to do if they catch you out in the woods at night,' Sin-Sin say.

'Miss Marius say she never did go back in them woods at night no more and she told us we better do the same.'

'Well, all I know is, I'm not scared of no Night People whistling and carrying on,' Sin-Sin say.

'What you gonna do if one sees you? Them people carry spears and can fly. What you gonna do if you come up against one of them?' I ask.

'Blue say Night People only bother people who bother

them or theirs. He say they ain't nuthin but old ones who've gone before us.'

'What he mean?'

'He mean Night People ain't nuthin but spirits.'

'Spirits . . . like ghosts?'

'Yeah. People that are there, but we just can't see them. Blue say spirits around us all the time.'

I look outside our house into the listening trees. I hear birds talking, leaves brushing against each other. I look at Sin-Sin's eyes shining in the light and I know I ain't gonna tell no more stories about Night People.

One time, after I tell all the stories for about a week and Sin-Sin don't say too much of anything one way or the other, I decide I ain't gonna tell another story till he take his turn. So we pick more leaves and grass for our roof for a while and then come inside our house and sit down. Sin-Sin wiggle for a while on his chair, but I still don't say a mumbling word. He finally sit still and look at me with a face that older than mine.

'The Night People come for me one time,' he say and wrap his skinny arms around hisself and start to rock his body side to side like Douglass do to calm hisself.

'What you say?' I ask.

He close his eyes and I lean up close to his face to hear.

'They come for me once and say they gonna come back.'

Sin-Sin look like I feel thinking about the Night People coming anywhere for me.

'They come to your house?' I ask.

Sin-Sin nod his head, slow-like.

'Come right inside and got in my bed, climbed right inside my head.'

'Huh?'

'I was dreaming. I was standing near the edge of the lake. Could hear the sound of water licking the rocks. Could hold out my hand and touch the lumps on a white stick laying on the bank like a long broken arm. The air smelled like mud.

'It wasn't real. The waves was moving like a million mouths opening their lips and talking. Talking to me.

'I stepped up, close to the edge as I could get without putting my feet in the water. The black water in that lake turned orange as a tangerine.

'I felt my daddy in there.

'I put one foot in the water and the talking mouths pulled me in and I fell inside that water and floated in the dream. Didn't hear nuthin but whispers. The shushing of the waves.

'Saw a shape drift by. Something tell me, that's him. That's my daddy. I follow the shape. Move my body in the water like it do. Something hold me. Something grab my arm, turn me round. Push something solid in my mouth. I swallow. My mouth taste like rock.

'I turn my head toward the shape I think is my daddy, but he gone. The mouths, the waves tell me to hush. They hold me by my arms and rock me. Sing me a song but I can't understand the words.

'I try to say, I want my daddy. I want to go with him, but they say no. I get mad. I say no and try to get away, but red wings fly toward me in the water. I feel a huge bird grab hold of my shoulders and lift me. Then I am leaving the lake, the dark orange water, the place where I felt my daddy.

'The bird take me up in the woods to a circle of tall, snake-haired trees.

'The trees whistle and open they arms. The bird drop me in the middle of the circle and fly away, red wings glowing in the dark.

'In the whistle-talk they tell me to climb inside the trunk of the oldest tree, say I should wait inside there.

'I climb inside the white-walled hole and look out into

the yellow-eyed night. I call on my daddy cause I feel scared.

'The trees keep whistling as they cover the hole and seal me inside the darkness.'

Sin-Sin crying when he finish his story, long salty tears that move down his face leaving slug trails. The only boy I ever seen cry was MC and he ain't nuthin but a baby.

I don't know what to do with Sin-Sin's tears. So I pick up a leaf and smooth it on his face.

'It ain't nuthin but a dream story, Sin-Sin. Nuthin but a dream,' I say while I smooth the salt into his orange skin.

'I ain't never gonna know nuthin about my daddy,' he whisper.

He turn his head and look at me close.

'You ain't never gonna tell nobody about the dream, is you?'

'What I want to tell that for?' I ask back.

'You gotta promise,' he say.

'All right.'

'No, I mean you really gotta promise. We gotta seal it with blood.'

I look at him close and say, 'I ain't sealing nuthin with no blood.'

'All right. A kiss then. A soul-kiss,' he say.

'What a soul-kiss?' I ask.

'Here. I'll show you,' he say.

Sin-Sin lean up against my face and put his lips against mine. I smell the green from the leaf in his face. It smell like green water. He push his tongue in my mouth. I start to bite, but don't. Sin-Sin taste like salt. He pull his tongue out like a snake sucking in.

'That's a soul-kiss,' he say, not looking old no more. 'That's as good as a bloodseal.'

I ain't thinking about Sin-Sin and his crazy story. All I think about is telling Lucille I got something she say I ain't never gonna get.

'Whatcha'll doing in there?'

We jump back in our seats at the sound of Blue's voice. Sin-Sin know him. I don't. All I know is stories I been told.

'Blue a wanga man,' Lucille told me one time. 'You know what that is?'

'No,' I say as she pinch my arm.

'It's a man can turn hisself into a snake or a lizard or a goat. Anything he want, he can change into.'

'How you know?' I ask.

'I heard some of the grown folks talking,' Lucille say. 'They say didn't nobody know nuthin about Blue, he just up and was one day. Miss Lomax's brother say he saw him coming up from the lake, no boat, no car, no nuthin. He just come walking into town from the lake. And you know there's only marsh and trees by the lake. I bet he turned hisself into a fish, got tired of the water, and then turned hisself into a man and come up on land to walk like the rest of us.'

I didn't believe her then. Now, I don't say nuthin. Just look at the beads and shells around Blue's neck. He got a piece of glass hanging on a neck rope, shining. When I look inside the glass, everything new and shaped funny.

I wonder if that's how he do his changing. Stretch out and fall deep inside his bones. Blood shifting around like sand till he's new.

He twist his head in my direction, then turn his long neck to Sin-Sin.

'You remember what I told you, boy?' he ask.

Sin-Sin nod his head, but don't look in Blue's eyes.

'Soon as you ready, you come to see me. You hear?' he say.

Sin-Sin don't say nuthin. He keep his eyes on the floor of our treehouse-on-the-ground.

Blue grunt, then he gone.

'What he talking about, Sin-Sin? You fooling around with a wanga man?'

'You believe whatever folks tell you, don't you?' he ask. 'Don't you?'

'No. I like to find things out for myself. Plenty of times grown folks are wrong about things,' he say.

'They wrong about Blue?' I ask. 'He ain't no wanga?'

'He's a man that knows some things, things most folks are bound to forget.'

'He didn't open up a chicken's neck and drink its blood?' I ask. 'He can't turn into a snake and make your mama's heart stop beating if you look at him crosseyed?'

'Your mama's heart need to stop if you walking around looking at folks crosseyed. Blue ain't no fool.'

'What you doing messing around with him? I bet Miss Dubois don't like that!' I say.

'He say he can teach me things, things I won't learn in no books.'

'What kind of things?' I ask.

'Things he say'll help me grow into a man, things my mama don't know nuthin about.'

'He seem all right,' I say.

'He is all right. He serious is all.'

'Is that why he don't smile at folks in town?' I ask.

'He thinks that's shining, shining for white folk, and he ain't never gonna do that. Blue say he stopped smiling the day they run his daddy into the river cause his daddy hurt the white man who hurt Blue's mama. And down in Mississippi, they was like most of the colored people up here. Couldn't none of em swim. They never found his daddy's body.

'Blue say he keeps that picture in the front of his mind: his daddy running out of the house and down the road, the high round behinds of the horses chasing him, running him down to the river and in.

'Blue followed the trail of red dust the horses left behind.

Then he hid in some bushes by the river and watched. He watched his daddy fall in the fast white water. Then he saw him stand with his legs shaking, but his back straight as he walked farther into the water, till all Blue could see was bubbles where his daddy's head had been. Blue stopped talking then. He didn't talk for five or six years.'

'He tell you that?' I ask.

'How else I'm gonna know?'

'What he want with you?'

Sin-Sin duck his head like he do when Blue come. He sit still for a while with his forehead wrinkled bad as mine, then his skin smooth out and he shake his shoulders like he coming out of a dream.

'He's gonna cut me,' he say.

'What?'

'He's gonna give me a man-cut, cut me like they used to do to make you into a man.'

'You crazy?' I ask. 'What you wanna let him cut on you for? You mama know about him cutting on you? I bet she don't. I bet this something you and Blue made up.'

'No, it's real. He showed me a picture of it in a book he got.'

'Blue cutting on you is gonna be your behind, I bet.'

'My mamma ain't never gonna know,' he say.

'What?' I ask.

'I ain't gonna tell her. This something women don't know nuthin about. He's gonna ask my mama to let me spend some time with him and that's when he's gonna do it. He's been telling me things I'm gonna need to know so I can be ready.'

'How come you can't just be a man like everybody else? How come you gotta get cut?'

'So I can leave childish things behind and be a grown man, Blue say.'

'Is that all you think about, being a grown man?' I ask him, frowning.

'What else I'm gonna think about?' he ask, frowning too.

'You better think about that cutting some more. And do some thinking about your mama. I know Miss Dubois ain't gonna stand for nuthin like this,' I say.

All he say is, 'She can't make me into a man. Blue can.'

III

That the last time I see Sin-Sin in our treehouse for a while. I see him in school some time, but he turn his head like he don't wanna see me.

I try to tell him one more time I won't tell Miss Dubois or nobody else. We could make a soul-kiss if he want. But he turn from me whenever he see me coming, like he turning from something evil in a dream.

I don't mind. I keep on going to my secret place, sitting inside the treehouse and telling stories to myself.

After a while, I stop worrying about Sin-Sin and his secrets cause Miss Marius got a note from a woman saying she my mama.

I bring it out here and puzzle over it sometime. Feel the loop-de-loop of Miss Marius's name on the paper and the other strange, dangerous name.

Dear Miss Marius,

Things sure do change, so do people. What goes around comes around in a hurry they say. I'm coming around there for my child.

Please accept these few dollars as my thanks. The words'll have to wait till I come.

Nola Barnett

1653 Cottage Grove South
Chicago, Illinois

Miss Marius say this my mama. And Nola Barnett say she coming here to get me.

That's when I first heard the whispers, the ones coming up from the ground. Heard a man voice and a woman, too. The man keep calling me, calling me his baby girl.

Me and Miss Marius was walking to the depot for the woman that say she my mama. We pass by Miss Lomax's and see her husband Mr Lomax sitting with his fiddle between his knees on his porch.

'How y'all doing?' he ask.

'Fine, Mr Lomax,' we say. 'How you?'

Even Miss Marius call him Mr Lomax. He long and skinny and like to fuss with Reverend Daniles. Like to call him a jackleg preacher that keep messing with people's minds. When I ask Miss Marius what he talking about, she tell me to stay out of grown folks' foolishness.

'Don't neither one of em know what they talking about,' she always say and keep on doing what she be doing.

Miss Lomax say that fiddling belong to the devil, so she get a brand new TV to run so Mr Lomax won't play. But he still do. Sit right up in the room and fiddle like it the end of the world, Miss Marius say. Even with that TV set on.

Miss Lomax act like she don't hear him, keep right on watching that blue light on the TV. Some nights you can hear them both, the TV and the fiddle going on into the night.

'I gots my fiddle back, so I'm all right,' Mr Lomax say as we pass.

'Somebody took your fiddle, Mr Lomax?' Miss Marius ask.

'Somebody tried to take it, but I'm too old and smart for that,' he laugh as we walk on down the road.

When we on the stretch of road between Miss Lomax's and Miss Dubois's, I hear them.

'What's that?' I ask Miss Marius, who keep on walking down the road.

'What's what?' she ask, still walking.

I stop dead in the middle of the road and listen. 'You hear that?'

'I don't hear nuthin but my heart beating in my ears from all this walking,' she says. 'You better hurry. We don't want to keep your mama waiting.'

I don't tell her I wait. All my life and I don't even know I'm waiting. Don't say, let her wait, let her sit there and think about things like I do.

But I keep hearing the voices, they start to build in my ears till I almost scream, but I don't. Miss Marius'd think I don't want to go see Miss Nola that say she my mama.

I don't want to go see her, but it's the whispers that stop me from moving.

The whispers jump up from the ground and settle in my bones till my body gets heavy like a big piece of wood and I'm stuck. A man voice calling, 'Baby girl... Baby girl, I'm here now, watching over you.' My legs take root and I stand in the road with my arms stuck out.

The whispers move through my body, a humming in my bones that circles round my waist tight as a belt and I can't breathe, can't move, can't even open my mouth to call out to Miss Marius.

'Baby girl. Baby girl,' voices say under the whispers. The whispers sound like white-capped water swirling round inside my head till I think I'm gonna fall from the weight, but I don't.

The whispers hold me still and fill up my head with an old watery sound... WHOOSHBEE... WHOOSHBEE... WHOOSHBEE... WHOOSH-BEE...

'Floating' is an extract from Charlotte Watson Sherman's novel *One Dark Body*, published by The Women's Press.

Bats

LEIGH KENNEDY

I didn't know much about bats until recently. I knew only frightening things about them – that they carried diseases and lived in spooky caves and slept upside down. That some of them drank blood.

The first bat arrived on Christmas Day. It was a sunny, crisp day and I was dressing more formally for the chicken dinner I had cooked for myself and a widower neighbour of mine, Mr Charles. From my bedroom window on the top floor, I could see the narrow strips of wintry grass and flower beds filled with the brown skeletons of shrubbery. Mr Charles was still pottering in his garden, inspecting his winter-flowering alpine bed.

My bedroom window was open because I was going to call out to my neighbour, to tell him that he could come around any time now. But something small and black whooshed past my head, banged into the bedroom door, fluttered clumsily around the room, then scuttled and scratched its way to the top of the old oaken wardrobe. Once it halted it made a small honking noise, like a little boy imitating a diesel engine, as it looked at me with tiny bright and beady eyes, wings outstretched and trembling.

The bat and I stared at each other. He was terrified. Even in my ignorance and own nervousness, I could sense his fear.

'Go away,' I said, feebly, looking around for something to shoo it with. I picked up a magazine and waved it at the bat. The bat made a sound like a stuttering micro-wail. If it had been the roar of a lion it wouldn't have made my heart leap higher. I jumped back, dropping the magazine. The bat folded its wings and settled.

'Out!' I said, shivering with disgust. 'Out!'

The tiny eyes blinked and looked beyond me, as if I had been assessed and he realised how un-dangerous I really was. The bat almost seemed to nod towards the window.

'What are you doing up in the middle of the day anyway?' I demanded, sounding like a mother of a teenaged son discovered out of school.

Something about the bat relaxing made me feel calmer too. I turned, thinking, I will have to ask Mr Charles. I leaned out of the window but the old man was gone from his garden. The sash window was stubborn but I managed to pull it down.

The bat began to squeak and flutter again, hopping from foot to foot. Just as I turned my head to look at him, a spot in the sky caught my attention. The spot was black in that damp, blue December sky. It grew larger. It was coming my way.

'No!' I screamed, too late to warn, too late to open the window, too late.

The black spot hurtled through my window. Glass and blood exploded into the room – carpet, bedcovers, pillows, a porcelain lamp splattered with crimson and sparkling slivers. I felt stinging cuts on my face and arms but no terrible wounds.

The second bat lay on the floor just beside my bed. It twitched and bled. I gently turned it over with the rolled up magazine but it was dead, or within a moment of death; glass shards speared its body, head and wings. I looked up at the first bat. He had turned to the wall, head drooping.

Mr Charles thought my story very odd indeed, but he couldn't give me any more advice than to feed the bat on my wardrobe some rat poison. He was a bit irritated because of the delayed dinner; however, he made absolutely no motion to climb the stairs to help me clear the mess when I explained.

So, I swept and scrubbed in the company only of the first bat, who turned around again to watch as the dead bat was rolled in a newspaper shroud. I studied the bat's face – ugly, it was, but not a stereotypical look. He had small, pointed ears and a long boar-like snout which ended in rippling nostrils. He returned the gaze from tiny, blinking eyes, then turned around and covered his head again.

'I'm not going to poison you,' I said softly. At the moment, I felt more kindness towards this unexpected visitor than to the grumpy man downstairs. But poor Mr Charles was not an animal lover; I had to forgive him for the suggestion because he had no experience of pets other than the cats his wife had loved.

After the Christmas meal, I phoned a local animal society to get some advice.

'Throw a towel over its head and toss it out the window,' the woman said, obviously annoyed that I had a problem on a holiday.

I couldn't. Somehow I just couldn't. Something about the way the bat looked at me made me feel it had chosen me for some sort of protection. A silly idea, but unshakeable.

That night, because I knew something of vampire bats, I shut the bedroom door tightly and slept on the sofa. The next morning it seemed to have disappeared but then I discovered it asleep, hanging from the clothes rail in the wardrobe. A pair of shoes was ruined from droppings but no other damage had been done.

I put some bread out for it which looked a bit nibbled the next day.

A man came to replace the broken window. He didn't like working in the room with the bat. Underlying all our communication, I could feel him thinking, 'Silly cow, why doesn't she just chuck the bat out?' But he was polite enough to me and got used to the quiet bat by the end of the job.

A trip to the library in the following days helped only slightly. I found a book which told me a lot about bats – diagrams of their skeletons, chapters on their echo-location and aerodynamics, the varieties and their habits. I decided that my bat was a hammer-headed fruit-eating bat, a native of Africa. I set a plastic bowl of fruit salad on the wardrobe that night before going to bed and the next morning it was gone.

But the book didn't answer the questions I continued to ask myself. Where had it come from? Was it an escaped pet? I noticed scars on the wings and wondered if it had been abused. What had terrified it so? Had it been with the second bat? Why wasn't he more timid of me?

He had grown rather placid – sitting up at night, little eyes like black beads in the dim light cast by the hallway light. I talked to him. I asked him the questions but he never answered. He never made a noise other than of movement.

Besides notifying the police, I phoned zoos and wildlife parks in the region. 'Have you lost a hammer-headed bat?'

'No, but let us know if you want to give him to us!'

New Year's Eve, nearly one week later, I stayed at home. Mr Charles was in a grump because I had declined his invitation to the local and because I hadn't taken his advice and poisoned the bat. 'Have you still got that horrible creature in your house?' he asked every time I saw him.

When the last minute of the old and the first minute of the new year met, I opened the window of the bedroom, hoping to catch some of the fireworks display from the top of Castle Hill, just visible from that window.

WHOOSH! *Whoosh!* I was nearly knocked back in the room by the two rockets sailing in through my window.

Bats! More bats! They flew in frantic circles around the

room, screeching and crying. One lit on the lamp fixture hanging from the ceiling, swinging it and crying. Another just flew around and around. In the dim light, I could see that these bats were different, with little mouse-like faces.

'What on earth is going on?' I shouted.

The first bat came to the edge of the wardrobe and looked calmly at the newcomers. Squeaks were exchanged. I moved towards the window. All three bats stuttered excitedly at me. I froze.

One more. Two, three, four more. Five. Six, seven. Seven more bats arrived within five minutes.

The following day, I contacted the local newspaper. A reporter came around. My bedroom was now covered in sheets to protect the furniture and things; bats sat on the bookshelves (cleared of books), on my chest of drawers, on the wardrobe, on the headboard of the bed. There were different faces – another hammer-headed bat, long-eared bats, horseshoe bats, a nectar-feeding bat, and two incredibly ugly leaf-nosed bats. Bats native to lands all around the world.

'Where did you get them?' the reporter asked.

'They just flew in the window, all in a panic. As you can see, they are calm now.' They were, in fact, sleeping.

The reporter looked over his shoulder at the window, where the curtains were drawn. 'Just flew in. Like bats outa hell, I suppose.' He laughed.

'Yes, I suppose so.'

You can imagine the headline. Me, my face stretched and distorted by a wide-angle lens, the bats on the bookshelves nodding above me. There had only been one photo – the bats had risen in a frightening chorus after the first flash and flushed the reporter back down to the kitchen.

The doorbell rang early in the evening on the day the newspaper appeared. A young, very pale, but handsome young man stood on the step. He was strikingly blond with translucent skin and a scattering of golden freckles on his face. He wore a green T-shirt, jeans, canvas shoes; carried a black cloth sack in one hand and had an easy amiable smile. 'Hello. I'm here for the bats.'

'Oh. You didn't phone . . .'

I found that I had to let him in the house even though I suddenly wished the article hadn't made it so clear that I lived on my own. As soon as the door had shut, I felt uneasy. He looked around, smiling, but there was something about him . . . like one about to practise discipline on the disobedient.

From upstairs, came a terrible commotion. All the bats were squeaking, hooting, whistling, crashing against the doors. The young man ran up the stairs and I followed. The bats were all at the window, which I had closed because of cold weather. The curtain rail had been torn down. All ten of the bats were at the glass, beating it with their wings and feet, trying to bite the slippery surface. The glass was smearing with bat dung and saliva. Crying and frightened, even my first, placid hammer-head, screaming with fear.

'Who are you?' I shouted. 'Have you ever abused them?'

'They're mine,' he said, smiling.

'Where did you get them? Do you have an import licence for them?'

He laughed, and reached for one bat, who went limp in his grasp and was tucked into the black sack.

'I won't let you – !'

He stretched his arms out and everything in the room seemed to be coated with a clear gelatine. I couldn't move or speak. I could see the bats, nearly frozen, stuck to the window in terror.

The young man moved easily, plucking the bats from the air, putting them in his sack. I was helpless to stop him. Motionless. I felt that my throat would burst from wanting to scream or cry. I felt desperately small against the power as he casually swung the heavy black sack over his shoulder and walked out of the room, down the stairs and away.

Even though only five minutes or so elapsed in that gelled state, it was enough. All was gone.

After recovering from the shock of having them taken, I began to realise how honoured I had been by their presence.

I could never explain it to the few people who later enquired – from animals groups, from a zoo I had missed, from someone wanting a bat as a present for his young son – or to Mr Charles.

My life was different after that, however. I know something powerful although it gives me no power. And I keep my window open wide enough even in winter, just in case they come again.

Plane Story

ELYSE GUTTENBERG

Susan couldn't help but watch. The tall woman in the next line over definitely seemed nervous – the way she kept glancing over her shoulder then turning back to ask the ticket agent what she'd said. Waiting for a husband? Susan wondered. Or what if it was the police?

She glanced to the sign above the woman's line: 'Advance Tickets' it read. The woman wouldn't be on her plane and with luck she'd end up on a reasonably normal flight.

Susan turned to another line and then caught herself staring.

She hated doing that, sizing up everyone in line, trying to guess who they were, where they were going. Except the truth was, she had no intention of stopping.

Maybe it wouldn't make a shred of difference, studying their faces the way she did. And maybe she should give it up. Stare politely at the collar of whoever was ahead of her.

But what if there really was something to it? What if it was true that the more reasonably average and sane her fellow passengers looked, the more they'd have a vested interest in making it safely back to the East Coast? And if enough people wanted the same thing didn't it stand to reason all their hoping would increase the odds?

No terrorists plus no nuts equals no plane crashes.

Susan knew it sounded like a formula but at least it helped calm her nerves.

The line had moved forward. Susan nudged her suitcase, closing the gap.

For all her worrying, things weren't going as badly as they might have. *It was only fibrillations*, her mother had joked on the phone. *Doctor says nothing to worry about. Nothing he hasn't seen before.* But she'd sounded terrible, her voice thin, so old. And the way she'd pretended she didn't care if Susan came before the heart surgery or after, then kept asking whether Michael – her ex-husband – could give her a lift to the hospital.

The line shuffled forward. Susan would be next.

Michael. She didn't want to start thinking about Michael again. It was always too confusing, trying to figure out which one of them had changed and when. Or whether it was the world that had changed and nobody had remembered to tell her. Whatever the case, she was done with all the analyzing. Their two daughters were in college and Michael belonged to another, younger part of her life. And wasn't it better if things just stayed that way?

The elderly woman in line ahead of Susan was hugging a friend goodbye now. Going to visit a sister, Susan guessed. Maybe catch a play in Manhattan. Ordinary, safe things to do.

And there on her right stood a husband and wife with two young children. Children were good. Susan liked having them on board. The younger one in pajamas seemed just the age to start in with a long, hard wailing. Not pleasant, but at least the parents didn't seem interested in a detour to Cuba.

But that was odd. The short, heavy-set woman behind her in line? Susan hadn't noticed her before. With those awful, wrinkled pants and the stretched out home-made sweater, she looked like someone who had lost her cart in a grocery store. Rumpled white hair. Red bifocals perched on her wide, grandmother-sized chest. Their eyes met and quickly, Susan looked away.

The woman had been watching her. Susan was sure of it. Something in the way she'd been standing, as if she was trying to catch her attention. Why would a woman like that be traveling? For family? Certainly not business. But she wouldn't be a terrorist either – not with that outfit, that gushing, toothsome smile.

God, but she hated to fly.

Squeezing down the aisle on the airplane, it was the same thing. Susan held her ticket, pretending to check the seat numbers while all along she kept scanning their faces. Middle-aged men. Well dressed business-type women. One glance, that was all she needed, just enough to convince herself they had jobs, lovers, family. Even a copy of the *Wall Street Journal* could be a way of saying yes, they wanted their stocks to go up as much as the next guy. Wanted to walk up one more time to a newsstand and buy a morning paper.

In the end, it was their voices that mattered. The effect of all their combined voices working to hold up the plane. Keep it flying. Almost like a prayer. Except Susan didn't believe in prayers.

She'd tried explaining it to Brian, her second husband, whenever he asked her to go with him to church. 'How can you expect me to believe in some white-haired gentleman on a throne in the clouds,' she'd said, 'when he won't even let a woman pray unless maybe it's a Friday night and she's standing in the kitchen with the candles and the bread?'

And now Susan remembered the time Brian had read her that article about the terrorist who handed his suitcase to his girlfriend, just as she stepped up to the counter. How careful the man had been never to tell her about the bomb inside. Never really explained why he couldn't meet her till later. And the girlfriend hadn't even suspected.

Brian had called it an unsurprising development. *Given*

the assumptions of fundamentalist thinking in the oil-rich Middle East . . .

Michael at least would have found something to laugh at in the story, laughed and known it for a tragedy all the same.

Susan had the window seat. She quickly reached over, tugged the plastic curtain as far down as it would go then tried not to think about the wing. All that steel, that weight. And nothing but a line of rivets holding it all together.

''Scuse me, honey. Looks like this is my seat.'

Honey? Susan looked up. The short, older woman who'd smiled at her at the ticket line shuffled her way into the seat next to hers. The middle seat. Not the aisle. Even though that one remained empty.

Susan rearranged her skirt then pretended to read through the safety brochure from the seat-back in front of her.

With her luck, Susan figured the woman would be just the type to start in with a coast-to-coast lecture on which kind of aspirin worked best for which kind of headache. Please, she thought, don't let her be a talker. Talking meant thinking and at 12:03 a.m. she was too tired to do any more thinking.

In the aisle, the flight attendant methodically pointed out exit doors, safety lights, emergency flotation devices. The one thing Susan asked was that if anything really did happen – please, whatever God there was – let it be over quickly. The possibility of those long minutes waiting, an oxygen mask clamped over mouth and nose, knowing you were going down, knowing it was the end – that would be worse than anything.

Next to her, the woman's clothes gave off the indistinct odor of too much time spent inside airport lobbies: a smell of air conditioning and other people's cigarettes. And another smell, something musty she couldn't quite place.

The air pressure in the cabin had changed. The plane was moving, rolling away from the terminal. She checked her seat-belt again.

Sometimes Susan wondered why she hadn't stayed in New York after she and Michael split up. At least that way she wouldn't have had to deal with this endless flying. But the simple truth was that airplanes just hadn't seemed a factor back then. Getting far enough away to make a new start had.

New start. That was a joke. Here it was only five years later, and she felt like one of those sandwich generation women she read about. Except that her sandwich had a fuselage for a filling with a wing on either side for the bread. On one slice an ex-husband and a mother about to go in for heart surgery; on the other a lecture position, two grown daughters and a divorced-after-only-two-years second husband.

'You know,' the woman leaned over. 'You don't have to be afraid to say it. I don't mind. Everyone does.'

'Excuse me?'

'You were thinking that I look like someone you know – right? A neighbor? A schoolteacher you haven't seen in years? Everyone's always saying how I remind them of someone. It doesn't bother me. My name's Beth. Beth means "house". Did you know that? Old house. New house. Any house. So it kind of fits, since everyone has one.' She held out her hand.

The woman was smiling, beaming actually, as if she'd said something immensely witty. Susan honestly preferred not to talk, but the woman had such a ridiculously inno-cent quality. Definitely she was someone's aunt. The spin-ster, candy-in-her-sweater-pocket aunt that every family had to have. 'All right.' She shook the woman's hand, returned the smile. 'You look like someone I once knew – a woman down the street from where I grew up.'

'You know I saw you in the lobby,' she said.

'Oh?' Susan wasn't sure she liked the sound of that one. She started fishing around for her reading glasses. Somewhere in her bag she'd packed a book.

'It's a game I have, trying to guess who's going to be on the same plane.'

Susan glanced sideways at the woman, tried catching a second look in her eyes. She hoped this house-Beth wouldn't turn out to be some kind of case. The night was going to be long enough as it was. And now that she thought about it, the fact that she was on the heavy side couldn't account for the way she kept shuffling, pulling at her sweater. She didn't have any carry-on that Susan had noticed, only the small overstuffed purse. It could have held a gun, but guns weren't supposed to make it though security. And people put bombs in the backs of radios and cameras, not in their lumpy pockets.

Trying not to appear impolite, Susan checked the forward rows. The plane wasn't completely full. If things got bad enough she'd be able to change her seat. Make up some excuse about stretching out. Trying to sleep. Surely a woman her age would understand.

The cabin hummed. A bell rang, rang again. 'Oh –' Susan started. 'We're up already. I hadn't even noticed.'

The woman seemed pleased. 'You don't like flying, do you?'

'No.' She opened her book, thumbed past the first few pages.

'Don't you worry yourself. I've got something real good for that.' She changed over to the aisle seat, rummaging through a sweater pocket, then brought out what appeared to be a small doll. Susan lowered her book. The woman was holding it out for her: a round, naked, chalky-colored figurine small enough to tuck inside her hand. 'Go on, you can hold her.'

'What in the world is it?'

'You see that belly? Here, feel how smooth it is. You

know how many times this ivory's been rubbed? How many thousands of years of rubbing? Abraham and Sarah hadn't even pitched their tents in the desert yet, and this sweetie was already ancient. Don't be afraid. You won't hurt her.'

Susan's hands remained exactly where they were. Under no circumstances was she going to touch that thing. The figure was definitely female: wide-hipped with huge pendulous breasts. So anatomically correct she didn't think the toy industry had a word for such things. Definitely not a doll. More like something you'd find in a museum. Next to the dinosaurs.

Michael would have liked it. It was just the kind of thing he would have brought home all wrapped up in a box with ribbons. For a joke. Tissue paper, card, the whole nine yards. Sometimes she thought that was what she missed most about Michael, his sense of humor, the little touches he added. Brian, on the other hand, would never have conceived of the idea. Economists. You didn't have to get any drier than that. But when she'd first arrived on the West Coast and met Brian that was exactly what she'd thought she wanted: someone different. No wonder it hadn't worked out.

'Are you married?' Beth asked.

'What?'

'Ah. Divorced. Is that what you're going back for? Try to patch things up with your husband?'

'Of course not.' Susan glared at her book. She couldn't believe the woman had the nerve to say that. A stranger. And a nut. She was seated next to a nut. Maybe the best thing would be to explain from the start, then the woman would leave her alone. 'Actually, it's my mother. She's going in for surgery and . . .'

'No, no no,' the woman stopped her. 'You don't have to worry about your mother, honey. She's going to pull through. She's got a good heart. Look at me – you think

I don't know? But tell me, what else is it you're worried about?'

Susan didn't answer. She was picturing Michael in that stuffy apartment he'd taken while they waited for the divorce to come through. He'd be staring out the window as he talked on the phone to her mother. A little hurt. A little confused. Pretty much the same way she felt.

Would this Beth person really understand? She was maternal enough, but it was hard to imagine she had ever been married. Widowed maybe. Divorced? Probably not, but then she was such an odd duck, the only thing Susan was sure of was that with this one, she shouldn't trust any of her normal guesses.

Beth reached inside her purse, pulled out a second then a third figurine. Two more came out of her sweater pockets and another from somewhere in her shirt. And then she started arranging them. On her lap. On the little airplane pillow. One she stood inside the ashtray in the seat arm – it was that small. And all the while she was nodding to herself as if discussing the situation, making sure they were as comfortable as anyone could hope to be, none of them arguing, the whole family happy.

Clay. Wood. Ivory. A few had bellies round as a hill. A few were streaked with reddish paint. Another was of a dark brown clay. Most had navels. One had black hair. Human hair. Susan was ready to swear it was human.

Beth leaned forward, followed Susan's gaze toward one of the figures. A chip was missing from one shoulder. Something that might have been a dress draped across the other. Beth picked it up, blew a speck of dirt off the front. 'You like her?'

Susan shrugged, tried not to look interested.

'There was this small grassy area, led off from a bend on the Euphrates in Sumeria. Good clay, fine. Wasn't gritty at all. They found that clay and they made hundreds of her. One after the other. They couldn't make them fast enough. But – ' Beth shrugged wistfully, 'that was then. Nowadays they're much harder to come by. Here, go on. You hold her. It's all right.' She placed the figure in Susan's hand.

Susan let it stay. It did have its own kind of beauty; not so primitive as some of the others. And now that she actually held it, the skin was wonderfully smooth, the breasts round – no one could claim it wasn't skillfully made. And the way it fit, molding itself to her hand, its head nestled between her thumb and fingers. With a warmth all its own. She could almost understand why Beth spoke of them the way she did. The way the warmth was rising. And a smell. Yes, she was almost certain. A smell of scented air and water. Sweet, clean water.

She stopped. The thing was too warm. Hot almost. Her hand stiffened. Quickly, she pushed it back. 'Here, take it. I can't look at this,' and she dropped it in her lap.

Beth shrugged then one by one, she put them back away.

The flight attendant pulled his cart up beside their row. He was a young man with deep blond hair that grazed the back of his collar. High forehead. Straight jaw. If anyone asked, Susan guessed he'd say he wanted to be an actor, that he'd tried Hollywood but things just hadn't worked out.

She gratefully accepted the tray then busied herself opening plastic-wrapped containers, pushing the food around her plate, sipping the brown-colored coffee.

Beth nudged her arm. 'The danish isn't bad.'

Susan tried a bite. What could a woman her age want with so many dolls? She couldn't be younger than sixty. Maybe she was an art dealer – that could be where all the talk about clay and Sumeria came from.

Susan ate, though she didn't finish. She tried reading but couldn't settle into the book. Tried closing her eyes but couldn't get comfortable. She would have opened the shade, except flying was always worse at night – the length of wing reaching out toward nowhere. Lights blinking their warning. She must have imagined the ivory figurine's warmth. Airplanes always did strange things to her senses. That was all.

The next time she looked across, one of the figures was half peering over the top of a sweater pocket. Another had its hair caught in the purse. Susan had to admit Beth wasn't doing anything more harmful that looking down the aisle. Drug runners were young men, tall and lean. And nobody would have left a woman like her with a bomb.

Beth turned, offered a smile. 'So what did you say you do for work? You're a teacher?'

'Well, yes. Communications,' Susan said. 'Small group dynamics,' then as if she felt she had to explain, 'speech,' she added.

Beth shook her head. 'I can never figure out how people study communication. You want communication go walk through a market. Listen to the old ladies arguing with the butcher about the price of chicken.'

'Yes but communications as a field has changed, become more specialized. Though you could also argue that it's very broad – ' She stopped. Beth was staring at her, her mouth open in teasing disbelief.

Susan grew annoyed with herself for answering, yet she did feel better than usual considering the circumstances. It must have been the smooth take-off. Somehow, she found herself willing to talk.

'Do you remember the first Superman movie?' Susan asked. 'The one that came out a few years ago? You know, the first time I saw that movie I think I was the only person in the theatre who walked out of there crying.'

'Now why in the world would you cry?'

'Because in that movie the president had Superman to catch his airplane when there was engine trouble. Lois Lane had Superman. But if my girls got hurt there wouldn't be any Superman to save them. If this plane went down, that would be it. For all of us. There is no Superman and sometimes it's just not fair. That's all.'

'You're right, you know. There is no Superman.'

For one moment it seemed to Susan they'd said something important. Profound. But then she heard that name 'Superman' hanging in the air – the way she said it then Beth repeated it – so loud all the people around them could have heard. She felt embarrassed. What was the matter with her to say such an absurd thing? And she didn't like the way this woman had listened, so interested, so serious.

Quickly, hoping to turn the conversation, she said: 'So, why don't you tell me about these things? You collect them? You have conventions, auctions or something?'

Beth smiled broadly, obviously pleased. 'Something of the sort, yes. Though most of the time I work freelance. It's much better that way. I'm not a palm reader, see. If someone wants easy answers, I haven't got them. And if you ask me, honey,' she lowered her voice, 'nobody else does either. So I stay with dealing. It's clean and it's fair. But I will tell you this: people have been carrying these little ladies around for an awful long time. After a while, you just have to figure someone knows what they're talking about.'

Susan nodded, but she had lost track of the point. She'd been worrying whether her mother had written down the flight number. Or if she had, what if she'd thrown the paper away by accident? They might miss each other at the airport. She could always call home. Take a taxi. But what if her mother kept waiting? 'Excuse me,' Susan said. 'I don't think I heard you correctly.'

Beth made a face. 'You know, you really do need to hear this. But let's try again. Look out your window. There's an airport down below. It's Denver.'

'I'm sorry. I don't like looking out.'

'All right. I have another idea. You like movies, right?' she pointed upward toward the front of the aisle.

Susan looked up. The screen had been lowered. There was a movie already playing. She felt a little miffed at herself for not having noticed before. And now there weren't any headphones, though she searched her seat. Whatever movie it was, the credits had long since passed.

From the look of the actors, their clothing, the cars, it had the feel of a detective movie, *circa* 1940. Susan watched a minute, tried to catch a face she recognized, a bit of dialogue.

Beth tapped her hand. 'That's him. Watch him now.'

'Who? Which one?' Susan craned her neck for a better angle at the screen. There was a warehouse. Lightbulbs dangling. Crates piled high. Colorized, from the looks of it. A tall, distinguished looking man in a dark trench coat stood under a circle of light.

'He's my ex.'

'Husband?'

'No. Not a husband. Lover,' Beth whispered. 'I always tell folks it's my work I'm married to. Anyway, he's a dealer too, but I won't sell to him. Not anymore.'

'Of course – ' Susan agreed, though she didn't have a clue about the story. Maybe if she called for headphones?

The scene changed. There was the same man, same trench coat. But he was in the desert now. Camels in the background. Tents. The special effects were quite good for an older movie. There was an excavation going on and the man was obviously in charge. A handful of turbaned workers were digging as he pointed. It was an archaeological site. Something to do with the ladies auxiliary in Beth's pocket, Susan guessed.

And now, a team of horses could be seen in the distance across the sand dunes. Two horses, then four, then six all harnessed together by twos. Galloping now. They were pulling a wagon, a covered wagon from the American West. Cowboys and Indians, that sort of thing. A woman sat on the front seat, bouncing and whipping the horses over the sand. She was small, like Beth, but thin. It was her, except she was young and glamorous. An actress. The camera panned the scene. She was wearing a bonnet, corkscrew curls flying out the sides, everything white except the pair of six guns around her hips.

Susan shook her head. 'Let me guess – she's the good guy? Is that you?'

Beth was delighted. 'I made that part up myself. Some things never go out of style. Anyway, he's the lover, like I said. And he keeps asking her to marry him. For a while she almost said yes, because she thought it was in the script. But then she realized all he wanted was a few more pieces for his collection. He had his own supply, an inheritance, but he ran that down. Sold out, is what I call it. So now he thinks I know something he doesn't. He sees me doing all right. A job here. A job there. Like today, with you. And maybe he's right, but he doesn't catch on. He goes through the whole movie trying to sweet-talk her, hoping she'll slip up and give away a few secrets. At least make a trade. But I won't. Not to him. I've got inventory to think about.'

'I see. So the woman in white is going to offer a bid?'

'Wellll . . . Maybe. But not exactly. Though he thinks it's all a matter of time. But I won't trade. He just doesn't have what it takes.'

Susan thought she could almost follow the story now. The man in the dark trench coat had his hands in his pocket. The woman had brought a small bag out from under her seat. It was lumpy and overstuffed, like Beth's. 'So what does she want, the heroine?'

Beth smoothed her sweater, pulled herself together. 'Make me an offer,' she said and now, though Susan hadn't seen her put it there, the clay figurine she'd held earlier was staring up at her from the empty, middle seat.

'Oh, I haven't got the kind of money a museum would have – '

'It isn't money, dear. You couldn't touch the kind of money it would take to buy one of my ladies.'

'What then? My first-born child?' Susan gave an awkward laugh. 'You're a little late for that.'

'Look, honey. Are you worried about this plane staying up or aren't you?'

'I don't have any idea what you're talking about. And would you please stop calling me honey. Susan. The name's Susan.'

'OK. But why else did you think I got on your line and not some other? It was because I heard you, plain as day.' She imitated her voice, almost too well: '*It's the combined will-power of every person in the belly of this beast that's keeping the thing up.* Your words,' Beth shrugged, 'not mine.'

'I didn't say that. Not out loud.'

'You thought it.'

'Everyone thinks it. It doesn't mean a thing. That woman over there, she'd say it. And that man with the baby sleeping in his lap, you think he's not frightened? Just because he won't admit it? They'd all say the same thing. But you want to know what I really think? I think you're a nut.'

'Nut?' she said. 'OK,' and she fished a shining bit of ivory out from her purse.

The carving was slender and beautiful and this time, Susan forgot to hide her interest. It was smooth and graceful. A female figure, but worlds apart from the others. She was shaped into an upside down U, fingertips and toes stretched to the earth, her back a straight bridge, breasts and hair pointing down. Susan turned her over in her hand, admiring the work, the delicate curve of her tiny legs, the black hair and painted eyes, wide and so perfect. 'What is she?'

'She's Nut. Just like you asked for.' Beth settled her arms across her wide chest. 'She's Egyptian. From Seti's tomb. I'm real proud of her. I traded her a while back for a

131

Peruvian, a lady with a bunch of snakes coiled round her arm.'

'Nut? That's her name?' Susan felt tired now. And very confused. 'I suppose I asked for that. No, don't answer. Don't say anything. If you'll excuse me, I'm going to find a seat where I can stretch out. I need to get some rest.'

Carefully, Susan squeezed past. She'd seen an empty seat up about four rows and on the opposite side. A fortyish looking business-type man catching the red-eye special sat in the aisle seat, his legs smartly crossed, a drink in his hand.

Susan murmured an apology, climbed across then quickly slid the plastic curtain down over the window. Half a minute later she was safely engrossed in her book. She reached the bottom of the first page, looked up as she started to turn.

The man was gone. Beth sat in his place, a pair of headphones held out toward Susan.

'How did you get here?' Susan asked. 'And what's that for?'

'You didn't want to sit with that guy. He's not your type. Worse than a talker. But if you want something to listen to – then go ahead. Listen.'

Susan sighed, took the headset and plugged it in. A woman's voice came clearly through the line: 'This is Linda Perry at Chicago's O'Hare airport. We're covering the collision between two planes this evening at . . .' Angrily, Susan yanked off the headphones. The plastic snagged her hair. 'Damn,' she cursed. Then 'No!' She threw them at her lap.

'What? What'd I do?'

'I want you to stop.'

'Look honey, I wasn't the one who said things had to balance. You did. All that nonsense about terrorists plus plane crashes – it doesn't work that way. Trouble with you is that part of you keeps trying to convince yourself the whole world's supposed to be neat and sensible, and the other part knows it's not going to be that way. Then you worry so much that all your timing goes out of joint. It's like your heart skipped a beat and the rest of you forgot to catch up.

'Let me tell you something.' Beth leaned into the arm rest. 'Back in the days when that ivory was still walking around on the hoof, they knew there weren't going to be any straight deals in the answer department, but folks did the best they could. And they didn't go around worrying about it. But there you were in that lobby, carrying on loud as if you had a megaphone in your mouth. So I figure . . .'

The color had drained from Susan's face. 'Not that way,' she jabbed at the headphones. 'I don't want any crashes. Ever. Nowhere. I don't know what you think, but this isn't funny. Airplane crashes aren't funny. And you're not funny.'

'OK. I'm sorry. I misunderstood. I was only trying to give you what you wanted.'

Susan was incredulous. 'Want a plane to crash?'

'No, not that. Besides, I wouldn't have done it. But see, I thought that you thought that there had to be rules. So if you think there has to be rules, and they have to balance, then you probably figure I can't keep this plane up for you unless another one goes down. You wanted rules, I was going to show you rules. If not, then no. Either way, see –'

'No. Don't explain.' Susan took a long breath. 'Could we please talk about something else?'

'Of course we can. Besides, this plane isn't going down. It's not your turn. So, tell me, why'd you get the divorce?'

Susan shrugged. 'Probably it was my modern thinking, like you said. I thought there was supposed to be more to life than what I had after twenty years of marriage.'

'Where's your husband now?'

'Which one?'

'Which one? How many do you have?'

Susan stared at her lap. 'Two.'

Beth seemed to consider that. 'Nah, gimme the husband. Not the lover you married. A lover's good for some things. But take my word for it, that one doesn't count. Not like the husband. Him you keep thinking about.'

Susan winced.

'So?' Beth waited.

'So Michael and I got married while we were still in college. It seems so long ago now. But, you know – they were pretty good times, most of them. We lived together for twenty years. Took turns putting ourselves through grad school. Brought up two girls. Music lessons. Orthodontics. The whole nine yards.'

She patted Susan's knee. 'So what went wrong?'

It took Susan a moment to answer. 'Life, I guess. Work. Arguing with teenagers. Mid-life crises. Whatever it was, we named it. Sometimes I wonder, maybe we read too many magazines. Believed too many bad television sitcoms.'

'You want him to call?'

'He's in New York.'

'I know, I know. You keep telling me you're not thinking about him. But the whole time there he is. Channel two. Clear as day. Only this time, it's not a sitcom and there's no advertisements coming. You just have to tell me what you want.'

'What do I want? How am I supposed to know what I want? I've read a dozen books, all titled: *How to Feel Good and Have a Nice Day*. I've seen a dozen movies, all titled: *Working Girl Goes Bad but the Boy Loves Her Just the Same*. The truth is, I feel as if everything these days is a how-to book only I can't find what page I'm supposed to be on.'

'You know honey, I like you. But let me ask you something. What do you know? I mean really know about this sort of stuff? You go to temple? No? What then? A church? Don't get me wrong – I don't care where you go. Just . . . Who's been telling you all these things?'

Susan looked at the window. The curtain was down. Nothing to see. 'No one.'

'All right. Then let me ask you this – what do you think these ladies are anyway?'

'Well,' Susan thought a moment. 'There are several types of magic. Sympathetic. And black magic, of course. In the first case the magic is used . . .'

'No, no, no, that's not it. That's not it at all. You're talking formulas again. I'm talking about *soul*. The big stuff. The real stuff. Here, let me show you again.' Beth set her bifocals on the bridge of her nose, pulled three figurines out of her bag. 'I collect these, right? I told you that. That's why I've been in Seattle. I had a piece of cedar I was hoping to trade and I'd heard that one of my older ladies had turned up at an estate auction.'

'Cedar? As in totem poles?'

'There you go, now you're learning. Of course, you aren't the Raven clan type or else I wouldn't have heard you in the airport. I do better with matriarchies. So here, pick one. All you have to do is give her a home. Permanent. And comfortable doesn't hurt. This is Myrine. She's good in war. And this is Erua, but I don't think you want any more kids. And this is Naila, for the sky . . .' she pointed to one of the smaller clay figures with a mounded belly and great round, pomegranate breasts.

Susan laughed. 'The sky, huh? As in airplanes? That would fit.'

Beth placed it in her hand, closed her fingers over it. 'Rub her breasts,' she said.

'Excuse me?'

'Go ahead. She won't bite. If nothing else, she'll help you sleep better.'

This time Susan felt it more quickly, the warmth rising out of the clay. She closed her eyes, allowing her fingers to stay shut around the tiny figure, feeling the warmth as if it were a caress moving along her arm, easing the tension from her shoulders, her neck. She thought of the word *beneficent*, then settled on *seductive*. 'Isn't there supposed to be something you say? Abracadabra? An invocation?'

'I keep telling you, forget the formulas. She'll work much better if you just kind of talk to me about your husband.'

'What do you want to hear?'

'Did you love him? Was he good in the sack?'

'Oh, come on – '

'No, really. Was he? I mean, I don't want to hear the details just, you know – were you guys all right together?'

'Well. I suppose we were.'

'Suppose?'

Susan smiled. There was a vacation they'd gone on. A drive, just the two of them. Funny, how often she found herself thinking about that drive. Up through Vermont into Canada, they'd taken turns at the wheel, deciphering maps, exploring antique sales and farmers' markets. The summer had been steaming. There was a river they'd discovered. And falls. Beautiful, cool, rushing waterfalls. 'Yes,' Susan laughed gently. 'All right. Yes.'

'So why did you walk away?'

Susan regarded the figure's exaggerated curves, the play of light colored clay and darker, incised lines. 'I don't even remember anymore exactly where it started.'

'And now?'

'Sometimes it's like flying, this business of being alone. When it's new you find it exhilarating. You're absolutely independent. Nobody knows you. There's no one else's schedule to worry about. Then somewhere along the line, things change. You start to notice that you're not just alone. You're lonely. There's a difference. And what's left?

Malls? Shop-till-you-drop bargain sales? I don't like it. I don't want to grow old alone.'

'There, there, honey. I know just what you mean. You miss him?'

'You want the truth? After five years – yes. I do miss him.'

'And if he meets you when the plane lands?'

'With an armful of roses, I suppose?'

'Not roses. No hothouse forced flowers for you. For you there should be wild irises. Streaks of purple and deep blue. The color of your eyes.'

'Highly unlikely.'

'But is it what you want?' Beth leaned closer, absolutely serious. 'Is that what you really want?'

'Like if I had three wishes, you mean?'

'Make it one and we'll call it a deal.'

Susan didn't answer. She kept hold of the figure, curious now, no longer tentative, following its lines, exploring with her fingertips. Naila – was that her name? The sense of warmth, it seemed to come mostly from the head, the stomach and yes – though she would have been shy to admit it, from the breasts also. They were pleasant to touch, seductive, the way they curved up then down again to the hollow between. And softer than she'd noticed before. So very soft.

It wasn't till a good while later that, reluctantly, she held it out toward Beth. 'Here,' she said. 'You'd better put her away. I wouldn't want to drop her.'

'Drop her? You just promised to take care of her. It's part of the deal. I thought you understood.'

'We made a deal?'

'She's yours now. All you have to do is give her a home. See, it's a trade: you do a little something for me, I do a little something for you.'

'So what happens now?' Susan pulled the figure back. 'I clap my hands? Tell you that I believe she's real?'

'You mean like Peter Pan and his fairy – what's her name?'

'Tinkerbell.'

'Yeah, Tinkerbell. I can never remember her name. But no. She's another one of those formulas I keep telling you to let go of. Back on the West Coast, you say how everybody's got to keep wishing to keep the plane staying up. Then you say there isn't any Superman. Except you're crying about it. You say you don't believe in prayers. But you want rules. Rules for love. Rules for living. Fine. But you can't have it both ways. Make up your mind.'

Susan fell asleep with her shoes kicked off, legs propped at an angle, the Naila figure safe in her hands. In the forward rows, only a few scattered reading lights remained on. No babies were crying. No drinkers flirted too loudly with the stewardess.

It was the first time in a long while she'd been able to sleep on an airplane, really sleep. And underneath the cover of the blanket Beth had brought her, there in the dark of her hand, the Naila goddess gave off the smell of a rich, flowering garden.

Susan dreamt of the trip she and Michael had taken together. There was the road meandering past long forgotten rock walls and lazy brooks. The girls were young again. Staying with an aunt in the summer cottage. She and Michael weren't kids but neither were they so old they couldn't find their way back to the waterfall. In the dream it was larger than she remembered, tumbling and gathering into pools, shaded and hot all at the same time. And quiet. Not a soul anywhere but she and Michael. Their clothing shed. Their skin slippery and warm. And the water, rising thickly round her calves. Her thighs. Drawing them in toward each other. Holding them in its current.

Susan opened her eyes. The pressure change in the airplane

had woken her, the sound of landing gear being lowered. Beth was gone. To the restroom she supposed. Except the NO SMOKING lights were on. She should have been in her seat. They'd be landing shortly.

She turned, saw that the curtain was still blocking the window. She tugged at it and it caught once as if rusted, then with a second touch slid smoothly open. Outside it was morning, the sun bright on the horizon. Somehow, she'd expected it to be dark. Clouds massed above the plane now, not below, great horses' heads rearing against a patient sky.

The Naila goddess lay nestled in her lap. Cool, until the moment she picked it up. Last night she would have said it was her own warmth the clay had borrowed. That maybe if she hadn't held it so long it wouldn't be doing this. Softening. Giving off that odd fragrance. She cupped it in her hands and waited, touching, but only lightly. Not stroking. Not yet.

No rules, Beth had said, but Susan wanted to get this right, wanted the timing to come out perfect, just this once.

Not until she saw the lights of the landing strip below did she turn toward the privacy of the wall. She raised the Naila to her face, inhaled deeply and held it, the scent of moisture and gardens so deep she felt intoxicated, so real it brought up a picture half remembered, half newly constructed.

And now the water was coming up at them, seagulls, a few scattered boats and then buildings, land. And then, crowding out the old fears, a different, lower sound: the ground taking hold of the plane, cradling them, carrying them along runways toward men who stood with arms raised, steering the plane closer toward thick terminal windows.

She caught at her breath, tried to still her racing heart. *Now!* Susan told herself. Beth wasn't coming back. There weren't any rule books. No hints of any kind. It had to be now.

Gradually first, then with a deeper motion, she began stroking the breasts, the soft, warm buttocks and pregnant stomach. There was no fear as she felt the tiny muscles gather and open at her touch. Only the sensation of skin against skin, a tingling in her fingertips, rising, as if the stroking was being returned. As if she was in her lover's arms again, Michael's arms, and they were holding each other, touching, sharing. And all the while she held the one picture in her mind. Clearly. The way she wanted it drawn.

A Hot Time

PAULA GUNN ALLEN

This story I have read and heard as a kind of 'little,' or 'grandmother,' story, that is, a humorous story for children and others on purely social occasions. Humor is an important part of Native American daily life. Without it, Indians could hardly have survived 500 long years of occupation. Humor is also a major aspect of traditional spiritual life for many Native American communities, where the sacred and the amusing are often combined in worship.

I think that Grandmother Spider, who is awesome in so many of her aspects, is also seen as one of us. Certainly, all the stories about her willing intervention on behalf of youngsters in difficulties beyond their abilities, and her unfailing good humor lend themselves to a view of her as capable of fun as well as of miracles.

I have incorporated some joking references to the overseriousness with which the stories of the people are often treated by mythologists and literary specialists – a bit of fun at my own expense, you might say.

Long ago the people were in the dark, and they were tired of not knowing when to go to sleep and when to get up. They didn't have Six Killer to pray to in the mornings when they went to the water to greet Long Man and prepare for the new day. True, there was a place of greater heat during some hours, and the air around them was more

gray than dark, but they didn't have much light by which
to work and play.

They were also yearning for a cozy fire to sit next to
when they told stories after the little ones went to sleep,
after the daily activities ended. Besides, they knew that fire
was very powerful, and they wanted the joy and growing
that came to people who had fire to grace their lives.

They really liked to pass the time companionably, and
the only reason they didn't do as much of it as they liked
is that when the darkness got a little darker some of them
insisted it was time to go to sleep. They believed that if
they had fire and some regular daylight, they'd be able to
spend even more time telling stories and gossiping and
being together. Maybe they would even have new cere-
monies to hold and go to.

The people learned about some other people in a distant
country who had firelight. They heard that those people
got to spend all day and all night telling stories, singing,
dancing, and generally carousing till all hours.

Well, they thought about all this for a long time. They
thought about what they needed and wanted. They thought
about those rumors, and they even sent some men to
see if they were true. They listened to each other's ideas
about what they might do if they had some firelight, and
they dreamed up all sorts of interesting activities. Even
those who liked to sleep early got caught up in the goings
on. They began to think that maybe they could sleep more
in light time, when there was true light, so they could also
enjoy the fire when it was very dark.

There were a few, of course, who had some reservations
about the whole affair. But aside from mumbling a bit,
mostly among themselves about possible dangers and haz-
ards from such a volatile and untested force, especially
when it was in the untrained hands of the would-be merry-
makers, they kept their reservations to themselves. And
this, of course, is how reservations first got started.

After a proper length of time planning and dreaming, discussing and surmising, mumbling and wondering had gone by, the people settled into the serious business of strategy. 'How will we get some firelight?' they asked. 'The people over in that other country who have some won't give us some. We tried.'

'H'mmm,' they sighed. They stopped discussing for a long pause.

'I know,' one of the people finally said. He was a tall skinny man who decorated himself magnificently with feathers. He was especially proud of his luxurious thick hair fashioned in a spiky style. He kept it in place with a nice sticky clay that came from the nearby clay bed. His name was Buzzard.

Buzzard uncoiled his lanky form and stood. 'Maybe someone will take a little jaunt over there long after it gets dark, maybe just before light, and try to snag some,' he intoned sonorously.

'Yeah, you need practice snagging,' someone hooted. The others laughed.

After the general merriment at Buzzard's expense subsided, it was agreed that Buzzard would go. When the first rays of light were just emerging over the saddleback rise near the village, Buzzard came limping in. He was definitely the worse for wear, his fine feathers matted and blackened. He sported a bald spot right at his crown. The hair there never did grow back. 'I blew it,' he said resignedly. 'Maybe someone else should try.'

Well, a couple of others went, but with the same result. Everyone was feeling pretty glum about how matters stood. They were trying to reconcile themselves to doing without the exciting firelight – which meant adjusting their plans, dreams, and hopes to fit their accustomed circumstances. Most were disappointed, except for the few who were relieved. They went whistling and giggling about their

143

tasks, relieved that nothing fearful and different was going to unsettle their equilibrium just yet.

But Spider got to thinking. She was always doing that. She couldn't help it, of course, any more than Buzzard could help swooping, strutting, and snagging. She spun out her thought and wove implications, extrapolations, and a few elegant day-dreams into a satisfying pattern. Her Dreaming done, she joined the folks sitting dejectedly around the empty place where they could almost see the firelight snapping cheerily on the sticks and branches they had carefully laid out in such anticipation just a few days before.

'Well,' Spider began softly. 'Maybe someone might try to get some firelight,' she said to no one in particular. She sat down carefully so as not to jar her fragile joints unduly. 'It's true I'm old and slow,' she continued. She paused again for a silence, breathing it in and out comfortingly.

No one looked at her. As was their way, they just kept on sitting as they had been, doing whatever they had been doing even if that was just brooding or wishing over their regrets. But of course, they were all attending carefully to what she said.

'It's true I'm a very small person and not very strong,' she said at last. 'But I think I could give it a try. My old body would appreciate some firelight at night sometimes. And I wouldn't mind having a little brightness to tend.' They sat companionably in silence after that, some wandering off, some coming over to join the group from time to time.

So Spider set out, much earlier than Buzzard and the others had because she was much slower. Along her way she stopped off at the clay bed and dug up some smooth, damp clay. She took some time to shape it into a tiny pot with a lid that she kept separately so they wouldn't stick together while they were drying. Her Dreaming had told her that the firelight would dry them more quickly and more finely than Heat Giver in the sky could. She had seen some fine potteries in her Dream, and she was looking forward to making and firing them.

The last one of her folks watched her make her slow way across the rise beyond the saddleback on her way to the Fire People's land. Her tiny figure soon disappeared in the grayness that met the top of the rise and clung to it like a *u'tinaatz*, a woman's short, light cloak.

As the next day was well advanced, the people saw her returning. She had a round lamp on her back and looked a bit misshapen in the gray distance. Their hearts fell to the ground in dismay when they saw this. 'Oh, no,' they said. 'It's one thing for Buzzard to get a new hairstyle, but if something so horrible has happened to Spider!'

They were too heartsick to finish the thought, but waited as calmly as they might, busying themselves with whatever came to hand as was their way when worried or anxious.

At long last Spider was close by, grinning a satisfied grin. 'Well,' she said, 'looks like I got it.' She reached up and took the clay pot from her back, revealing a change such as they had feared. For on her back pulsed a bright red-orange design that hadn't been there the day before. But it was a very handsome and wise design, one she had dreamed of herself, and it exactly matched the one her pot lid sported, and she seemed happy to wear it.

She set the tiny pot down in front of her, sighing a small sigh of satisfaction as she removed the lid to reveal the bright glowing ember she had carefully carried so far. 'Look,' she said. 'Firelight.'

And there was a hot time in the old town that night.

'A Hot Time' is an extract from Paula Gunn Allen's collection of stories *Grandmothers of the Light: A Medicine Woman's Source Book*, published by The Women's Press.

Ash, Wood, Fire

PATRICIA A MCKILLIP

Black, her eye said. Cinder black. And smooth. Black moved under her eye. She moved, too, pulling her face out of the crook of her elbow, into dawn. Grey light spilled over everything: grey stones, grey hearth, grey ashes on her hands. The black moved, bumping against her arm. She sat up quickly, making a grating morning sound in her throat. Black beetle, slow, and long as her thumb. The stones had grown cold under her. She flicked the beetle on to its back, watched it wave its legs, crawl on air. Then she blew it upright. It lumped away towards the hearth where it would blaze like a coal in her fire. She straightened, yawning, pushing matted ribbons of hair into her cap. The beetle disappeared under the grate.

She blew embers alive, piled chips and sticks, and blew, piled more sticks and bark, and blew, and then the wood. Something tiny wailed and snapped, sap bubbled. She burned hearts, bones, black beetles. The warmth touched her face; she closed her eyes. The warmth seeped into her; she was the warmth, warm. Warm, she thought; warm, she breathed. Almost warm enough to come alive. Sap in the wood, seed in the earth, warming . . .

A beetle lumbered, loud and black, grumbling behind her. She hadn't burned it. Or she had, and in the fire it had grown enormous.

' – at her, dreaming, with fires to be . . . fires . . .'
Fires.

146

She moved to other hearths in the vast kitchen, blowing, coaxing, growing fire in the stone ovens, under great kettles of icy water that ham-hands, red with cold, hung to sway in front of her face. The kitchen filled with the sound. A kettle heaved in front of her, splashing water on to her flame. Ash hissed, smoked. A word licked at her ear; a hand, wet and hard, felt for something under her apron. She made a noise, twisting, picking a smouldering stick out of the fire. A haunch nudged her; she sprawled on stones.

'Nothing but bone; dogs wouldn't sniff at you, they wouldn't bother. Kitchen scraps have more on them.'

'Leave her alone, the Beetle said in her flat, harsh, rasping voice. 'Leave her to work, then, or I'll toss you to the hounds, you pale horny toad. Slug. Get those kettles hissing. You. Girl. What is her name?' she asked, exasperated, of the hanging sausages. 'Does she have one?'

Every morning, every morning.

'Anastasia.'

'Rosamunda.'

'She never said.'

'She can't speak.'

'She can.'

'Isolde.'

'I can talk,' she said, her back to them all. 'Talk,' said the fire. 'Talk,' said the dripping, hissing kettle. A face, in its shiny, battered side, looked back at her, distorted in the dents. The nose dipped sideways, the chin veered, melted into a pool.

'Talk, then,' someone said. 'Tell us your name.'

The face had no name. She sniffed instead, swiped her nose against her shoulder. Pots laughed, knives snickered in the bacon; an oven door screeched, clanged shut.

'My name is Ash,' she said. 'My name is Wood. My name is Fire.'

'Her name is Patch,' someone said, high and grating,

through his nose. 'Patch, from Thickum Spinney. Salt. Salt, over here.'

Salt ran behind her, little light steps on the stones.

'No,' argued a furiously stirred pot. 'That was the last fire we had. This one's new.'

'Naawoh,' a spattering pan said derisively. 'This one's been here forever. You're new.'

'Five years,' Pot huffed.

'That's new. Fire's been here forever.'

'Then what's her name?'

'Fire!' the Beetle snapped. 'Over here!'

She made, she made, until the kitchen grew thick, sultry with smoke and steam and smells. Perfumed maids, black flowers, scented the steam as they picked up copper water cans; black stalks of gentlemen appeared and disappeared into the mists, then came back again, for vast silver trays upon which Flower, mute and stunted man, laid a single rose, a white carnation. The argument flared intermittently, little flames here, there, springing to life, sinking.

'The other was shorter.'

'This is the other. She grew.'

'That high? Overnight?'

'You don't notice,' the Beetle said abruptly. 'In here. Faces always coming and going. Chopper! Apples, apples, keep them coming. You. Onions. A mountain of onions. A swimming sea of onions. Chop them small as babies' teeth.'

'The other's hair was light.'

'How could you tell? She's ash, head to foot. She drifts, hearth-creature. Puff at her and she'd waft apart.'

'This one's too tall ...'

'Pepper!'

She tried to think back. Had she been smaller? Or had that been someone else? Fires content, for the moment, she took fresh hot bread from a basket, wedged herself out of the way in a corner of wall and hearth, pushed close to the warmth, and tore at the bread. Stone and fire, stone and fire, nothing else but that, no matter where she looked. Grate and ash, wood, armloads of wood, winter wood, summer wood, each with its smell of snow or sun. Nothing more. Fire never counted years, neither did she. Still, dusted with breadcrumbs, warm, nodding a little against the hard warm stones, she saw her hands, fingers grey and black with ash and char, nails broken, knuckles split with dryness and cold, an old mark or two where the fire had tried to eat her. Her hands belonged to fire. Had they ever done anything else? Had they been born smelling of char and sap?

They were what hands looked like that belonged to fire.

She had no other hands. None that had peeled an apple, placed a flower on a tray. She was Fire. What did years matter to fire?

'Fire!'

She moved, dodging around elbows, across floor slick with apple peel, her eyes searching, finding the discontented flame under a vast pan hung on a triple chain, heaped with butter and onion. Eyes stinging with smoke and onion, she heaved wood, built it up with her bare hands, angled this log on that, until the fire itself – billowing, snapping tree-bones, boiling tree-blood – drove her away with its hot breath.

Fire. Wood. Ash.

The black flowers began to return the silver trays, littered now with crusts and cold bacon fat, crumpled napkins, flowers withering in brown pools of tea and chocolate. A hillock of scraps began to grow in a great bowl for the Kitchen Dogs, the Beetle said, though there were no Kitchen Dogs, only Kennel Dogs, fed as carefully as princesses. Salt and Pepper and Choppers, Stirrers and Scrubbers passed and repassed the bowl; dipping into it, swift as birds, pecking away at the mound, a dart of hand, a suddenly rounded cheek. Fire ate only bread, finding tastes – the flood of salt, the sweet tang of orange peel – confusing, disturbing. They brought words into her head; they made her want to speak, though the words that pushed into her mouth were all in some peculiar language – the language that silk spoke, or perfume – and she could neither shape nor understand them.

'Fire!'

In a breath, between meals – the plates scrubbed from one, the quail braising for the next, onions and apples browning in butter, Pins rolling out pie crusts all down a long table, bread out and cooling – the argument flared again.

'She was a little bit of a girl, with no front teeth. This one has teeth.' This from a Sauce so lovingly stirred it might have held the last cream, the last sugar, the last rosewater in the world.

'Teeth grow.' This from the Kitchen-Beetle herself, huge circle of hips, round and black from behind, a circle of back, a small circle of black head, hair pulled into yet another circle at her neck, so fiercely and unshakeably round it might have been carved of stone. Her heavy cheeks were cream threaded with veins of strawberry, her brows as pale as the marble pestles, her eyes shiny black insect eyes, that saw everything and had no expression.

'Not so quickly as all that.'

'How often does anyone look?' Pastry, pressing rings of beaten egg-white out of a funnel, flung up his arms. Egg-white squirted high; Salt watched, open-mouthed. Falling, it just missed the Sauce. 'No one would look unless she wasn't there making fires. She didn't have teeth. She has teeth. Who has time to look?' His free hand pounced under the table, drew out a Chopper, small and dark, cheek full of something, his eyes and mouth clenched tightly shut, his body frozen by the hand at his neck. 'Look at this one. Does he have front teeth or not?' The Sauce shrugged.

Pastry pushed the Chopper back under the table. 'Who knows? Who cares? None of them have names.'

'I have teeth,' said the table. 'I have a name. All of us have names.'

'What's hers, then, rat?'

'Fire.'

Pastry stamped under the table. 'Cockroach. Get to work.'

'She's too tall,' muttered Sauce. Steam enveloped his face; he inhaled rapture, and forgot Fire.

Then the nut pies went in, and the quails stuffed with apples and onions; the kitchen rats reeled, drunk with smells. She hauled wood constantly; going out to the snowy yard, piling it in her arms, taking deep breaths – not of the wild, golden, spicy air – but of pitch and wet bark, the inner smells of trees, as varied to her as their names. She had no names for trees, only the pictures in her head that each wood-scent conjured: some were dark and bristled, green all year; others stood pale and slender, wore leaves like lace and rustled with secrets at every breeze. The ovens set within the stones ate wood, ate forests. Pitch boiled and wailed, trees gave her their fragrances, their memories, clear to her even in the riot of kitchen smells, so that, kneeling at the grates, sweating, balancing logs, dodging smoke, brushing burning cinders back into the fire with her hands while the kitchen clattered and chopped and roared behind her, a green wood grew around her, the ghosts of trees.

'Fire! Where's that girl?' the Kitchen-Beetle snapped. 'She might as well be a block of wood, for all she hears you. Where did she go? She was just there – '

'I'm here,' she said, from the heart of the wood, and the trees faded away.

'Fire!'

They descended from the upper world, the stately bearers of silver and copper, flowers and food. They bore away entire woods full of quail, whole vegetable gardens of salads, and came back for the nut orchard, and the cream from the milk of a hundred cows. They returned carrying bones, crusts, herbs trapped like green wings in hardening sauce. Scrubbers and Pluckers and Choppers snatched cold leftovers; Cooks, Bakers, Sauces and the Beetle herself ate hot seasoned quail dripping with sauce, nut pies crusted with brown sugar and butter. Fire, dreamy with heat, ate bits of bread charred with ash, chopped apples that had hung on trees, food going grey in her fingers until it seemed she ate ash. The Kitchen-Beetle's eye, bright and thoughtless as she gnawed birds, swivelled aimlessly and fell on Fire. As always, other eyes followed.

'The other spoke more.'

'This one is the other. She's turning.'

'Turning?'

'Becoming,' the Beetle said impatiently. 'They do. They all do. They put out leaves. They begin to dream.'

'Her?' Sauce snickered. 'She's disappearing, more like it. She's growing ash on her thick as bark. She can't think much, she's put together like twigs. Twigs for bones, wooden thoughts.'

The Beetle looked at Fire, great white teeth tearing at quail, her eyes black as the underside of a pot, and as flat. She made a sound, between a snort and an inquiry, and tossed the bones.

'It's in the air,' the Beetle said. 'She smells it. In the wood.' She heaved to her feet; Scraps ran among all their feet, collecting what they had let fall. She raised her voice. 'Pluckers!'

Geese, this time, their long white necks lolling across the thighs of Pluckers, trembling at every touch. Their feathers blew everywhere; fire scorched them, Sauce cursed them. Scraps leaped after them, snatching them as they floated. A snowdrift rose between the Pluckers; flurries of down, the last winter storm, swirled around Fire when she opened the door to bring in wood. The kitchen snow confused her; outside, in the melting snow, she smelled gold, she smelled water running slow and warm through still, secret woods. Inside was fire and snow still flying, through the tender green smells of wood.

Mushrooms simmered in butter and rosemary over the flames; geese, headless, impaled, turned slowly on spits – the fires hissed and spattered with their fat. Cauldrons of potatoes and leeks boiled, spilling frothy water into the flames. She made, she made, coaxing drenched fire alive here, there, building and rebuilding next to ovens full of bread shaped into swans, of airy towers spun of egg-white and sugar hardening in the heat. Chocolate and raspberries frozen all winter, and hazelnuts pounded fine as dust, melted together under a flame, never high, never too low, teased with titbits like a child. The world turned fire under her eyes, her busy fingers; she shaped potato flames, raspberry flames, geese flames, as if she were remaking everything out of fire, while pots were stirred, whisked away, others hung, and the voice of the Kitchen-Beetle wove the clutter and chaos around her into supper.

Then she found herself dreaming in a darkening kitchen, a piece of potato half eaten in her grimy hand. She leaned against a cooling oven. A solitary Scrubber splashed among the last of the pots. All around her, fires were burying themselves deep into heartwood, in the darkening hearths. A coal fell, a heart snapped – sang. The Kitchen-Beetle sat in the shadows, still and silent, watching, listening to the small noises. Fire watched her: the circles of her knees, her breasts, her darkened face. Cinders fumed. A pot settled on the rack. A flame sprang up, hid itself again. They sat, Fire against the oven stones, Kitchen-Beetle in her chair, in the heart of the fire, listening to the kitchen speak.

The Beetle dwindled, went small, small, a moving bit of dark in the darkness. Fire dreamed of fire. An eye opened among the coals. It was green as leaves: her eye. Another opened. Another. The ring of hearths watched her out of her eyes. A flame danced, spoke. Her voice, her word. She stirred against the stones, murmuring. Her cap brushed off; hair tumbled down, dark as wood. All her eyes watched the beetle crawl toward the hearth. It spoke as it passed her: a sudden gleam across its dark, polished back.

'Fire,' it said, and she breathed the word, felt it dance across her heart, light as leaves, whispering, whispering. She rose finally, brought in wood, and water, and began to make.

Morning found cold grates everywhere. Cooks, Sauces, Bakers milled bewilderedly, betrayed, calling, 'Fire! Fire!' and never seeing her, while beside the door a young woman stood watching, tall and sapling-slender, her eyes as green as new leaves, her hair shiny as the beetle's back, perfumed with wood. The lowly Scrubbers saw her first, and the Choppers, and Scraps and Stirrers; they flashed their teeth, or lack of them, grinning in wonder, as she opened the door to light.

'Fire!' the Kitchen-Beetle called peremptorily to no one, to anyone, as if a ghost of ashes might rise out of a hearth, a little, smudged, graceless bundle of twigs, and begin to kindle herself alive, while Fire passed out of the kitchen into Spring.

The Mermaid's Legs

JEAN BUFFONG

I have never heard anything like it in all my life – never.
If teacher Marion knew the old lady would of carried on
like that she would not of invited her to the church. Then
again the lady is really stubborn, you know. If they tried
to get her to stay in the house with the food and things
she might start quarrelling and saying it's because people
don't like her. They jealous because her granddaughter
getting married. I don't know ... everything nice and
peaceful then, just like that it sounded like the devil himself
was in the church. The priest ... you should of seen his
face. I was right in front, so I was able to see everything.
I made sure I had a front pew because it was the first time
that I been to a proper wedding, so I didn't want to miss
anything. I don't mean that I never been to a wedding like,
but was the first time I been in the choir and able to see
what really went on at the altar. The priest was busy busy
performing the service ... said some prayers and things.
Said some nice things about the two teachers. That didn't
surprise me really, because they were two of the nicest
teachers the school ever had. Well, the priest did all his
business and just as he got to the most serious part, then
things happened. As he started 'I now pronounced you
man and – ' he didn't finished. One 'O Gawd, Lawd have
mercy' broke out in the church. 'Lawd have mercy Am
way bacay oye me belly me belly O Gawd'; well I tell
you, even now it's hard to describe the atmosphere in the

155

church at that time. The priest looked up, his colour changed as if all the ashes on Ash Wednesday fell on him. I tell you it was the loudest screech, not just loudest but funny like, as if it was not from a real person it came. That was the funniest thing I heard since Aunt Sar died and Tanty Mildred hollowed out when she realised that her sister dead . . . really gone for good.

I can hear the sound in my head after all that time. Sort of deep deep down in my head I can hear the bawling. Sometimes I think I have special hole in my head storing up all these things. At the time Aunt Sar died we were accustomed to when people died to hear others bawling all kind of papa bunjay oye and saying all kind of things. Sometimes as if they confessing all their deeds, perhaps hoping that the dead person would forgive them, but this time was something else.

We knew the lady was old and expect her to die anytime. I mean me, Fatima and my cousin Verna, although we were little, yet we were accustomed to death, you know, not because our family always dying but if there is a death in the village everybody was around helping and thing. So when Aunt Sar died it was nothing to us. We practically lived with the three women, even when Uncle JJ was living there. They had no children, so all the children in the village were theirs.

As I was saying, as children we were not afraid at all. We were in and out of the room where she was laid out on the bed ready to be bathe, dressed and put in the coffin. She laid on the bed flat on her back like if she was sleeping, but we knew she was dead because for one thing she never slept on her back and the other she was too quiet. She always tossing about and talking as if she and somebody fighting. Anyway, to us children she was old and died. We were sad and cried a little, but to begin with we were more interested in the rice tea and saltfish souse during the wake. Tanty Avis and Tanty Mildred, well, that was something else. At one time I was afraid for them; worried that they would fall down and die as well. Although they were old that would still of been a lot of trouble. When they started holding their belly and falling down all over the place, that was really scary. Tanty Mildred seemed to be in another world. These two women bawled and bawled. I don't know where they got the eye-water from. They moaned from the time Aunt Sar died right up to the eight days' prayers, and even after that was as if they went funny in the head. The night of the eight-day prayer Tanty Avis got a hammer and started pounding the house, saying she mashing down the damn place because the house too big for them now. After a while things started to settle down, people just carried on, but as I said it was not the same for the two old sisters. I supposed in a way was just as when Janice died. It's been a long time now, but sometimes it's just like yesterday.

Even now sometimes, Mammy look at me as if her eyes screaming at me. I used to think that she blamed me for Janice death. To tell the truth when she first died I used to prayer to God to forgive me, because I used to think it was my fault that my little sister died just like that. Just so.

We shared a bedroom. Had one big bed. Sometimes we used to fight to sleep in front the bed away from under the window in case spirit came in on us in the night, especially after the time Mammy got up with a big round purple mark on her leg. She said was a pipe mark. It was just like the mark that my friend Sonia mother had on her arm a few weeks before. According to Sonia, her mother said that was Mr Joshua who used to lived in the pasture that put it there. I didn't know how she could say a thing like that, especially as the man was her godfather. The man looked harmless, he can't even slap mosquito biting him, but according to Sonia he was the biggest lougarou in the place. Me, I don't know. To me if anybody making nastiness is Miss O'Brien that living in the little house next to Mr Joshua. That woman is something else. Everybody 'fraid of her.

One day, me and Sheila was going up Cacoben Hill; sun hot for so. When we reached by Miss Eva house one strap of my slipper burst. It was a bit dry rot anyway, so as if the hot sun finished it off. Well the pitch hot like fire, the bush on the side of the road just as hot, I can't walk with only side of slipper on my foot. Sheila said Caryle, that's Miss Eva son, does repair shoes so he wouldn't mind tacking the strap for me. We stood in the gap and called Caryle. We called and called but no answer, but we heard as if there were people talking on the bottom side of the house down by the sea. To be honest I don't know why Miss Eva built her house on this precipice. If another hurricane Janet pass, before the wind start to blow, she and her family end up straight out in the ocean. People say when she wanted to build the house she had a lot of problems getting carpenters to help her. Nobody wanted to work on that precipice. Not only how the piece of land bad, but they said Jasper used to meet the devil under the gru-gru tree over the road and sometimes under the big tambranch tree. Some people say they meet him up in all different ways around there in the middle of the night.

I think was two years ago, one thing broke out. Nobody really knew what really happened. Was around harvest time. The Catholic always make their harvest in the big school, and then have a big dance in the night. Anyway, was after midnight when Reynold and a set of boys were coming home from the dance they saw this thing. They said as soon as they turned the corner coming towards the gru-gru tree they saw a shadow. Some of them said it looked like a beast, some said it was only a shadow. They were not sure because it happened so quickly. Only Carlton said it was a naked man; these boys lie so much you don't know what to believe. What was for sure was something left from under the gru-gru tree made one dash across the road; when it reached on the spot where Miss Eva house is now, it stopped, looked at the boys, then threw itself down the precipice. They said everything happened so quickly, nobody had a chance to say a word. Was as if they turned to stone, until Carlton let out one piece of 'O Gawd bunjay oye', and by the time they catch themselves only his white pants foot they saw pounding the road in the darkness. When Carlton reached his mother house, he gave the door one boaw doaw boaw and pelt inside. His parents jumped out of bed. All ask his father, asking, 'What's wrong?' He can't answer. His eyes popping out of his head, his tongue rolling about in his mouth. Same time his mother got the bottle of bay rum mixed with cacajab and started rubbing him down.

Aye aye one bacanal in the place the next morning. Some people said it was jumbie going home. They reckon the jumbie lived in the silk cotton tree by the side of the tambranch tree. They say it could be because Carlton disturbed it, that why it wanted to turn the boy into a dummy. Others said it was Jasper doing his nastiness, and he wanted to make sure they don't talk. People always said that man does turn into all kind of things, even wedding cake. I don't know how human being could turn into beast and wedding cake to dance in the road in the middle of the night, but in this Grenada the more you live the more you hear. Whatever it was, from that night everybody was afraid to walk up the hill. When we went to school we used to walk fast fast. About a year after that Miss Eva built her house there. It was a good thing, though, because we were not afraid to walk up there anymore. Anyway, as I was saying, me and Sheila stood in the gap calling Caryle, hoping he would sew up the slipper for me. We couldn't hear any sound in the house but there was a sort of noise, a sort of mmmmmm ... mmmmmm coming from behind the house nearer to the sea. It sounded like two persons talking but not using proper words like ... a kind of mmmmmm from one person and a sw–ish swiiiiish from the other. Sheila such a coward she started pulling my skirt for us to leave, but the pitch burning under my foot like fire so I wanted the slipper fixed.

I kept on calling Caryle, at the same time moving a few steps in the yard to peep round the back of the house down by the sea. Well; this time I was the one ready to run. I couldn't believe my eyes; the woman was standing on the big stone in the sea. She was lucky the sea wasn't rough. Everybody was afraid of Miss O'Brien; is now I understand why. She was wearing a long black dress and a nylon black headtie. She had her arms over her head, her eyes staring straight up to the sky as if she talking to God. The 'voices' we heard was her and the waves. She was there as if pleading with God, or perhaps asking Him to put curse on somebody. I'm sure it wasn't God she was talking to, though. I always heard people saying that the woman hand is never clean, now I understand what they meant.

The way she stood out in the sea reminded of the time the river took Miss Sagoo. That is something I would never forget until they put me six feet under. To see how me and Sheila shouted to the woman to come out of the river; shouted to her that the river coming down. Shout; bawling to her you know, before she even looked at us. She didn't believe us at first, because no rain fell at all that day. Rain didn't even set up, the mountain was bright bright. The sun having hot gossip with the ground, like the usual Lenten season. Some places so dry not one green leaf on any tree, just parched ... brown dry. Some of the trees so naked you could see clear clear from one place to the other. When I stand up on the big stone behind the kitchen, I see the big boucanoe tree way up in Mr Touse land up Mt Plaisir. The day the river take Miss Sagoo, me and Sheila was in the river washing. We didn't have rain to study, then all of a sudden the water started to look kind of dirty dirty. I say all of a sudden because it was as if we dipped the clothes in clean water, lift it out of dirty water.

Sheila first noticed it; not how it was dirty but how the water was getting deeper. She was in the deep water hole bathing when she shouted to me. I heard Sheila saying something, but I did not pay attention to her. I heard her shouting but kept on scrubbing under Mammy working dress arm with a corn stick.

'Flora,' she said. 'Flora, listen. Hear that tumbaying up Mount Plaisir. It look as if the river coming down!'

What you mean river coming down?' I said. 'You always with your stupidness. You ever see river come down without rain fall? Perhaps is blast they blasting up in the hills.' While I talking I dipped the dress in the water to rinse it out; it was then I noticed the colour of the water. Not only the colour but I realise the water was reaching up to my shin.

'Bunjay Sheila,' I shouted. 'The water look dirty!'

'Jesus Christ. I see what you mean. It look as if the river coming down. The water coming up to my knee.' Sheila jumped out of the water like a cricket. We raced about, picking up our washing where we had them spread out on the stone and bush by the side of the river. 'Come come, make haste. Make haste; let's get out of the river. Let's cross on the other side.'

We dashed about, picked up the clothes as quickly as possible. Some wet, some still dirty. The water was almost covering the flat stone we used to jump on to cross the river. Leaves and bits of rubbish floated down. The water became like when you dig potato and wash out the mud.

As we reached the bank I looked back to see if we left anything behind. 'O Gawd,' I gasped. 'Lawd Sheila, look. Look, Miss Sagoo down there. She don't hear the river coming.'

'Bunjay!' She gasped, and started to shout to the woman.

'Miss Sagoo, Miss Sagoo,' she shouted. 'The river coming. Miss Sagoo make haste, the river coming down.' The woman carried on cho-chooing the pair of old dungarees. The only thing that mattered in the world was she and the dungarees. Me and Sheila shouted and shouted. All the time we could hear the river rumbling, tumbling down the mountain.

'Run down there and call her, Flora,' Sheila shouted. 'Run, quick. The river coming fast.'

'Miss Sagoo, Miss Sagoo! The river coming down. Quick, pick up your clothes,' I shouted, as I raced to where she was. Waving my hands about like a mad person. 'Miss Sagoo, the river, the river coming down. Please hear me.' I was shouting and pleading with her in my head to hear me. At last she lifted her head, as if coming out of a dream.

'Quick,' I said. 'The river coming down. Cross on the other side.'

'What you say gal? Who coming?'

'The river! It coming down. Look how the water dirty!'

'What you mean river coming down? Whey de rain for river to come down?'

'I think it fall in the mountain. Hurray up,' I shouted. Doop, doop a doop ruck a tuck tuck, the water was tumbling nearer and nearer. I was getting panicky, because what I was saying did not really soak in the woman head.

'Aye, aye,' she registered at last. 'Aaye but look how the water dirty nuh! The river look coming down for true. I better hurry up.'

'Make haste and cross over,' I prodded. 'Hurry.' At last, at last, she noticed the water. I felt relieved. She dashed about as if she had spring in the body. In one last sweep she bundled the washing in the basin and dashed on the bank to safety. I went back to meet Sheila. We put our basins on our heads and started dwaddling home. Just as we reached the damson tree, I don't know what made Sheila look back, but I heard her bellow: 'Oh no!'

I turned around to see Miss Sagoo's basin on the ground and she in the middle of the river heading for the other side. The heavy water was only a few yards away.

'Miss Sagoo, don't go,' we both shouted. 'Come back, come back.' We tried to shout above the noise of the rumbling water.

'I going for me petticoat,' the woman screeched. 'I forget me petti –' She did not finished what she was saying. The water rushed on her like a tidal wave. She raised her hands in front her as if trying to hold back the water. One woosh shoosh goosh – right in front our eyes she was swallowed inside the bowel of the water. Swallowed up ... gone ... gone ...

Sheila and I screamed and bawled and screamed and bawled. Crowds of people were quickly by the river. Some were on the bridge, few yards further up. They saw the whole thing. Men began running down the bay road towards the sea, peeping and searching as they went. Others used long bamboo to poke into the water as far out as they could reach. Everybody searched and searched. Some women were crying. Children running between everybody trying to see what was happening. After the first few minutes, me and Sheila were dumbed. I felt dead inside. I closed my eyes to stop seeing Miss Sagoo's face as the water swallowed her. The only thing they found after all the searching was a nice white frilly petticoat hanging on a black sage bush.

Three days later Mr Joe going to raise his fish pot early in the morning, down in the stone hole between Marigot and Blackbay, noticed a piece of cloth tangled up between the stone. He said he thought it strange because he was sure that it was not there when he set the fish pot the night before. Anyway he rowed his little boat nearer and had a little poke inside the hole with his oar. He said at first his body felt sort of funny. He could not say exactly how, but he knew something was not right. He said he used one of his hook and sort of pull out the piece of cloth, was then he noticed something like a person foot. Well he never rowed a boat so hard in all the years he fishing. He pulled up in Marigot bay and bawled out that a body was stuffed in the stone hole. Was like the whole place catch a fire – Concorde, Marigot Grand Roy, the whole place. To begin with they started saying is somebody who killed somebody or the other and stuff the body down there. Quick quick they started saying is Jaspar that kill somebody to pay off the devil. At first nobody thought about it being Miss Sagoo because was miles from where the river took her away, so nobody would think that she would be dragged so far, all the way from Grand Roy.

That was one of the strangest thing that happened in Grenada. Years later people still talked about how the river take the woman high dry season. Imagine, Lent season – everything parched dry, sun splitting earth, farmer want to burn their lands but 'fraid to light fire in case it get away and no water to put it out. No rain for weeks and just like that river come down . . . even after that still no rain. Everybody said it was a sign . . . Papa God coming. Church people started preaching louder that people must repent . . . make peace with God. Every day a different preacher turn up in the foreroad. Some Sundays there are about three or four different groups preaching. Miss Sagoo's daughter came from Trinidad. People didn't even know if that woman alive or dead. Me I didn't know Miss Sagoo had any children. Apparently the woman left Grenada and went overseas years ago, first to Venezuela, they they say she lived somewhere in the Virgin Islands before she settled down in Trinidad. She only came back to Grenada once to see her mother, then she went back, saying Grenada too slow for her. The woman face looked like an old horse and she stupid like some old donkey.

Me and Sheila suffered from shock since the death. Sometimes in the night in bed I hear the river and when I tried to close my eyes is Miss Sagoo I seeing. That was bad enough, but when that woman came and saying is we caused the river to take her mother, well I tell you I almost turn a mental case. She said we should of seen the petticoat hanging on the bush and go and get it instead of letting her old mother try to cross the river again. She went on about how we waited until the river was near before we called out, knowing that the old woman was deaf as bat.

With that woman coming from Trinidad and running her mouth and other people saying how they see the dead woman standing on the river stone, I became very sick. All I did was think about what happened. Always having headaches.

To make matters worse, about three months after all the ruction a woman came from Happy Hill telling Mammy about how she had a dream about me, and Mammy must let her bathe me. Apparently she had to boil all kind of bush, take me to the busherie foreday morning before first cock crow and bathe me. She said that she had special power to drive out evil spirit. She said if Mammy didn't do what she says something bad would happen to me. Mammy run behind the woman. Told her not to bring her damn stupidness in front her door, if anybody had evil spirit on them, was her . . . If is she nastiness she to want to practise, she better go and find somebody else. Then the school children started teasing me and Sheila saying we have lajabless on us. It affected me worse than Sheila, still when her mother said she'll send her to Tivoli to her cousin for a while she was glad to go, because she didn't like school anyway. Me, it was different because I liked school, so even when Sheila said I should ask Mammy to let me go with her, I said no. I didn't want when I come back for the girls in the class to laugh at me because I did not know the subject. I knew they didn't like me already because they say I was too small to be in the same class with them. Some of them have fifteen and sixteen and still in standard four, so was shame they shame because I only had twelve.

Some of them, especially Shirley and Norma, used to make see a lot of trouble. When all these things with Miss Sagoo happened they even used to beat me up. For months afterwards I was not happy at all, not at school, not at home. Mammy was really worried that something would happen to me – especially when people started saying how Miss Sagoo haunting the place. Miss Mae, who lived behind Miss Moore, by where she used to keep the school, said she saw something. Miss Moore had the little private school there for a few years. She used to take in children under five. That was a very good thing because some mothers didn't have time to look after the little children, so for at least during the morning they would go to school where they would learn to write the A B C and get something to eat breakfast time.

The lady running the school good good. As soon as her husband come from America he made her close it down saying he don't want her mixing with all those common people. I don't know who he think he is, because he come from a big country he want to show off on people, thinking he better than even the people he used to go to school with. The trouble was although he didn't want his wife to even talk with the people in the village, it didn't take him long to start running after all the young girls. Joanna, Sheila's sister, the girl was working in a Syrian store in town good good, helping out her mother with the house and thing, after a while I noticed I didn't see her; when I asked Sheila for her she said I too damn farse, I must mind my own business. I was surprised. I didn't find that was farseness at all; I don't go about minding people business, and I told her that. A little while afterwards she told that her sister making baby for Mr Moore and they send her to stay with a godmother in Grenville. Not only the young girls he used to interfere with; that big woman with all those children behind the post office. I don't know what was going on between them, but the woman used to go in the market on Saturdays with Miss Mae – all of a sudden, as if she turn big shot, she don't even want to talk to anybody. Not just that, when Miss Moore used to run the little school, she used to help out Miss Margaret, sometimes giving her two days' work to help her out with the children, even taking the smaller ones on the school without money because the mother could not afford it. Then what happen, eh? What happen, next thing people started talking how is at Miss Margaret Mr Moore does sleep. The woman don't have any shame, she even go to the man house and curse his wife. I never see that before.

Anyway, as I was saying before about Miss Mae seeing something! Was early on Saturday morning she getting ready to pick up Lago Pride for the first trip to town. Everybody trying to go down early to catch the sale, especially as the tourist boat came in the Friday night. That morning Miss Mae sent Anson ahead with a basket of provision. She was only two minutes behind him. She said, as she reached a few yards before where Miss Sagoo had put down the basin to go back for her petticoat, she saw this white thing in the road. At first she thought was Mr Boyce goat that broke the rope. Then as she got nearer her head started sort of swelling up and perspiration started pouring down her back as if she had a bucket of water leaking on her head. She said she felt as if somebody was walking beside her. She had her eyes fixed on the thing in the road. Somehow she knew it was no goat. She got so frightened she could not move. She did not even blink her eyes, yet the thing disappeared ... just like that. One second it was there, the next it vanished ... gone. Then when she sort of glanced out of the corner of her eyes to the river, she saw the shadow of a woman flash in the water. Miss Mae said she had to say five 'Hail Mary' and three 'Our Father' before she could move. Was a good thing Anson did not see it. He sure would of mess himself.

When she reached by the road and told the people what she had seen, they said she is not the first person to see the dead woman. They said because of the way she died her soul was restless, she needed prayers to help her to rest in peace. One of the women said that one day she was washing on the big stone on the side of where the accident happened. She said she was alone in the river, but she heard a cho koo choo chook chook as if somebody scrubbing clothes. When she lifted her head she saw Miss Sagoo plain plain as when she was alive – same red check dress with the old straw hat on her head. It took her a few seconds to remember the woman was dead... by then she had disappeared. People started to be frightened to go to the river so they decided to make a prayer for the dead. After that things settled down.

Our home is sort of sandwiched between the mountain and the sea. When it's really hot the breeze from the mountain and the sea helps to cool the place a bit. Being more or less on the coast, the main road from Sauteurs to St Georges passes through the village. The road narrow, narrow like snake belly. It's like one long silver-black snake coiling in and out... slitty, slittering up a little hill, down a dip. Sometimes between thick provision and fruit trees. Travelling from Palmiste to Gouyave although you on the main road in between provision, you still near the sea. Whether you walking or driving, you could look down into the sea water and see little fishes swimming about. If the sea is rough the waves wash right in the road. Anybody passing have to time the waves and run or get a good soaking. Say you going to Sauteurs by bus from St Georges, it's like you doing all sort of dance in one. One minute the bus bend this way, next it twist the other way.

Before you blink your eyes zuish, cruish, you flying up one hill then jukotoo juk you rolling down another. One minute you by the sea, the next you in the bush belly, and you still travelling along the same main road. For instance, once you cross Grand Roy bridge and go around Boawden corner, it's the sea to left and rocks and thick provision and things on the other side, even over your head.

In the rain season the rock is covered in nice beautiful green clothes. All sort of vines twist itself to form a hot blanket. The vines are all sorts. There are fruit vines like the nice juicy yellow water lemon. Nobody take notice of it until they start riping and falling in the road. There is the stinking-toe. Same as the water lemon, you don't know the tree is between the vine until the hard-shelled fruit start to fall. Not everybody like stinking-toe, they say it make news like mandarin. The shell is hard as coconut so you have to take a stone to pound it open. If you not careful, all the dry powder inside fly up in your face and on your clothes. Even when you eating it, it makes news. Once it's in your mouth, if feels like wet flour, sticky sticky, and messing up your face. Not only that but the name describe it just right ... because it smells strong. Apart from fruit vines we also get skipping rope between the bushes.

If someone wants to really enjoy a nice refreshing walk along the sea front early morning is the best time. That's the time when the sea breeze cool and refreshing, and as the birds would be getting up to hear them singing is just wonderful. A stranger taking a walk would find it hard to believe it's one main road that runs all round the island. It branches off all over the place like centipede legs, but you can still follow the one road. If you in Grand Roy and walking, to say, past Victoria, when you leave Boawden gap, walk across Lapoutree to White Gate and you'll pass under the big silk cotton tree. People afraid to walk there in the night; they say in the trunk is the devil and his disciples' workshop. I don't believe all that stupidness. I more believe it's the owners of the gardens behind the tree that trying to frighten people to prevent them from thiefing their food and things, especially the fruits. Right by the side of the tree is a big mango Rose tree. When it's in season the owner hardly get one mango to make remedy. School children stoning the mango, even before they start to ripe.

There are plenty of other fruits as well. Lots of guava trees. When they riping and the sun hot, the sweet smell of those big yellow guava hit your nose like essence. Sometimes it smell as if guava jelly or cheese cooking. The thing with guava is not only children love it, but snakes too. You see a tree branches spread out covered in juicy yellow guava, then you notice holes in the fruits. When you look closer you have to run because what you see is a long silver snake sliding and twisting among the branches. It move about just like the bus on the road, in and out around and about. One minute the head is one place, next minute it's on another branch and you hardly notice it moving. They say the snakes are not dangerous. They reckon it is more afraid of people than the other way round, but I'm not going close to find out, especially if the sun splitting earth. Some stories have it that in the heat the snakes get vex and fly.

Not only in the guava trees snakes live but in the silk cotton tree as well . . . snakes and great big black and white, and sometimes red, serpents. They twist up, twist up around the branches of the silk cotton tree. Could be why they believe the devil and his disciples are happy there. Some of the things you hear is really hard to believe. Sometimes again it's hard not to think about them, because for instance look how the silk cotton tree shape. It shaped different from the other trees. It sort of stands like a house on four posts, and boarded up on three sides with a door on the fourth side. It's the tallest and biggest tree along the road. The trunk is big and thick, not like a big mango tree or anything like that. If you peep inside it's like a big dark room. The branches spread wide all around like an umbrella, covering the road and over the sea. Its shadow shades straight out to the big white stone in the middle of the water.

That's another thing. They say that a mermaid lives under the stone. Certain time of the year in the middle of the night on a full moon night she would come out and sit on the stone combing her long hair. She always sit with her back to the road. Nobody ever saw her face clearly. She sits in way that only the top part of her body is out of the water.

Mammy told me a story that happened a long time ago. It's a long time but the man is still alive. He in the poor house in Mileweze now. His sister is old living somewhere in Shantimel. Anyway, Mammy said one Friday night moonlight bright a gang of young boys were walking from Victoria to home. They stayed liming in Victoria until it late and they couldn't get a lift, so they decided to walk. As they got near the silk cotton tree they smelt that sweet sweet perfume. Nice lady perfume. Because of all the stories they know about the place, smelling perfume this time of the night was something to make the hair in their head raise up. Caryle started shaking like a leaf. Same time he grabbed Matthew hand saying, 'O gawd boy. You smell it. Mus be lajabless going home. We done tonight ... we done.' They were about to run when Amos noticed a shadow on the stone.

'Aaye; all you look. Look. I think is the merrimaid perfume. Look she on the stone.' He shouted out. Stand up plamp under the cotton tree.

'What you on about man?' Cecil shouted to him. 'Come on run ... run.'

'Look ... Look!' Amos pointing to the stone. 'I always

hearing about the merrimaid, I never see her. Is six of us; she can't do us anything.'

'Amos, Amos you stupidy,' Matthew shouted. 'Come on before she get you. Amos, come on.' Amos took no notice of his friends. He was fascinated by the figure on the stone. He stood on the narrow wall separating the road from the sea, still pointing to the figure. The shadows of the leaves were like dancers on his face.

'Look; all you look. The moon bright I could see her good good. It's the mermaid alright. You all too damn coward. I want to see her legs.' Amos started to jump behind the wall.

'Amos you idiot! Come back. She don't have legs. Amos, come back. She don't have legs, she have fish tail,' Caryle shouted.

'Yeah, what leg. You ever hear merrimaid have legs? You can't even see her face properly. You think is her legs you go so,' Cecil added. 'Come on, let's run.' The young men have moved from under the shadow of the tree and were limbering between a brisk walk and full scale run.

'Is woman you want. Go on, is woman you after.'

Gordon who was quiet all the while added, 'You smell sweet perfume in the middle of the night. You see merri-maid sitting on the stone for you to run like hell. You on about you going to see her legs, you good day oui!' With that last remarks the boys started to run. A now excited Amos was foot searching for safe place to approach the beach to have closer look. The last thing the other boys saw of him was the shadow of his white jersey half way on the shore like a spirit.

About half past three the next morning Miss Mina wake up to get her things ready to go to the market. She expected Amos to get up when he hear her in the kitchen. She busy busy in the kitchen, packing the baskets and things. No Amos. This boy so lazy, she muttered to herself. 'He so damn lazy. Last night he go and wet his tail in Victoria, this morning he can't get up to help me.'

She went around the house to his room. Opened the door, pushed her head towards the corner where his bed is. 'Amos,' she called quietly, not wanting to wake his sister in the next room. 'Amos, time to get up.' No answer. She went inside and was about to pull the cover when she noticed that the bed hadn't been slept in. Everything was just as she left it when she made up his bed yesterday morning.

Miss Mina started quarrelling, saying how Amos is a good for nothing. He know is Saturday morning and his father not home. The boy knows that. He knows his father still in Trinidad. These Trinidad people is something else. Always mashing up people business. All the time for them to strike they don't strike. They wait until the nutmeg co-operation meeting finish and the people have to come back to Grenada to close down Piarco airport. Now the man can't come home until Sunday morning. Amos knows that ... he knows; you know. Instead of coming home to help to bring the load by the road and go in the bush early to change the animal he following woman frock tail. She was real vex, but something inside her sort of telling her something else, as if somebody trying to talk to her. She went back inside the room and looked around. Nuh, something wrong. Something wrong, she thought. She shook her head. 'Mavis, Mavis get up,' she called her daughter. 'Get up, girl, you brother didn't come home last night.' She went to the girl's room. 'Amos! Mavis you hear me girl, get up. You hear what I say. Amos didn't come home last night.'

Mavis was four years younger than Amos, but since Amos came to live with them after their grandmother died, they were very close. If Amos meant to sleep out he would tell his sister. He usually tell her most things he did in the village. When she heard her brother didn't come home,

Mavis jumped out of her sleep as if she was pushed out of a dream.

'You brother tell you nuthing yesterday?' her mother ask. 'He tell you he go sleep out last night?'

'No Ma'am. What you mean?' Mavis was wondering about the girl up the road that Amos told her about. He better be careful. These people and them don't make joke with their girl children, you know.

'What you mean, what I mean? I tell you he din sleep in his bed.'

'Amos don't sleep out, Ma. Perhaps he went to the garden early.'

'Nuh, girl, something wrong. His garden clothes hang up on the nail.' Miss Mina stood in front of Amos room, one hand crossed in front her, the other cupped her mouth. Her piercing eyes seemed to be boring into the door. Mavis came out to meet her. It was then about four o'clock.

'Don't worry Ma'am, he soon come. Perhaps they sleep in Victoria, he soon come.'

The same time they heard footsteps on the gravel in the front yard. Mavis laugh, 'See what I tell you? You wake me up for nothing. I tell you he soon come.'

'Amos. Amos,' a voice called in the front yard. Quick quick Miss Mina followed by Mavis went to see who it was. Outside was still dusky. They could just make out Caryle standing like a spirit in front the door.

'Caryle, whey Amos?' Miss Mina asked. 'I thought he went out with you last night, eh? Whey him? He din sleep in his bed last night.'

'Marning Miss Mina,' the young man said.

'Whey's Amos?' Mavis asked.

In the half darkness he looked even darker than usual. He started scratching. His hands went to his head, then his foot, then to his back.

'Caryle, where is Amos?' Mavis asked again, seeing his movement. 'What wrong with you?'

'I thought he came home, Miss Mina. I thought he came home. That's why I come and call him to go in the bush.' Caryle was jumpy as if jumbie was playing with him.

Miss Mina was not actually looking at the young man. She was looking at his dim shadow doing a sort of African war dance as he scratched himself.

'Amos didn't come home,' Mavis said. 'What was the last time you see him last night? You all left him in Victoria, eh Caryle? You left him in Victoria last night didn't you?'

'O Gawd Bunjay oye,' Caryle bellowed. With that, before Mavis or Miss Mina can open their mouth, he turned and run towards his home. The day was beginning to brighten up. The reflection of the sun was over the mountain. The neighbours were getting up. Miss Mina heard Mr Baptiste talking in his house. She called him and tell him that Amos did not come home last night. She babbled on what happened a few minutes ago, but Mr Baptiste was not listening.

'Perhaps he find a young lady in Victoria,' he joked.

She went and stand behind her kitchen where she can see Mr Baptiste in front his door. She related again the incident with Caryle a few minutes ago.

'True. I saw them going up last night. Was Amos, Cecil, Caryle and Eddie two boys. Did Caryle say where they left Amos, or where he was when they last saw him?'

'The boy din say nuthing. Just started bawling for papa bunjay and running. Mr Baptiste, someting happen to Amos. Someting funny happen to my boy. I going in the police station.'

'I coming Ma'am. I coming,' Mavis said.

Mr Baptiste left his wife preparing the tea saying he going to the police station with the neighbour. By that time Miss Mina was half way down the road, her two hands on her head bawling, and Mavis behind her also bawling. By the time they reach the station Caryle was there dancing like he had pougatae in his skin. Although it was very early morning people was by the road, already wondering what's happening. Miss Marcia, that's Eddie's wife, came and hold up Miss Mina. Cecil's mother and father was there. Cecil behind them looking like a spirit. Miss Mina and Mavis bawling how something happened to Amos, without even knowing anything at all. How the rumour reach up Mt Plaisir so quickly nobody knows, but Amos aunty, the one he couldn't get on with, she come running down the road screaming how they kill her nephew.

In the confusion that followed, the police managed to get a story from Cecil and Caryle. Some people found it very funny . . . they couldn't understand how Amos could be so stupid . . . or why the other boys didn't drag him home. But then some said the mermaid already had Amos marked out, there was nothing anyone could do. A group of men decided to go and look for the boy. Miss Mina wanted to go with them, but they told her to stay in the station. Mavis stayed with her but her aunt went with the men. When they reached around Boawden corner they saw some of the bay men coming towards them. The way they were shouting and waving their hands it was obvious they were not talking about fish. Three men were sort of carrying a bundle. It was Amos. Apparently after the men from Allen cast their net, the lookout man spotted a person sort of folded up between the stone hole under the silk cotton tree. He called out, but the person did not answer. He then shouted to the others on the shore. That's how they found Amos, naked apart from his tear up jersey in his hand. All what they asked him the only thing he kept saying was: 'She prutty prutty prutty.' That was hot hot news for a few weeks. They teased Amos, teased Amos. They even made carnival song on him. After a while, people don't bother with him. He was just there saying nothing but: 'She prutty prutty prutty.' One thing for sure, for a long time those boys never stayed in Gouyave late.

The Mermaid's Legs

Even now, people say when they pass under the tree you could smell either sweet sweet woman perfume or strong medicine like a doctor shop.

'The Mermaid's Legs' is an extract from Jean Buffong's novel *Under the Silk Cotton Tree*, published by The Women's Press.

Evolution Annie

ROSALEEN LOVE

For Roy Lewis who nearly got the story right, but not quite.[1]

You know all those stories of origins, those myths of our beginnings. 'A group of animals lived in the trees,' they'd start, and continue with the saga of how one day, down we came, we discovered the plains and the joys of upright posture. We stood up, looked around, and decided to stay.

I have to tell you something. That story is a myth. That wasn't how it happened, not how it happened at all.

I suppose you've read all about the importance of the dominant male in this early group, the primeval Father, and how civilisation began one day when a group of his sons got together and co-operated for the first time in rejecting their Father's authority. They killed him and ate him, or so the story goes, and that was the beginning of it all – guilt (naturally) and civilisation as the oh-so-thin veneer covering the beast within, and since incest had something to do with this version of what we did to Father, this dark deed of our early days led (allegedly) to bonding outside the family group. For the greater good of the gene pool, some say, though I think that is stretching the evidence too far, imagining we knew all that back there in the Pleistocene, when of course we were just doing what came naturally. We had the trick of moving on to higher things. We had other reasons for doing the old man in.

Another story has it that we suppressed all knowledge of this dirty deed, sublimating it instead into the act of going to church on Sunday.

I ask you, does that sound a likely story? Just because it's complicated, and inherently improbable, doesn't mean it has to be true. Take hold of your own common sense in these matters. It sounds improbable because it is.

Call me Annie. Evolution Annie. Come listen to my tale. Let me tell you the story of our beginnings.

We didn't decide to come down from the trees as an act of free choice. We fell out of the trees and had to make the best of our new circumstances. It wasn't Father whom the boys killed and ate one day in the (alleged) first act of ritual communion. It was Mother who decided someone had to go, so she . . . but that is getting ahead of my story.

I am Annie, a diminutive prosimian, or so they will later describe me. I can tell you I am neither ape nor monkey, but something with the edge on both, as far as brains go, and their use in the skilful manipulation of what brawn I possess. Diminutive I may be, prosimian I am, but never underestimate the sheer animal cunning, the near-human intellect of the humble small prosimian. Look at the merry dance our bones have led you all, look at the clever way we've let fall a hint here, a hint there, that we were far more than we seemed.

Call me names, I can take it. Come on 'Ape-like ancestor'! Ya, heard it all before. 'Primitive' – ouch, that hurts, that really hurts. I am what I am, and proud of it. 'Primitive' is a relative not an absolute term.

We know it now, though we didn't know it then – that we didn't need to progress much further along the line we were taking when we first fell out of the trees, but nobody could predict it, back then. Least of all Mother. If only she'd known she'd have made us climb back at once. Her death was to be a triumph of the simians, her rebirth a source of inspiration to us all. What we learned from Mother was that the bigger brain has not been worth the effort.

When we first fell out of the trees there was great consternation.

'This is it,' said Father. 'This is a sign from above that we must embark on a long and dangerous journey. Clearly the moment has come to get up on our two feet and take a long walk. We shall meet danger, and suffer discomfort, and we shall be sorely tried along the way, but we must go on, upwards and ever onwards.'

'That's a good idea, Edward,' Mother agreed. 'Why don't you and the boys go off and do all that, and we'll stay here in the long grass under this shady tree, and wait for you to return?' So the boys went off with Father, and some of them returned, after tests of fortitude and endurance which Mother agreed would surely have been too much for me, Annie, and my various aunts and cousin and sisters and their babies. While the boys battled raging torrents and the common cold from the icy blasts from the north, and sandy blight from the hot desert winds from the south, and lions, tigers, killer ants one way, the woolly mammoth in the opposite direction, Mother just sat underneath the tree. She taught us all she knew: sewing, rope-making, splicing, basketwork, the practical things of life, though she did not neglect our higher natures. Along the way she also devised the first alphabet, a fairly primitive affair in the light of what came later, but the little ones picked it up quickly. She baked a few clay tablets, for the cuneiform, she said vaguely, though she never did much with them, being busy at the time with plans for her funeral. Not for her the old ways, where we chewed the deceased around for a bit, and threw the bones out of the trees. She wanted something more for herself, a small burial chamber inside a largish pyramid, to keep out the hyenas, and our Father, for eternity. (Though this was a passing phase. Later Mother decided the pyramid was not really her.)

Mother stayed at home and developed tools and the skills of reason. Father and the boys went out into the world and got cold and wet and suffered broken bones and fell into chasms and some of them survived frostbite, crocodiles, tigers, giant leeches that fell from the trees, snakes that rose up from the earth, poisonous berries (soon to be so labelled by my mother, the experimental botanist), killer crabs with giant pincers, elephants, and worse. So many ways for a primitive prosimian to die out there, but we were protected from all through Mother's care and foresight. The male of the species, we knew it even back then, is more prone to accidental death. Staying home under the trees made excellent sense to us girls.

Fire, now, I'm sure you've heard their version of events. How Man the Hunter strode to the edge of the spitting volcano, bravely dodging the hissing dragons, the smoking sulphurous fumaroles, the lions and bears that stood between him and the precious new discovery. Man the Brave strode to the edge of the bubbling lava, thrust a stick into the fire from below, and took it back, overcoming all the trials and tribulations of keeping it alight. Man harnessing an unruly Nature to his own ends. Man bringing Woman the tools of cooking. Man pointing the way to the Division of Labour, with Man the Hunter of Fire, and Woman the Grateful Recipient.

No. These are stories they tell, but they are truly myths of our beginnings. They are the yarns men spin around the camp fire to make them feel good about things.

Father didn't bring fire from the volcano. Fire just happened. One day there was a great storm, and a lightning strike, and fire came to the grassy plains of the veldt, and we ran before it, until it veered away from us. It left behind a few burning logs, which we kept alight out of scientific interest in manipulating and controlling our environment. Father was away doing something else at the time.

I don't want to make too much of it. Fire happened, that's all. It was an event in our lives. Fire, from which, when we lived in the trees, we frequently had to flee, but now we lived on the ground, we could discover the value of the firebreak. Properly under control, fire could become a hearth, and with the hearth came the possibilities of a true home, in the sense we now know it. We couldn't do that when we lived in the trees. The forest would burn, taking us with it.

When Father first saw the hearth on his return home from what he and the boys liked to call hunting, but I call mucking around in the bush, the first thing he said was, 'Why did you have to ruin a perfectly good camp site by messing around with fire?'

Mother said, 'OK, you take it back to where it came from then. You and the boys, see that volcano over there? Kilimanjaro? Why don't you take this burning brand – mind you keep it alight all the way – and run up to the smoking crater at the top, and throw it in. Propitiate a fire god or two, and you'll feel a lot more comfortable.

Father and the boys took some of the fire back to heaven, and they felt all the better for it, while Mother and me and the rest of us girls just got on with learning the finer techniques of cooking. Meat with the inside quite raw, and the outside thoroughly blackened, the way we like it best.

Then Mother figured out a way to divert some water from the river down a channel and across the savannah, so that we had reticulated water and the beginning of a sewerage system.

'What are you doing, ruining a perfectly good camp site by bringing water to it?' asked Father on his return, minus one or two of the boys. 'Dirt is perfectly natural, and we should all be rolling in more of it, such is nature's way.'

So Mother gave Father a goatskin full of water and told him to go off and find the source of the Nile, and return it to the Earth our Mother and then everything would be all right.

Before he left this time, Father called us all round him and gave us a lecture on the division of labour. 'It works like this. You women stay home, now we've got this hearth, not that I approve of fire in the house, the proper place for fire is in the volcano, but be that as it may, you girls stay here and make this place as nice as you can, in preparation for our return, and we'll go off and become the specialists in our field.' Father waved regally at us as he prepared to leave. 'You may, if you like, gather a few berries while we are gone.'

Mother saw it differently. She was developing the hearth-based multi-skilled workforce. Like Leonardo da Vinci who was to follow her so much later, Mother kept churning out the ideas, and some of them worked, and some of them were years before their time.

'Running around after wild animals will mark a dead end in evolutionary development,' said Mother, as she fed grass seed to what she called her chicks, small feathered creatures she encouraged round the camp site for their eggs. They had to be good for something, Mother reckoned. Burnt feathers tasted quite revolting.

'Without effort there can be no improvement,' said Father, kicking a chicken out of the way.

'I agree,' said Mother. 'After the Nile, you could try Mount Everest, and after you've done that once, you could try it a second time, without oxygen.' She was careful to remind him as she rescued a couple of eggs from in front of his feet, that if he was going to try Everest, he had better remember to take long strips of gazelle hide to wrap around his feet as moccasins.

Father's trips gave Mother the peace she required to get on with the work of her gravesite. She was quietly persistent on the topic of the afterlife. 'It will be a time of peace and quiet. Calm after the storm. Rest after work.'

'What about the boys, Mother?'

'There will be boys,' said Mother, 'but they will be changed. They will be more like us.'

Naturally we scoffed.

'The savannah will bloom, and the lion will gambol with the dove . . .

My sister, Sukie, fell about laughing.

'And if you don't believe me, you can go down there and help with the digging.'

We said we believed her all right.

For the afterlife, Mother knew she would need a new kind of dwelling place, but she never could work out in her own mind what it should be. She moved on from the pyramid to the barrow, a pre-dug affair, basically a hollow chamber under a mound of dirt. 'Get cracking,' she'd say to the boys, first thing in the morning on one of their increasingly shorter sojourns in the camp. 'Hollow out those shelves there for the sacred relics.'

'Sacred relics?' Father would snarl and stamp off, but we noticed he used to slink back and listen when Mother explained what she meant. 'I'll need food,' she said, 'if I'm to set out on a long voyage into the afterlife. And I'll need a few of the comforts of home, a vase or two, and a pot for the unguents.;'

'Unguents are unnatural,' said Father. 'We were born to eat pulverised cockroaches, not smear them on our bodies.'

'Take no notice of your Father. You'll all miss me, when I'm gone.' The little ones burst into tears, and Father and the boys could stand it no more, and went off to explore the ancient continent of Gondwana.

The invention of alcohol took all our female skills. Who

else but Mother could take the grated root of one cassava, a few juniper berries and a handful of banana skins, and make something drinkable from it? Father would have us all dead from using the wrong cassava, the poisonous variety. Mother was the one who was rock solid reliable in all botanical matters.

The problems really began when the boys came back again. They returned from the life of action and started sitting round the fire drinking gin and causing trouble.

This time they proved more than usually resistant to Mother's plans to send them to China across the overland route. 'The Himalayas and the Gobi Desert. You know, over there.' She waved her hand in a direction in which they hadn't yet gone off. 'Spices, tea, trade. That's where the future lies. The Orient and its mysteries. Why not give it a go?'

'No,' said Father firmly. 'Pour me another gin, Giselle.'

Though Giselle spiked his gin with a deadly nightshade berry or two, Father survived, while crying feebly, 'Pour me another gin, Giselle. That last one packed a wallop.'

Mother called us girls together. 'Those boys will be the death of me,' she said, staring into her half-completed barrow.

How could we all combine to keep Mother out of her grave that little bit longer? Especially when some of the boys were getting rebellious. 'If she wants to go on a trip to the afterlife, why stop her?' they said. 'It's time she started going on one of those long trips she's so fond of sending us on. Let her see what it's like. And while we're about it, why not give her a shove along the way?'

Of course the girls told Mother, and she kept the boys on short rations for a week.

'I'd like a nice grave facing the sunrise,' said Mother. 'Or perhaps the sunset. The sunset over that part of the savannah I always find particularly entrancing. Perhaps some idols in my grave, images of frogs, fish and snakes, to ensure regeneration after death, and propitiate the Archetypal Feminine?' She kept the girls busy inventing sculpture.

It marked the turning point in the evolution of the prosimians, the way we were tried and tested again and again, whenever the boys came home with Father. Back they'd come and settle into the joys of the hearth and home, and though Mother said she was listening to the travellers' tales, she often had that faraway look in her eyes, as if she was preparing a speech to which one day they would all have to sit up and listen.

The boys came home, some of them, and rolled around the rush floor wrestling, and they took the mickey out of Mother for her funeral plans, and Father sat down in the least windy corner and expected to be waited on, and that was the first time in human civilisation that women realised how much better off they were when the men were off and away doing their own thing.

The first act of human co-operation was when we got together, Mother and the rest of the women, and worked on plans to send the men away. We held what was probably the first Council of War about it. (This was before we came to the conclusion that peace was the way to go.)

'Annie,' said Mother, 'see that tribe of *Homo habilis* over the hill?'

'What, that lot that eat giraffe?'

'They're gross,' said my sister Sukie. 'Giraffe!'

'The eating habits of *Homo habilis* may not be our own, but that is purely because they have developed the stone axe, while we are specialising in the refinements of civilisation.' Mother recognised that the stone axe gave them an edge on us with respect to carving a haunch of giraffe, but she could see further than this. She could see the potential uses to which a pre-chewed thigh-bone of giraffe could be put.

War, for example.

'How'd you think they'd go in a battle with Father?' Mother had to explain what she meant. 'First one of them picks up the thigh-bone, and hits his neighbour over the head with it. Of course, the neighbour soon gives as good as he gets, and so it goes. It's called war.'

I shall always be grateful for the things my mother taught me. Though she soon decided that war was for the future, she was the first to recognise the possibilities, and the problems. She knew that if we went down the evolutionary path to war, the boys would take to beating up the neighbours, but she could think the whole thing through. She knew that once they got the knack of it, they'd soon take to beating us.

'Murder and mayhem are thoughtless, uncivilised, backward-looking activities, leading us one way only, back to the trees,' said Mother. She stuck to the peace, although she knew the threat of war.

Instead of warfare, Mother substituted cricket.

'See that thigh-bone of giraffe?' Mother asked my sister Giselle. 'I want you to go and get it for me.'

'What, go down into the valley with all those *Homo habilis* yoicks?'

'Now. This minute.'

'Why does it always have to be me? I always have to do everything.'

'Because you're so good at it,' said Mother, sending her off down the hill with a cheerful shove.

My sister Giselle was always the great whinger of the family, and the effect of whingeing on human evolution has never been studied, as far as I know. Whingeing doesn't show up in the bones, so no one gives it any thought, but my sister Giselle was the first and the best at doing the least work round the camp and making the most fuss about it. Giselle whinged, and the more she whinged the more jobs Mother gave her to do, to take her away from the trees and out onto the savannah where the boys chased after the gazelles.

Man the Hunter, Ha! Man the accidental-tripper-over of the lion's leftovers, that's what those boys were. According to Mother, all this hunting business was merely a temporary aberration, useful for keeping the boys busy but useless to anyone who wants to maintain an orderly camp routine centred around hearth and home. Someone has to mind the babies, and Mother regarded hunting as a device invented by Father to get out of his regular child-care duties.

Man the Killer Ape? I suppose when Giselle was sent off to get the thigh-bone of the giraffe (and Mother was right, Giselle did get it; it was thrown at her when she moaned and groaned about her wretched lot) the idea was perhaps then in Mother's mind, Man the Killer Ape. Hit Father over the head and be done with him forever. But Mother being Mother, as soon as she saw the possibilities of shaping the bone into a bat, and a lump of chewed gazelle tendon into a ball, we became instead 'Man the Cricketer'. I have to hand it to Mother. As the ball was sent flying off across the savannah and various scores called 'runs' were marked up on the wet clay tablets, the boys made use of their enormous stock of energy and their oversupply of hormones, and we found a new use for the cuneiform.

As the shadows lengthened, and the seasons changed, and the chill wind blew from the ice, Mother knew that the cricket season had come to an end. Cricket, she wanted to believe, was the game which would best inculcate the team spirit, show the boys how to be good losers, and teach them that eye-hand co-ordination so necessary for lead-

ing them gently on to the higher pursuits of reading, writing, weaving and sewing.

Alas, Mother's fond hopes for the civilising influence of
cricket on the prosimian male were doomed for the start.
Father and the boys soon adapted the game to their own
ends, and cries of 'Up yours!' and 'Howzzat?' delivered
in an aggressive and unco-operative fashion, the ball hurled
down the pitch with the intention of hitting the batter
square in the goolies, the ferocity of attack when the bat
connected with the ball, the way it sailed high in the
treetops and fell to earth on some innocent toddling prosimian, all these innovations were too much for Mother.

Worse, much worse, was to happen once winter started,
and cricket gave way to football. The neighbouring hordes
wanted to join in, and our pleasant camp site was invaded
each Saturday by groups of loutish *Homo habilis*, who
introduced the custom of spectator hooliganism and
punching up the umpire.

As she began to realise the unintended consequences of
her actions, Mother grew quiet and spent more of her time
uncharacteristically brooding in front of the fire. It was
then that it started to sink in on us that Mother was growing old. Her fur was tinged with grey, her eyesight was
not as keen as once it was. Sooner or later, Mother would
lie in her grave, and we knew how much we would miss
her, when she was gone.

These thoughts marked the beginnings of philosophy.

The way they tell it now, back then we suddenly discovered ourselves the possessors of rather large brains, so
we used the surplus grey matter for thinking.

No. That's not the whole truth. The brain was still a bit
on the small side when we first fell out of the trees, but
down on the ground the hands soon grew strong and

skilful in their weaving and sewing. It was the skill of the hands that drove the brain on to bigger and better things.

Try telling that to Father. He simply will not listen. Father believes in brain-led innate male superiority, because he has, by sheer weight of comparative size of everything else, more brains.

'Mere quantity alone,' muttered Mother, 'means nothing. Consider the case of the elephant. Huge brain, no sense.' She explained the steady growth of the human brain as the result of co-operative acts. It takes groups of people working happily together to erect grass humpies, to dig gardens, to create agriculture and a settled pattern of existence. The skilful use of tools in turn affects the neural connections of the brain, as new habits of life are forged, in ways not yet really understood.

Mother only knew that social change must give rise to physical change, and the prosimian brain did not lead this process. It trailed far behind.

We all knew that Father's behaviour was never any kind of argument for intelligence in diminutive prosimians, at least, in the male of the species. The females were different. There seemed some reason, in us, for the existence of sex-linked individual differences. We had the common sense. They had the wanderlust.

There were plenty of other differences.

'Is it, as Father suggests, that there is a good Father in the sky, who will guard us from harm, if we set about approaching him properly?'

'No,' said Mother. 'There is a good Mother in the earth, who asks only that the system of natural cycles of matter and energy go their own way, unhampered, through the systems of air, water and earth. It's like this, Annie,' my mother would often say to me, for being the youngest in the family I was often about her furry knees, 'Annie, this life must be but a pale shadow of something quite other than it seems. There has to be something more to it than the endless round of gathering food, eating it, and using the sewerage system for its newly designed purpose. What are we training the little ones to collect berries for? For food, I know, but there must be another reason for our existence.'

So Mother reflected on the connections between things. She noticed the pathways in nature, how the berry changed its form and nature as it passed from the bush to become first food for the birds, then ready-mix guano fertiliser, then the new plant germinated from the seed, to berry again. Mother was the first to think this was about nature's bounty, the first to try to keep things moving round, to keep the carbon and nitrogen cycles in some kind of order. She was the first of the great recyclers.

In the rare moments when they were together, Mother and Father agreed on one thing only – the importance of stories for the moral development of the young, to encourage the young into proper patterns of good behaviour. 'Heroic behaviour,' said Father. 'Warm, nurturant, co-operative, sharing behaviour,' Mother would retort sharply, wanting to instil in her brood from the beginning the virtues of co-operation over the sin of competition.

So when Father told the littlies the story of prosimian Lucy and the big bad paleontologist who got the story of our beginnings quite wrong, and the bloodthirsty fate that befell poor Lucy when her bones were later dug up and displayed on TV, Mother told tales of daily life centred on the composition of the good compost heap. And if the eyes of the littlies glazed over somewhat faster with Mother's stories than with Father's tales of goodies and baddies, at least Mother's stories served the function of getting them off to sleep in a reasonably short period of time.

Mother's stories told them what Father's left out, that winning the race to be fully human was not really what it was all about. What matters is the kind of human being we develop at the end of the race, nurturing, caring, someone who will properly respect their mother's gave, when she is gone.

Sitting around the camp fire, combing each other's hair, catching the odd louse, tick, flea or other parasite, gazing into the fire, there we were, a group of happy prosimian women with but one problem in the world, what to do with the men?

'It's them!' said Auntie Elsie, as the dust on the horizon signalled a herd of stampeding gazelle, one sure sign that the men were on their way back to us, making the maximum amount of noise. Back from the away match in the camp down the road, and stoned to the gills on poisonous home brew.

'Why don't we . . .' said Auntie Elsie. 'When you think of it . . .' She pounced on another louse at the back of Mother's furry neck. 'Why don't we just move on ourselves, leave the home fire burning and the empty cradle rocking gently, and the shelters deserted, leave a mystery behind, and just go off and set up camp somewhere else? Leave the camp to the boys. Just walk out and leave it all, leave the stuff of mysteries behind, leave, just leave.'

'Elsie, you always were a hopeless, mooning romantic,' said Mother. 'What, leave my lovely grave?' and we knew we couldn't ask her to do that.

'The way I see it, men are some small use. In youth, when female passion outstrips common sense, reason, intellect, and whatever, and our hormones send us racing in their direction for those few short heady moments of passion which lead we all know where.' To the babies playing around our feet. 'But with age comes wisdom, and the recognition it's not really been worth all that trouble. The way I see it, we still need them, for the moment, to propagate the species and replenish the stock of babies, who, you know, fall all too easily to the marauding leopard or the rapacious fox.'

Ah, those long-lost days of the primal horde, before women invented the incest taboo. It had been all the same to us then, whether it was our brothers or our fathers whom we used to create the new batch of babies. We lived, unawakened, in a state of primitive promiscuity, not realising the future harm inbreeding might cause the human species. It's not true, what they said, that it was Father who unwittingly, through the manner of his death, instituted the custom of exogamy, of marrying out of the family. No, it happened well before Father met his fate at the hands of his sons. (You remember that story, where the boys were so furious when he ordered them away from their sisters, that the boys killed him and ate him? Afterwards, it was said, they felt sorry for what they had done, and were consumed with a guilt so strong that from that day on they did what Father had ordered back when the fracas started.) Sigmund Freud invented that story, but only to conceal his own dubious motives, to hide the guilt he felt about inventing the crazy story in the first place.

No, the practice of marrying out of the horde into which one was born was the invention of Mother. When she sent Father and the boys off on their long and dangerous pilgrimages, the smartest boys soon got worn out with it all, and dropped off at neighbouring tribes along the way, where the local girls congratulated them on their cleverness, and begged them to stay. Some of the boys settled down happily, far from home, spreading their smart genes through a wider population. Genetic diversity, that's the key to evolutionary success, though we didn't think of it in quite those terms then. How could we use those words, when we barely knew the relationship between copulation and conception? Except that whenever the boys were home, conception happened all the time, and when they went away, we got a bit of a break from the child-bearing side of things.

From time to time Father came home, to replenish the supply of young males, and to take the next batch of boys on his travels. Occasionally, we girls would try to get our brothers to see the light, to encourage them to think that they, too, could be weavers and potters and writers like us, but no, it was in the blood, the urge to follow a male leader, even if he led them up mountains and through bogs and into immense hardship, at all times testing their endurance to the limit.

What us girls wanted to know was, why did they do it? What were they running away from? Us? What were they trying to prove? These questions remain unanswered, to this day.

According to Mother, the men could come and go, grow up and leave, after various fashions, but it was Matriarchy which provided the solid core to society, the handing of camp fire sites down through the female line to the women. It made eminent sense to her. Through the institution of the matrilinear descent of property, Mother knew she could achieve respect in life, and exercise some control beyond the grave. Marrying her daughters out to the horde made sense, when she started to think about it in terms of real estate. It multiplied the number of camp sites all over Africa, and round all those camp sites people would sit, and remember the tales of her exploits. Big Mother, the first of her kind.

Everyone knew the camp site belonged to the women, while the men bequeathed necklaces of hyena's teeth and similar useless objects to their sons.

With respect to the housing crisis of the Holocene who, except Mother, back in the Pleistocene, made moves to protect their descendants in this way? Big Mother, the first and best of them all.

*

How to explain it, the bond that developed between us sisters as we went about our daily tasks, the feeling that arose in us, for the Earth, our Mother, of which our own dear Mother represented the living embodiment of all the caring, nurturing features we held most dear, the source of warmth and nourishment, rest for the weary, unguent for the harassed soul. We developed a feeling of unity with the bare earth under our paws. We learned to feel special, because we alone stood upright, our eyes fixed on the stars, our feet planted on solid earth.

If only we could get the boys to see things our way. Mother was starting to work on her plan, except we didn't know what was happening, until it was over.

It was too good to last. The practice of exogamy, together with the invention of team sports, combined according to some relentless inner logic that Mother could hardly have thought through, to present us with problems on a large scale. How to stem the tide of aggressive mindless violence at sporting occasions, and increasingly at weddings, that seemed to be accompanying the widespread adoption of our customs across the savannah? Alcohol contributed, too, and towards the end of her life Mother grew increasingly sad at the use to which her bright ideas were being put.

She made several attempts at civilian control. The police force was brought into being, and the institution of human slavery helped get rid of the worst offenders, but Mother could see that Paradise could never be regained, not in Africa. The years slipped by, and Mother increasingly just sat by her barrow, waiting for the moment when she would enter it for the last time.

'The boys will see it our way, when I am gone.' She believed to the end that with her passing the religion of God the Mother would begin.

When our Mother said her time was come, we knew what those words meant. We knew what we were expected to do. She had grown steadily weaker, and now she could barely move from her bed of rushes to greet the new day with her customary invocation to the sky and the sun, the bringer of warmth, and earth the bringer of nourishment.

We took her announcement to mean that she wished Father to prepare the drink from the cassava root, and ferment the juniper berries for her last meal. We knew what that entailed. Father would get it wrong, for he never properly worked out the difference between the safe and dangerous plants.

Father was pleased to be trusted with a simple action of the hearth. He didn't notice when Auntie Elsie poured the rest of the drink on the ground, once Mother had taken her cup.

Afterwards we laid Mother to rest in her barrow grave, and placed round her offerings she prized, pots of cassava flour, a jar of sloe gin, a few dull heavy stones that she predicted would be called 'gold' in the afterlife, and last of all, her precious tablets of slate and clay, with the mysterious marks of the cuneiform upon them.

According to Mother's instructions, we refused Father's offer of help in eating the remains, and we made sure we sealed up the door with heavy rocks the way she wanted it done.

That is why we are here, today, and why we worship our Mother, the earth, and why we still drink gin.

That was the end of our Mother. Our Father met with a somewhat stickier fate, but that is another story. He may now be the tallest tree in the forest, and you should pay him your respects as you pass, but don't expect an answer from him. He is too busy pursuing the thrills of the chase in that happier hunting ground.

As you pass by the smallest flower in the forest, pause and reflect that it may be our Mother. Speak kindly to her, and avoid trampling her into the dust. She has moved on to a more reflective future.

Evolution Annie

Who knows, with this simple act of your consideration the earth may spring a little under your step, your hair may lift with a cool refreshing breeze, and your travels may be a little more joyous along the path, because of her.

1. The story 'Evolution Annie' was written in part as a response to the very one-sided view of human evolution portrayed by Roy Lewis in *The Evolution Man*. (This was first published in 1960 under the title *What We Did to Father*.)

'Evolution Annie' is from Rosaleen Love's collection of stories *Evolution Annie and Other Stories*, published by The Women's Press.

One Dark and Starry Night

SARA MAITLAND

Once upon a time, long long ago and far far away, there was a young queen in a tower.

Lest you should get the wrong idea about this story I should say at once that this was not a standard model fairy-story princess with goldy locks and a simpering smile. On the contrary, this was a dark witch queen, tall and slender and sternly beautiful, and the tight curls of her hair, which was cropped very short in the fashion of that place, broke like waves on the broad black beach of her forehead. She was very sad. And she was very pregnant.

Nor was she a prisoner in the tower; she had climbed the three hundred and thirty steps freely and now leaned against the solid parapet and looked down, trying not to think, not to remember. The tower was in the centre of the city. I do not know if you have ever been to great Zimbabwe, the ancient ruin which is the heart and mother of that brave new country. The huge walls there are thick and solid, the entrance ways are narrow and welcoming, but despite the size they are made of millions and millions of tiny slivers of rock, dry stone, and bonded by their weight and the skill of their masons. The walls curve round, vast and embracing. I think this young queen's city was like that. And inside the walls it was part busy market, part safe haven, part great palace and part strange temple, and above it all, at the very centre, rose the tower; high above the busyness it reached up towards the heavens and at night its shapeliness was a darker black against the dark black sky. The people of the city had built the tower, with love and labour, so that anyone who wished could climb up and watch the stars, for in that city, unusually, it was judged nobler to be a magician and astronomer than to be a warrior or a king.

But now the queen did not want to look at the stars. She did not want to think about stars. She did not want to think about her husband either. For the young queen had a husband whom she loved very much, and she was right to do so, for he was merry and wise and very beautiful and his eyes sparkled not just in sunlight but in moonlight also. But now she did not want to think about him, nor about the stars.

So instead she looked down on the great courtyard, where in daylight there was constant activity; where the long caravans from the east met the traders from the western forests and exchanged goods and gossip, wares and worries, merchandise and magic; where the people of the city, serene and dignified, listened and learned, taught and told the old stories. Now, under the pale lemon moon the courtyard was still and calm, but the memories caught the young queen unawares and she could not help but remember.

She remembered the evening, only a few precious months ago, when her husband had come leaping down the tower, his scarlet cloak flying, swirling around him, and his earrings gleaming gold. He had snatched her from her work, laughing, loving.

'Come,' he had said, pulling on her hand in his excitement, 'come and look. I have found a new star.' And she had run with him up the tower, nearly as light and lithe as he, for all she was five months pregnant. And there, in the navy-blue band of sky low on the eastern horizon, pale and pure, a bright white star.

He said, 'That is a star for the birth of a king; a greater

king than the world has ever known – a king who will be for the rise and fall of many nations.' And he looked at her with love and passion and awe. He knelt at her feet and kissed her belly, just below the navel; and the child inside her wriggled with appreciation and delight and the three of them were full of joy.

But then . . . but then . . . how to account for, how to remember a changing so gradual that it may just be the fears and tremblings of pregnancy, and at the same time is so sturdy and real that there can be no return? Over the next few weeks her husband had withdrawn from her, had gone away inside his own dreams and would not talk to her. He was busy all the time. He spent long hours in his manuscript room, poring over his maps, and star charts, and ancient documents. And he would not talk to her. He spent wide spaces of time in the incense and myrrh factory, talking to the old spice mixers – women so skilled and industrious in labours that even after bathing their fingers never lose the faint aroma of holiness. And he would not talk to her. He sent out long letters across the whole world; from her room she could see, if she chose to look up from her own star-casting and spell-weaving and daily business, the messengers going out, running or mounted, across the wide plain beyond the city walls. He sent messages to his old friend, the Arabian desert ranger, whose people's camels bestrode the great golden sand dunes beyond the hills of morning. He sent messages to the mage king of the northern mountains, whose people lived half the time in darkness and whose land mourned the vanishing of the sun by covering itself in moon dust, white and cold like a funeral robe. They sent messages back and he would not meet her eyes and he would not talk to her.

One morning she had come out from her chamber and found the great courtyard frantic with busyness. There were pack ponies already laden, and the guides had gathered to a summons she had not known of, and were there leaning on their spears with their leopardskins already tossed over their shoulders ready for a departure. His great white stallion was brought out, harnessed for the long road and eager for the travelling, and she heard the shrilling of her own black mare left behind in the stables.

Then he came out, solemn, dressed for a journey. He still did not meet her eyes. He kissed her, formally, for a long parting, between the breasts and said, 'Well, I must be off.'

'Off!' she cried. 'Off where?'

'Off on my journey,' but he had the grace to look embarrassed.

She clutched at the baby in her belly which turned and lurched. 'Now?' she cried. And hearing the shriek in her own voice and hating it, fearing that he would think she would limit his freedom, she said in a calmer voice, 'Why now, just at the worst time of the year?'

'I'm off to find the baby king,' he said and looked proud and excited.

'Well,' she replied with a forced smile, 'if it's baby kings you want, I have one right here for you.'

But he did not smile back; he looked irritated and said, 'Don't be trivial. This is history, This is important.'

And after that she said nothing more, because there were no words that could ever put right so great a betrayal.

Then he went.

So now the young queen was in the tower, trying to think or to remember, not knowing whether she was sad or angry. Then suddenly her body was shaken with pain. Then suddenly she found that her ankles were soaked with warm water and her face was soaked with warm tears. Then suddenly she did not think or remember him any more, because she had her own important thing to do.

She half-ran, half-groped her way down the tower and into the arms of her midwife, who was also her old nurse and her friend. And there for a while she was comforted.

But much later, in the long hours of the night, struggling and weary, she called out for him and her need of him was so great that she blamed herself for his absence.

'Men,' muttered the old woman, wiping her darling's face. 'They're like that. Always under your feet, and never there when you want them.'

But the young queen had gone on a longer journey even than her husband's, and such gentle irony cannot reach to the dark country where she sojourned now. 'No. No. No,' she cried and the unborn child, hearing her and misunderstanding, felt rejected and sulked and made the pain worse.

'I want him, I want him,' sobbed the young queen. 'I want him. Why isn't he here?'

'Husha, husha, my lovey,' said the crone. 'Haven't you learned yet? They can think of the silliest thing – destiny, politics, history – just about anything to get out of doing the difficult and important work.'

'No,' she said, and wept. 'It is me. I am not good enough for him. I don't deserve it. I am too silly and trivial and stupid. My child is not good enough for him, I do not deserve him. He is too big for me. He and his friends, they're right to go. They know things; they are important, wonderful, wise.'

The old woman laughed; cackled from her stomach. 'In one generation? In one universe! *Three* wise men. You've got to be joking!'

And after that they settled down to the important task of birthing her baby daughter.

'One Dark and Starry Night' is from *The Man Who Loved Presents: Seasonal Stories*, edited by Alison Campbell, Caroline Hallett, Jenny Palmer and Marijke Woolsey, published by The Women's Press.

Murder in San Miguel

MARY WINGS

'El Circo!' cried an ad in the local newspaper of San Miguel de Allende in the state of Guanajuato, Mexico.

The circus. What would a Mexican circus be like? Certainly more fun than standing here waiting in front of the hotel. Mrs Eleanor Shoulder read the Spanish newspaper with intense concentration, trying to understand the words and guess at the possibilities that lay beyond its pages while she waited for someone to show up at the hotel desk. She fiddled nervously with her silver conch earrings and stared at the advertisement. The Circus! Eleanor had always loved circuses as a child. The clown face was the only clue to what might be under the striped canopy of the big top.

Eleanor peered closely at the newspaper, following the Spanish words, trying to make them have a sound in her head so she could make sense of them. She was the kind of person who needed the *sounds* of words to understand them.

She heard Harold lowering himself on to a bench in the reception area. Harold groaned as she rattled the pages of the newspaper.

There were two marijuana field raids, and a theft at a church. Saint Anthony of Padua missing, Eleanor read. But he wasn't really from Padua. He was from Lisbon. But his relicware was in Padua. And, it was said, in San Miguel de Allende. Hidden in a little golden statue of the Saint and his pig, was a piece of his ankle bone. Tobillo. Or was it his shoulder bone? Triza. Shred or fragment. That was the most sense she could make out of it.

Not likely any of Saint Anthony's bones made it this far, Eleanor thought. But despite the ensuing centuries the people of San Miguel believed that their Anthony was the granter of special favors, she continued reading in the paper. And now he was gone. Someone had submitted a well worn photo of the beloved Saint's pet to the newspaper. She could see that the snout of the Saint Anthony's pig had been rubbed over and over again by those who believed.

Another picture showed a little empty niche, high up on a wall. There was some speculation about the renovations that were being done in the church. Foot traffic. A lot of ladders. Escaleras. At least that what she thought was going on in the article.

A new Saint Anthony would shortly be installed beneath the high niche. Something bigger, and probably cheaper. 'To make the love of our Saint ever clear,' remarked the priest. The town was in deep mourning over the event, that was obvious.

An old woman was bringing some dolls made of yarn out of her bag to sell to Harold, when the hotelier appeared.

'¡Lárguese!' a silver-haired man with deep brown skin and blue eyes grumbled, his large foot threatening the hem of her skirt. The old woman scurried off but not before Eleanor pressed some pesos into her palm and collected a few dolls. The hotelier controlled a grimace, introducing himself. When Eleanor looked up into his face his smile became wider. 'Larry Welsh,' he grinned. 'What's the name?'

'Shoulder,' Eleanor said, looking behind him at her husband, Harold, who had collapsed on the bench, feebly wiping his brow with an old handkerchief. His face was pinched in pain. Eleanor's back wasn't feeling so hot either.

The golden years. Harold and Eleanor Shoulder had been planning this trip to San Miguel de Allende for almost three summers now. A colonial monument town which housed a large expatriate community. San Miguel's official status as a monument ensured that the cobblestone streets and brick facades remained frozen in a time centuries old, unlike its population.

'You have reservations?' The hotelier spoke perfect English. Underneath his brown skin Eleanor saw he was North American. She presumed he was one of the expatriates of San Miguel. The place was famous for its foreign community, mostly North Americans, some British.

The hotel had come highly recommended, despite its being so cheap. It had a waist-high wall all around it, a spectacular garden and was rated with three stars. Hotel Dolores. *Dolores.* Pain. Hotel Pain. Eleanor's back was starting to ache. The lower lumbar region. What time was lunch, she wondered.

She'd read in the brochure that the food was vegetarian. Harold had stopped eating meat last year, as part of an arthritis treatment. He was thirteen years older than she and Eleanor was starting to worry about their age differences.

When she was a woman of twenty-nine, a spinster in those times, the forty-two year-old Harold looked distinguished with the wings of silver hair that flew above his ears. Then they were intellectual and physical equals.

But fifty-nine and seventy-two were different realities. Harold's physical problems seemed to have geometrically increased. They attended more and more funerals every year, the funerals of *his* friends. Eleanor's feet itched to travel, even as they burned in the morning's heat, travel before it was too late.

Eleanor brushed away some gray strands of hair that

escaped the french bun at her neck and had caught in her shell earrings. She wasn't that far from totally silver herself.

She looked at Harold with irritation and pity, each emotion compounding the other. The way his heavy body made him sweat. Harold was trapped inside his body, a body that had trouble traveling, Eleanor thought. Eleanor couldn't wait to see everything in the world, explore the nooks and crannies of the globe. Their outlook and energy levels seemed worlds apart.

'Spell the name please?' Larry said.

'S-H-O-U-L-D-E-R.' Eleanor played with a rotating rack of postcards which showed the main features of San Miguel. The famous pink church, the central jardin. The hotelier frowned, looking for the name. Behind his back Eleanor noticed a few bulky objects. Crudely carved figures, standing in wooden boxes, or nestled in crates among sawdust and excelsior.

Eleanor saw several youths hovering in a back door expectantly. The hotelier looked up suddenly, following her eyes.

'¿Qué diablos quieren ustedes?' 'What the devil do you want?' he barked and the boys retreated quickly to the dusty bed of a beat up old pick-up truck. He thumbed through some papers clipped neatly together and frowned and Eleanor watched his distaste as he flipped through the cards, reading handwriting he hadn't written. Clearly he was not used to playing receptionist.

' "Shoulder," got it,' the hotelier sighed. 'Apartment 37.' He held out the keys and Eleanor noticed that the office behind him featured old primitive paintings of religious events, people praying. A young man in black pencil leg trousers and a white nylon shirt appeared and started hoisting the luggage into his long muscled arms, listing slightly to the left as he led the way burdened with their baggage. Always noticing the way people walk, talk, always spying, listening in, her daughter Iris used to accuse her.

Eleanor took Harold's arm even though he didn't have trouble walking. Not arthritis, not a heart problem this time. Harold had shingles.

Shingles. It didn't sound so terrible. Like athlete's foot, tennis elbow, grannie's tartan, the recognizability of the name seemed to imply that it wasn't serious. Shingles. Something that goes on the roof. Asphalt shingles. Clay shingles.

Shingles. A herpes infection of the nerve endings. Eleanor had a case of it herself last year. After a while you just sort of let it become part of the whole picture. Like white noise, the sound of waves.

But Harold didn't seem to have access to the 'off' switch which Eleanor had developed. She tried not to be a snob about it. She tried not to think he liked the attention. Enjoyed it, even! It was a special bond. Florence Nightingale of matrimony. The devoted wife, the devoted mother, forever nursing! Eleanor was not one for that.

Nevertheless she felt guilty. She was blaming Harold for his pain. She felt it was very clearly wrong to do so. But now, damn it, they were in Mexico.

Helping him through a garden lush with banana plants and jacaranda trees, she talked to him soothingly.

'I'm calling the doctor as soon as we get in the room, honey,' she said. Dipping under a bougainvillea vine which grew over the door Eleanor Shoulder noticed Harold's face, feeling his pain as she saw him flinch.

There was no treatment for shingles. You just had to endure, sweat it out.

The small apartment, thank God, was beautiful. Rough white tiles with bluebirds lined the walls in both the kitchenette and the bathroom. The beds looked hard and good for her back, the linen was clean and crisp. Perforated tin lamps were set with colored marbles. The place looked like Christmas. But then Mexico looked like Christmas –

Christmas with flowers – every day of the year. She couldn't wait to get out on the streets.

Eleanor tipped the young man and watched Harold painfully sink into one of the beds. She sat the two yarn dolls on the pillow on the other one. Harold didn't bother smiling anymore and Eleanor Shoulder was glad. She picked up the phone to call a doctor.

Her Spanish was good enough to locate a physician. Doctor Alacá asked if Harold had some *Zovirax*.

'Si, si, but it does nothing for the pain', Eleanor explained and the doctor gave an empathetic mutter of agreement.

He prescribed morphine. *Morfina*. The word was the same in both languages. They still prescribed actual morphine in Mexico, none of the fancy pharmaceutical synthetics had made their way to the mountain-top village of San Miguel. The doctor suggested a pharmacy. He would call and give the order over the phone.

Consulting the map, Eleanor Shoulder agreed. La Botica Allende was near the Hotel Maria Dolores, just past the Instituto. She readied herself to go out and took stock of her physical condition.

Her culottes were sticking to her, and her feet sloshed inside her tennis shoes. She felt dipped in the grime of her own sweat. After she got the morphine for Harold she could make herself look more presentable, she thought.

She splashed cold water on her face, ran a rough washcloth over her neck, arms and into her armpits. Cooler now she slipped on a fresh T-shirt and strapped on a small black leather purse around her waist.

Out on to the veranda, into the colorful garden and through the brick portal was her route to San Miguel.

She walked on the grass to the closest edge of the wall, stood on her tiptoes and looked down at the cobblestone streets. This was going to be hell on the lower lumbar region. Tearing off her shoes and running her toes through the cool green grass would be a better idea.

The streets of El Centro San Miguel were narrow and roughly paved with cobblestones. To call them cobblestones was complimentary. Rocks, the size of softballs, or pointed like small footballs, had been dumped along the streets and Eleanor could feel every one through her shoes as she balanced herself with each step. Ah to have a footbath. She noticed that all the local women wore flats and walked in the streets aiming their toes at the larger flatter stones. She put her hands at the small of her back and stretched backwards. Ah.

Eleanor looked up at the stone wall to check the painted letters. Yes. *Caja del Correo*. Right turn.

San Miguel was certainly eclectic, Eleanor Shoulder thought as she stepped into a grove of trees. What went on through the streets and behind the walls was a late twentieth century melange of cultures. Some would call it colonialism, Eleanor thought, noticing a North American women her age, strolling the grounds with a big sketchpad under her arm. The woman was strangely gotten up in a tomato-red Mexican peasant dress, her yellow petticoat hemmed with wavy silver rick-rack.

A walking piñata. Her hands were tinseled over with expensive silver jewelry and even a big straw hat and papier-mâché flowers. Underneath a withered face had been coated with pancake makeup and two sagging eyelids were bright jewels of blue over piercing aqua pupils floating in yellowy whites. She peered at a small boy holding a balloon and quickly began to sketch him.

An Indian woman nearby watched her. This piñata woman was a festive skeleton, a day of the dead tourist! The villager with her wrinkled brown skin and gingham apron looked at the sketch that was forming on the paper. She smiled. The piñata woman had marvelously reproduced the child's expression. What an eye! Eleanor stopped to buy a paleta, frozen fruit on a stick, from a ten-year-old seller on the street. Fresh strawberries, crunchy white ice.

Sidewalk sellers. A series of canvas stalls caught her eye and refused to let her go, their wares ever attractive in their glitter and color. Children's toys, multicolored balls, balloons in glittering Mylar, dolls in yellow dresses and miniature wrestlers in plastic. From underneath the shelf of a booth she heard the delightfully tormented laugh of a baby being tickled.

Elaborate combs and ponytail binders in lace, studded with pearls and sparkles lashing off the gold of earrings, bracelets, anklets, and necklaces. A child cried out and the throngs in the square stopped and looked up at an escaping balloon. It floated towards a bright blue sky until it was caught in one of the topiaried trees of the square, engendering laughter among the strolling crowds.

These trees, pruned into ovals as neat as Lego toys, they obediently marched around the square. Toy trees. Eleanor quickened her pace through the crowd towards the end of the square where the toy trees parted.

Finally, there it was above all of them, a pink confection, a sugar cake stalactite, pointing into the sky. La Parroquia. The church. The signs of renovation were everywhere. Between her feet and the entrance large concrete slabs shot into the air, displaced tiles and paper candy wrappers. Scaffolding ran across the pink exterior of the church and a black ribbon hung in the door, presumably an indication of the theft of Saint Anthony from the place of worship.

She remembered the story of this church, La Parroquia. Guiterrez, the eighteenth century Mexican architect, had copied Gothic arches from a European postcard. The towers arched and soared and pointed to the heavens like any Northern European model, but Guiterrez interpreted the surface in high Mexican baroque, *churrigueresco*. The swirling pattern of flowers, geometric shapes and rotund saints was worked out in bright pink stone from local quarries. The postcard, Eleanor thought, must have been in black and white.

She waited with an Indian woman and her two small children for a Jaguar sedan to pass. San Miguel certainly was a melange. Indian farmers, ejidatarios, rubbed elbows with expatriate Americans who came down for the climate and the cheap real estate. They owned businesses and busied themselves writing good and bad poetry, doing yoga or giving parties. But, Eleanor thought suddenly, would any of them go to the circus?

More circus signs appeared amid the ice cream vendors and flower stalls. A long pink wall which curved for a quarter of a mile seemed to house something grand. Perhaps it was the back of the Instituto, Eleanor thought, consulting her map. It seemed to run in the correct direction to La Botica. Eleanor checked the map and continued walking, the stones became rougher and the large blazing initials of political parties on posters pasted to the wall, so emphatic, so foreign, seemed to frighten her. Her feet were aching, and she began to wonder if this was a good route as she saw the end of the wall. At last, back into civilization. But she was wrong.

Eleanor stood at the edge of a deep green field, inhabited by two tattered, blinking ponies. They were listlessly grazing in front of a circle of shabby vehicles drawn around a huge striped tent.

So here it was. The circus. A real circus. Eleanor thought, not part of an entertainment franchise or a movie set. People who got lost from other lives and found a way to live on the road. The circus, a foreign legion for gypsies, acrobats and people who were differently abled. Living out their lives in buses, entertaining town people under the big top for small money and thunderous applause. People whose lives Eleanor could only imagine. She shouldn't linger, wondering.

But she did. The lettering on the banner was in English, **The Circus!!!** it proclaimed with extra exclamation points, in case the reader wasn't excited enough. The big old-fashioned letters were like fluffy pastry. Outlined in three colors, they vibrated in the sun.

Underneath the banner an aluminum trailer held the cut-out portrait of the clown Eleanor had seen throughout the village. Big tufts of red hair shot out above his ears. His eyes seemed to look hysterically at the rest of the world. Eleanor took a deep breath.

The morning coolness had vanished and heat was setting in. All was quiet on the field of El Circo. Two small boys played at the empty gate to the right of the trailer. Inside a cyclone fence seven or eight vehicles had drawn themselves around the tent. All painted the same color of bright blue, they guarded a strip of grass between themselves and the tent. Behind the vehicles Eleanor could see two or three women moving silently among the ropes. Circus women doing their wash.

Eleanor started towards the periphery of the tents, ropes and cars. She was walking into their living room, she thought, moving quickly past one of the tattered looking ponies. It took a few lethargic hops away from her. She drew closer.

She looked at the curious vehicles which circled protectively. Two Winnebagos that had seen better vacations, and three school buses. All had been quickly painted over in the same bright blue paint, the surface chipping away to reveal other colors and former occupations. A cyclone fence kept the compendium of ropes, platforms, tents and vehicles secure. Everything was still. Only the pony rustled the grass. Bolder now, Eleanor circled closer, approaching the first school bus which had seen much better days.

With odds bits of cloth flapping out of open holes, broken glass plastered over with silver duct tape, there wasn't much left of its original windows. Misshapen letters managed to spell out, El Circo! on the side, and a big dent in the back revealed the yellow and black paint of a former school bus. A flowerbox with flourishing purple and white pinwheel petunias spilling out of it hung beneath a window.

'Hallo!' A greeting called from behind the bus. Eleanor came closer. 'Hallo!' No. The voice came from *under* the bus.

'Hallo!' she called back. The voice seemed to be body-less, but cheerful. Laughing at her!

Eleanor squatted down, looking under the vehicle and saw two naked feet, on either side of a bucket.

'Hallo!' A face appeared. Upside down. With dark brown skin, long black strands tangling with the grass on the ground. A young girl who was bending over back-wards, sticking her head between her legs and laughing. 'Come to the fence!'

Eleanor obeyed and gripping the cyclone fence, she saw the girl had resumed her seat over the bucket and was squeezing the clothes out, her brown fingers flashing in the soap suds, her long brown arms stretching into the water. She wore baggy knee length shorts that were all the rage among teenagers these days. She threw her long hair over her shoulder with the universal gesture of young women confident of their beauty.

'Where you from?' she said. Her teeth were crooked and her mouth a deep red and Eleanor wondered if that could possibly be her natural color.

'Los Estado Unidos.'

'No, obviously. But where?'

'Walnut Creek, California.'

'That anywhere near the Fresno?' Her accent was intriguing. Nothing like Spanish.

'Sort of. Your English is so good, do you have relatives in Fresno?' What was that accent?

'What does it sound like to you? I've been all over, you know. Where is the place you were born?'

213

'Your accent doesn't sound Spanish, were your parents from Eastern – ?'

'I asked you first. Hey, I like your purse.'

Eleanor looked down at the black leather pouch strapped to her side.

'Where'd you get it?' The young woman squinted into Eleanor's eyes.

'In California. So what do you do in the circus?' Eleanor asked, imagining the young girl being sawn in half or flying on the trapeze.

'You know,' she ignored Eleanor's question. 'Pretty soon I'm going to work in a *bank*.'

'A bank?'

'Yes, teaching English. I'm very good, you see. I know what is the secret to teaching language. I know the different parts of the brain. I speak to just the right place.' She held up a hand dripping with bubbles and pointed to her head. 'The words has to be about sound and at the same time seeing and the feeling. It has to come from a place of being. This is language!' She dipped her hand back into the bucket. 'It's very different than the usual approach. It's because I speak five. My grandmother, Hungarian, my mother, Brazil and my father ... Well never mind my father. Let's just say he was a teacher.'

'Have you taught before?'

'Teaching? It's very new for me. But already I am excellent at translation. You see I can exist with the two parts of my brain at the same time. After a while, it becomes very easy. My approach is so unique, however, I don't think they pay me right now. Could you lend me a little money?'

'No. Sorry,' Eleanor smiled. She liked the pleasant sing-song of the girl's voice and grinned widely as she turned and started walking away.

'Wait – '

'I really have to go now, thanks. And good luck with your English lessons,' she called.

Again Eleanor started across the field away from the buses and tents slowly.

'Hey, hey! Don't walk away! Besides you don't walk so easy either, I think you're wearing the wrong shoes!'

Eleanor stopped and looked back at the bus.

'Come back,' the girl called. Eleanor turned. 'Come back, please,' the girl said, her voice softer. Through one of the windows, behind a cloth, a brown hand stretched out and waved at her. The girl was suddenly inside the bus now. And Eleanor wanted to see inside. She came closer and the features of the girl became clearer.

A big smile, real, not like the clown's. Misshapen teeth, tight brown skin and eyes that didn't blink. She looked Eleanor up and down slowly, and her smile got wider.

'I didn't mean to offend you,' she said. 'But you must forgive me. I ask *everybody* for money. That's the way, you see. I will have to stop asking for money like this when I work in the bank and get a salary. So for now, I like to ask for money. Pretty soon I won't be able to any more.'

'Well I'm not giving you my purse, so you can forget that.'

'Maybe you could give me something else.'

'I'll come and see you in the show.'

The girl laughed. 'You won't do that. It's only the people of the town that come to see us. You Norte Americanos are too worried about fire! Rules this, regulations that. I know, I have an aunt in Fresno, California. I visit her a lot. But our circus is not allowed to make happen in the United States.

'There aren't many traveling circuses around anymore anywhere I guess. Do you meet other circus performers along the way?'

'Yes, I know some. The employment rate is terrible for

circus performers in the States. And also not so easy for you, I expect. Hard times, huh? You are something like a civil servant, maybe a librarian, or a schoolteacher.'

'Yes. I'm a teacher. I *was* a schoolteacher. Retired.'

'Ha-ha, ha-ha, I told you, didn't I!' She leaned backwards and Eleanor could see that the interior of the bus was filled with columns of crates which held empty green coke bottles. Behind them big fluffy bags of popped popcorn stuffed the first two rows of the old school bus, like white balloon people waiting for a ride. Dark shadows in the background suggested figures, puppets.

'You see I told you, that's how I'm so good at languages. I know it, even if I don't already know it.'

'You're very good,' Eleanor said, coming closer, peering ever deeper into the interior of the bus. But the girl moved towards the front of the window and blocked her view.

'I know exactly what yo-o-o-o-u n-e-e-e-d,' she said, emphasizing the last two words slowly. You need. The words hung in the air where she had intended them.

'How could you know what I need.'

'I just know. I see how you walk over here to the circus. Tell me, where are you going – '

'Actually, I'd better get going – '

'Yes, your husband. I knew you for a married lady.'

'Not a hard guess. I have on a wedding ring.'

'Yes, but you have just arrived here, I think. He's not with you. He is resting, ill maybe,' she absently started plucking some of the dead petunia blooms off of the flowers in the little crate hanging out of the window. 'You don't walk like a woman who is a person alone in travel. You're used to having someone. You walk through the field like it is something new. You look at everything, at the circus, the sky, at me. And your feet hurt.'

'OK. Now if we're finished with my diagnosis, how about yours – '

'I'm telling you,' the girl ignored her, 'I have exactly what a lady of your age – '

'I just can't get you to stop selling me, can I?' Eleanor laughed despite herself.

'Let's not be sensitive, be in the way of not knowing. You are old. OK, that's that. But I can show you the possibility of a better life, Madam. You're also in your prime! You feel like a young woman because now you have the eyes of a young woman. But not the thoughts. Like a kaleidoscope your thought sees many patterns because of all the years you have lived,' the girl intoned.

'Flattery will get you nowhere.' Eleanor said.

'You have some many and interesting thoughts, I think.'

'I've lived with them a long time so now I'm used to them. I like the thought. Nothing surprises me anymore.'

'I can surprise you,' the girl said simply looking up from the flowers.

Eleanor glanced at her watch, thinking about Harold.

'It's up to you, Madam. I offer you – ' she paused and looked over at the ponies, as if giving herself time to make up her mind. She looked deep into the purple pinwheel of a bloom just under her chin. 'Yes. For you a footbath.'

The ponies chomped on the grass, their big teeth made gnawing sounds which entered the silence between Eleanor and the girl.

A footbath from the young circus performer. Eleanor's feet seemed to swell and pound inside her hot damp tennis shoes.

Eleanor loved footbaths. She hated to admit it, but next to sex, a footbath and massage was one of her favorite treats. No, it was more than a treat. She desired it, the feeling of the hands which stroked her arch, gently twisting her toes –

Eleanor looked back at the woman. She wanted this footbath. But she had to hurry for Harold's medicine.

'I have the traditional and secret knowledge of gypsies

who have wandered two continents, Madam. I can promise you a different kind of knowledge that has never been put to work for you, Madam, for your feet. I prepare for you the footbath of the recipe carried by Emperor Sigismund and passed to the brother of my grandmother Valask, the Greek, for which he paid with his life.'

'For a footbath?' Eleanor looked at her.

'You will feel like you walk on air again. I promise. My unique footbath of herbs, essences and some of the minerals from holy places, ground to a fine powder, personally I am the one to supervise. And it goes deep, the spirits from the mountain enter your bones, and the tonic of turmeric will – '

'It's OK. I don't need the menu. But I could use a footbath. But I want the whole treatment. Hungarian grandmother, the Greek – '

'Taught me all things I know – '

'Brazilian father – '

'I give you the footbath you will not be disappointed for having.'

'OK. What's your price?'

'One half hour grandmother of Prussia footbath essence coppers of Rúsore, Ungersore, in exchange for your earrings, Madam.'

The earrings.

'May I have them now?' She held out her hand. Eleanor came forward to better look into her eyes.

'When are you going to wear my earrings? You're welcome to them, but surely they're inappropriate for the circus. Don't you need something big and theatrical, long dangly curtains of bright red beads that are visible under the big top?' Eleanor needled her. She looked up and saw, indeed, that the flesh at the bottom of the young woman's ears was very stretched, the holes in her earlobe were pulled into slits.

'For the bank, Señora, you forget. I will need a completely new wardrobe for the bank. I suggest you get back to your husband now. And rest. Return to me after my last show. Around ten and one half. But you don't want to give them now?'

'Earrings upon delivery of footbath.'

'Whatever you prefer, Madam. There is more than one kind of medicine in Mexico, Madam, perhaps this will work well for you.'

She gave Eleanor a final smile, revealing little or no dental work in her history, and closed the window of the school bus.

'Goodbye,' Eleanor said. She hoped she could get Harold doped up so he wouldn't mind when she went out later to collect her footbath.

Eleanor left the field under the watchful eyes of the two ponies. She circled around the other vehicles quickly. Time to return to get the medicine and bring it to Harold. Every moment of discovery for her was a moment of pain for him. He couldn't help it.

All was quiet. Perhaps the performers were resting, getting ready for the show. Rounding the corner of the last school bus she came upon the silver trailer, its new bright aluminum and professional lettering pronounced 'Mexican International Circus', in English.

Underneath was a picture of a fire eater, flames circling his lips and a cloud of smoke issuing from his mouth. Floating on his charcoal breath was a woman. Her great ostrich plumed headdress could not hide her strange posture. She wore her head between her knees, her neck a kind of snake. 'La Muchacha Flexible!' proclaimed the script above her knotted body.

Her face was done in loving detail, the dark brown skin and the broad knowing smile of La Muchacha Flexible. The Elastic Girl would soon be in possession of Eleanor's silver earrings and giving her a footbath.

And Harold was suffering at the hotel. Christ, what was

she thinking? Eleanor turned away from the painted face and twisted torso, wondering which direction to go. She decided left and was rewarded at the next corner. A look around the edge of the stone wall showed her the establishment she was looking for. La Botica Allende.

La Botica Allende was a tiny shop which seemed to cling on to a series of buildings at the end of a steep hill. Little yellow shutters protected the windows which were beautifully etched with flowers and plants. The names of local physicians in old fashioned type were floating in the middle, the capitals ending in curlicues. Posters of the laughing circus clown bedecked the entire wall beside the shop door.

As Eleanor stepped inside it seemed to her that she stepped back centuries. The walls were lined with scores of white ceramic canisters. They marched around the periphery of the room, decorated with Roman soldiers on either side of orange and blue flowered shields. The brilliantly colored shields sported names which were almost familiar. Latin.

Ignat Amara. Gem: Popoli. Axumg. Opium. A grouchy looking woman, the farmacéutica, in a white apron stood in front of a screen set with pieces of etched glass. Behind her a marble work table was busy with canisters and powders, and behind that a dark pantry which led out on to the street.

La farmacéutica waited on a teenager with a bad complexion. Acne was so painful for teenagers; Eleanor looked at the young girl's face, her otherwise smooth brown cheeks alive with red festering sores. She thought about her daughter – and then just as quickly put her out of her mind.

La farmacéutica dumped some brown powder from a canister into the stone bowl of a mortar dish. *Manzanilla* Eleanor read from the shield. That would be, perhaps, something like camomile, she thought. La farmacéutica hoisted her round torso up a ladder to another ceramic canister, the Roman soldiers and their shield turned so Eleanor could not read the name. Then a few drops from a tiny brown bottle and la farmacéutica brought out her pestle.

La farmacéutica's strong sure hands grasped the handle of the round tipped stone and pushed it hard into the bowl, rolling her eyes at the pimple-faced girl.

The scraping and the blending of the ingredients on the stone surface almost hypnotized her. Scrape, scrape, scrape. Sighing, la farmacéutica lectured the young blotchy faced customer in a quick Spanish tongue.

Harold, I'm coming, dear, hang on, Eleanor thought, remembering his wheezing little whines of pain. At least he didn't make the whimpering noises at night.

'No puedo comer nada hecho con agua helada,' the young woman shrugged, pointing to a pimple on her chin.

'Si, si, y los bombones,' la farmacéutica said sternly handing her a package. If the customer didn't eat ice cream and bon-bons her face wouldn't erupt was the disapproving message of the pharmacist. Eleanor's eyes moved over the canisters on the ledge, *Chlorato de Pottasso*, Potassium chloride. Didn't they make bombs out of that stuff?

'¿Señora?' The woman in the white smock snapped her to attention. The teenager had left and Eleanor Shoulder stood alone before her, hoping her performance of Spanish would make the transaction quick and painless.

'Buenos tardes, mi doctor –' oh shit, the past tense for 'called in', 'este, uh telephone –'

'¿Cual médico?'

'Necesito algo para –'

'Which doctor?' La farmacéutica said in cold, perfect English.

'My doctor, Señor Alacá, called in a prescription for morphine –'

'¿La receta?'

'No, no tengo la receta –'

'We cannot possibly fill your prescription without a receipt from the doctor.'

Did her eyes almost look triumphant, Eleanor wondered. Or maybe it was her own paranoid feeling of being punished. For being angry with Harold for his illness. If only she could get the morphine she could at least put them both out of pain.

'The doctor – Dr Alacá called in! ¡Es urgente!' Eleanor protested.

'Go to the clinic. Seventy-five Insurgentes. Get a written prescription from the doctor and I will fill it.' La farmacéutica seemed to be looking Eleanor up and down disapprovingly. Did the woman think that she was a drug dealer, Eleanor Shoulder, a fifty-nine year-old joy rider in a panama hat? Eleanor fingered the bun at the nape of her neck nervously. Maybe she did look a bit like an aging hippy.

'Adios,' the woman said with finality, turning her back.

'*Nos vemos*,' Eleanor muttered, not without pride that she knew the colloquial expression and didn't used the touristic 'hasta la vista'. *I'll be seeing you*. But whatever the expression she hoped someone *else* would be on duty when she returned with the goddamn receta.

'¡Lárguese!' She heard la farmacéutica say angrily.

'Jesus Christ,' Eleanor muttered, 'What did *I* do?' noting the extreme bad temper of the woman. She pulled out her map. A seven block walk. Should she go back to tell Harold? No, better try to make it back to the clinic and bring him the stuff. That would be all he would care about. Oblivion.

Eleanor traced a route on the map, muttering an incantation of the names of streets, and looked up to check the sky for direction. She chose her route and set out across town.

'Psst!' Eleanor turned her head. How did she know that hissing sound was meant for her? She saw the brown eyes aiming clearly at hers. A thin young man dressed in a jaunty sailor jacket and wide Chino pants came up and limped alongside the ledge. He'd been hanging out by the pharmacy door. The pharmacist's '¡Lárguese!' must have been intended for him.

'You need help, Señora?'

'No, no,' Eleanor said. The map was stuffed firmly in her pocket.

Did she look like she needed help? Eleanor thought, watching with dismay as the young man strode on the street beside her. He had a very bad limp. She wondered if he had an artificial leg or foot. He was thin and his eyes were nervous and brittle.

'You want some pre-Columbian artifacts? Here, look, fertility goddess –'

Eleanor looked down at the torso of a woman that was all belly and breast. No head. 'No, no thank you.'

'Original –'

'Yeah, original like you and your friends make in the back yard and bury for a year. Now if you don't mind –'

'Lady,' his voice was softer now. 'I heard you in the pharmacy,' he explained. 'Someone you know is sick, right?'

Eleanor didn't say anything. She didn't need this interruption on the way to the clinic. She willed her feet to move faster along the ledge. Her back was really killing her now.

'You have a problem, maybe I can help?' A car rode up behind him on the street and he jumped. He was on the ledge now, walking just behind her.

'How do you know I have a problem?' she said over her shoulder.

'Getting these drugs, sometimes it's a foolish bureaucracy. You are in pain, or someone you know, maybe your

children, or your husband, is sick and you come to a new
city – '

'¿Qué es lo que quiere?'

'Oh, you speak Spanish, very good! But I am worried
for you, you see, because this clinic is very far away – '

'It's right on the map – ' Eleanor saw a woman approaching her with a huge bag on her back full of the sweet
bollillo rolls. There must have been two hundred rolls in
there, Eleanor thought, jumping into the street. But why
was she explaining this to him? She shouldn't say anything.

'The doctors, they go home early, then you cannot fill
your prescription!'

'What's your solution?'

He cocked his head and stepped back into a side street
and then into a doorway. She turned and saw him fumble
in his jacket even as she forged ahead.

Eleanor concentrated on the rocks beneath her feet and
then she started imagining the footbath. She started to
make better time. He was nevertheless behind her again,
gesturing and smiling, refusing to believe she didn't want
what he had to offer. Then, out of the side pocket of his
sailor's jacket he pulled out a packet of white powder.

Ignat Amara. Gem: Popoli. Axumg. Opium. Harold was
suffering back in that room. And here was an answer. But
this, this limping boy was offering death.

'Only two hundred – ' he grinned evilly.

'Scram! ¡Déjeme en paz!'

'Two hundred and fifty dollars and no pain, I promise
you, no pain at all.'

'¡Socorro! ¡Policía!' Eleanor yelled. But not too loud.

That got him. His face drained of color and she watched
him stop dead in his tracks.

'You are a fool, Mrs.'

But she was no fool. Heroin? Even if she did decide to
consort with criminals she could overdose Harold without
meaning to. She looked at his young, angry fuck-you face.

Eleanor knew something about junkies. She was the mother of one.

Eleanor's daughter, Iris, had been addicted to heroin for years. The wrong time in history. The wrong crowd, the wrong attitude.

But not the wrong mother. While Eleanor refused to blame herself Harold took it pretty hard. He was older and it was harder to for him to understand. Young people and drugs.

And then Iris disappeared. Nineteen. And gone.

Eleanor and Harold did Missing Persons. Neighborhood Crime Awareness training. Private Detectives. Parents of runaways.

After a while she pretended that Iris was dead. Eleanor even made up an obituary, a newspaper article. It was supposed to be therapeutic. It worked for a while, for a few hours. And then Eleanor just gave in to living without knowing. To living with all the possibilities of what might have happened to Iris. Dead in a ditch in Des Moine? Crashed out in a flophouse in Tangiers?

Eleanor walked more quickly until she came to the edge of the park where the clinic was located. She entered the cool crowded park thinking about Iris. Before she knew it she was at the clinic and had taken her place in the line with the waiting patients. Her hands resting in the small of her back for support, her feet aching on the hard tile floor, she patiently waited her turn.

Eleanor's heart sank after waiting twenty-five minutes to hear that Dr Alacá was not there. Not at the clinic. The doctor, she was informed, was at his office. Caja Homobonos. Possibly he was there. No, the young man nodded sadly at her, they couldn't call his office. They couldn't give her la receta for morphine either.

At least they didn't suspect her of being a middle-aged dope dealer. Or buyer.

Homobonos. She looked it up on her map. Right around the corner from La Botica! No! Well, shit. The whole trip for nothing. Damn la farmacéutica!

Eleanor crammed the map into a ball and stuffed it into the pocket of her culottes.

She hurried back through the park, the large white egrets squawking against the chirping of swallows.

'She's angry, she's angry,' she heard the big birds screaming and laughing at her. 'Give her the *receta, receta, receta*,' the little swallows replied. Bump, bump, bump went the basketballs. Clowns jeered from every poster.

Through the park Eleanor could see the junkie leaning on a fence. He called out to a passerby. She sighed and walked quickly out of the cool park into the heat and sighed again.

Finally on the steep street where La Botica stood, Eleanor checked the map again. The doctor's office should just be around the corner. She started the steep descent down the cobblestones to the door of the doctor's office.

Cerrado. Closed. That fucking farmacéutica! Eleanor savored the word. Surely both the doctor's office and the pharmacy would be open later. Just midday and lunch to get through.

Maybe Valium would help? Eleanor still had some left over from her own back problems. She slowed her pace to the Hotel Dolores. She wasn't anxious to give Harold the bad news. And she did feel badly for him. She remembered in the hotel two nights earlier, seeing the little red dots swelling up, as if they were crawling out of his navel, and around the soft tender skin on his side, and right up his spine.

Meanwhile she was still on a street in Mexico.

Mexico d'oro. Mexico was gold for Eleanor. She became a different person in Mexico. Slower, kinder, happier. But she was worried that Harold's condition would end their visit. They would have to go home, and she would have only had a moment in Mexico. A few twinkles of glitter, one plaintive chorus of a mariachi band, the cry of an egret and a lot of heavy walking. Maybe one footbath.

'Yes, yes, but the Aztecs believed that the gods only existed on human blood. Priests tore out the hearts of sacrificial victims and dedicated them to the gods while they were still *warm*,' Larry Welsh sounded patronizing.

Eleanor and Harold had been invited to lunch at the behest of the hotelier, Larry Welsh. They were taking their lunch in the dining room. The place was booked full of North Americans, a few of the piñata variety, others dressed just as cheerfully in pastel sports separates. Eleanor tuned out of Larry's voice and listened to them.

They were taking classes. And teaching classes. Any kind of classes. Painting classes, yoga classes, Tai-Chi, learning Spanish at one of the many schools for foreigners. A retired accountant teaching English to some local teenagers, he commented on how diligently they studied.

The busy bright bunch of retirees were in their last energetic moments, Eleanor thought, detecting the limp wrist of muscular dystrophy in one man. A woman thin as a skeleton crossed legs riddled with red blotches. They chatted and twittered away, mutual compliments all around, a balding woman with thin red hair with stark white roots did a spontaneous tango to the laughter of old men.

These North Americans weren't rich or even spoiled. But they had small pensions and disabilities that made Mexico a place to pursue last interests with waning pocket-books and abilities. It would be the kind of place she and Harold would be visiting from now on, Eleanor thought. She tuned back into Larry's voice.

He was regaling them with stories about how he'd gained the property, the problem with clearing title, the small personal armies landowners sometimes resorted to down here. He clearly saw himself as a new breed, a sort of colonial cowboy. And he had a lot of bloodshed to talk about with Aztec rituals. It seemed to be a favorite topic, the primitive bloodthirsty past of the natives.

'When the incessant wars and human sacrifice were abolished, it destroyed the core of Aztec religion, causing the Indians to abandon their belief that the gods depended on men for food. What an improvement! It's the first commandment after all,' Larry Welsh continued. 'You don't kill your own. The Spaniards, they brought civilization. Christianity.'

'The Christian God was any better?' Eleanor said, irritated. 'The green cross of the Inquisition is right down the street!'

'But that was for heretics – '

'You're defending *the Inquisition*?' Eleanor found herself smiling. Larry the unlapsed Catholic!

'Aztecs feared their gods, but did not *love* them,' he said almost coyly trying to catch Eleanor's eye.

'I think I'd better be getting back to the room.' Harold, whose white face seemed drained of blood, did his best to sound apologetic. Eleanor and Larry looked at him a bit surprised. He hadn't been present for most of the luncheon conversation. But he hadn't missed much, Eleanor mused. Larry Welsh had a thing about the Catholic colonization! He was defensive about it, and Eleanor couldn't imagine why. Unless he identified with the colonizers of 400 years ago.

'I – I think I'd better go back to the room,' Harold repeated and stood up suddenly. 'The heat – '

'Do you want me to go back with you, honey?'

'No, no. I'll be OK. I just want to take another pill and lie down.'

'How many are left?' Eleanor asked.

'I don't know . . . I . . . I didn't look, I – '

'That's OK, I'll go to the doctor's office and the pharmacy is right next door.'

'No it's really all right, honey. I think I have enough to see me through the night.'

Eleanor looked at Harold, at his trembly smile. He wasn't going to last too much longer in Mexico. Pills and pain at the Hotel Dolores. He'd be better off at home.

She looked back at Larry. She didn't like the way he just sat there during her whole interchange with Harold. Illness is a private thing between a couple.

'Do you want coffee?' Larry asked her, hailing the waitress.

'Yes, thank you.' She didn't want to linger in Larry's company but there was such a lovely view of the garden from the dining room.

'I hope you're enjoying it here.' He waved at the garden beyond the terrace. Apartments nestled under the tiled overhang, open corridors where the linen ladies pushed big white carts of sheets between flowered tiles, flower pots and flowers.

'That's my apartment there,' he pointed to a big square atop the main building of the hotel, cantilever balconies with pots of red and yellow flowers on a roof terrace. 'The penthouse.'

'So what's it like to live here in San Miguel?'

'Oh, it's wonderful.' He leaned forward and behind his tan Eleanor could see that he was older, older than she'd thought. 'Many people come down here and fall in love with the place. You will fall in love with it too,' he said with a twinkle in his eye.

'Well thank you very much for your company at lunch,' she said automatically and Larry smiled, his eyes traveling up and down her. She didn't like it.

But then his eyes flickered over the lawn, back towards the carport which was filling with the dust. A figure waited there, a shadow limping away.

'I think I'd better lie down before I make another trip to the doctor's office,' Eleanor explained. 'If you'll excuse me.'

'No tengo.' La farmacéutica looked blandly at the receta for morfina in Eleanor's hand. 'No tengo.'

Three hours after her nap Eleanor had found Doctor Alaća, gotten the receta and now la farmacéutica was telling her that there wasn't any more! They were out?

'Señora, I came here earlier this morning, you said just to get the receta and now –'

'¡No tengo, Señora!' La farmacéutica spat the words on to the marble counter and retreated behind a glass screen to start grinding something with her mortar and pestle.

Eleanor stood and looked at the curlicue letters, watching the woman bustling about. Above them the Roman soldiers guarded the shields on the canisters that lined the walls. *Ignat Amara. Gem: Popoli. Axumg. Opium.*

'Fuck you!' Eleanor said almost loudly enough for la farmacéutica to hear. Eleanor didn't care. Two older women entering the store seemed to laugh at her.

She stepped out on to the street. It was dusk, but still warm, and a few stray hairs had escaped and were sticking to her cheek. She brushed them away quickly, imagining the 'Psst!' of the heroin dealer, who, in fact, was nowhere to be seen.

Eleanor walked to where she had seen another botica. She found it, but it was closed. She returned to the hotel feeling defeated.

Harold was a sport. He swallowed a few Valiums and encouraged Eleanor to go to dinner. He even remembered a patio renowned for its chiles en nogada. Chiles en nogales! Harold managed to smile. It was one of her favourite dishes. Eleanor sighed, was this what old age was going to be like?

Once when her back went out she dreamt she was Frida Kahlo. Or dreamt she was in one of the paintings anyway, caught on canvas, skewered with a steel rod. Bleeding. Eleanor looked over at Harold. Hardly Diego Rivera. She'd better hurry up before her back really became bad. She took out her two silver conch earrings. Silver. She'd gotten them almost thirty years ago. Before anyone else had pierced ears. Even Iris. Pushing the posts through her ears and affixing the backs behind her earlobes for the very last time, Eleanor picked up her big Mexican sarape purse and stepped into the night, happy to note on her map that the restaurant was close by.

¡Chiles en nogales! The dish patterned after the Mexican flag, the stripe of cream sauce, the green roasted chillies, the field of red pomegranates awaited her at a nearby restaurant. Two glasses of vino tinto gave Mexico a certain glow. That, the altitude and the anticipation of a footbath. Eleanor paid the bill and left the restaurant, negotiating the pavement with feet still sore from travel, her sarape purse banging against her hips as she made her way along the pink wall, wondering what exactly she was doing, and suddenly missing Harold.

Eleanor approached the circus slowly, a little unsteady on her feet. The main tent was just emptying and the performers would probably still be in their dressing rooms, congregating in their caravans.

Weaving her way under and over thick hemp ropes that held up the big top, Eleanor stumbled on stakes until she saw the windshield of the school bus where Muchacha Flexible lived. And then she saw her.

A golden woman inhabiting the feathers of a bright

purple bird. It was La Muchacha Flexible, her face crowned by a fan of feathers two feet long, a large purple fan framing her tiny hips. Even her purple leather ballet slippers were adorned with the long floaty feathers. The little pony stood by her side, munching out of her hand. 'You come late,' she was saying. 'Just give me a minute.'

La Muchacha walked over to a young moonfaced man with a necklace of shells around his somewhat pudgy neck. She stroked his arm, they exchanged a few words and La Muchacha returned to Eleanor.

'Now I am ready, Madam. I am going to work on your feet.'

'I'm ready too.' Eleanor walked uncertainly across the grass, avoiding candy wrappers and pieces of popcorn, holding on to her big open purse. La Muchacha Flexible led her over to where she had been doing clothes earlier. She pointed to a stool. Eleanor sat carefully on the hard wooden seat, the legs of the stool sinking into the damp ground.

'Oops.' Eleanor grabbed the sides of the stool and giggled, her purse collapsing next to her on the ground as it slid off her shoulder.

'I think you have been having a nice time with the vino tinto this evening, Madam.' The girl walked off towards a big trough near the fence and returned with a bucket of brackish water.

'If you think you're going to get my silver earrings in exchange for putting my feet in the elephant's water for ten minutes,' Eleanor said, 'then the deal is off.'

'You don't worry, now, I tell you.' She put the bucket down. 'All is OK, really.'

'Are you really going to wear my earrings? It's all a story about the bank, isn't it – '

'I like your earrings Madam. And I like you. Everything cannot be costume, circus people, entertainment, do you think? Sometimes we performers have to hold back something for ourselves, don't you think that's fair?' She had her hand in the bucket now and was moving her fingers around in the murky water.

'I want your Hungarian grandmother's recipe – '

'Yes, yes.' La Muchacha pulled out a small plastic sack with a rubber band around it. Inside was a bright pink granulated powder, just like the cheapest brand of laundry detergent. 'You are going to be a lot of fun, Madam.' She smiled and put her face close to Eleanor's and jiggled her head back and forth so her hair shook. 'I am going to *like* giving you this treatment!'

And then Eleanor's feet were in the dark water with the pink bubbles floating on top, and La Muchacha was squatting in front of her, her purple feathers floating just above the grass. She dunked Eleanor's feet in the water, and brought them up again, looking them over, Eleanor's toes, her soles, her ankles. Fifty-nine years of walking.

Eleanor closed her eyes. Despite her position on the stool she was relaxing. She seemed to feel La Muchacha's look upon her feet, but no, it must be a massage. Tension flooded out of her feet.

Oh, that was good. And there. Yes, that very long spot in the arch, so deep now the pressure. Little toes, tiny treasures now in La Muchacha's hands. And the silver of Mexico flashing behind her eyelids.

La Muchacha said, 'It's over now.'

Eleanor opened her eyes. The pink bubbles in the bucket had turned grey in places and there was a dark soap scum on her ankles.

'That was pretty good.'

'Feels even better in five minutes. See all this grey and brown here in the soap. That's a bad spirit, it's all come out now.'

Bad spirit? Eleanor closed her eyes. Her feet were humming, shivers of pleasure shot through the sole of her foot to each tingling toe.

'Whatever it is, it's a fair exchange for the earrings.'

Eleanor took the earrings out and held the two little shells in either hand and moved them up to La Muchacha's face, as if visually trying them on her. They would look wonderful next to her dark skin, those earrings. The young woman sat patiently, watching Eleanor's hands approach.

She took the earrings from Eleanor with a delicate thumb and forefinger. She nodded carefully, looking at them and then back to Eleanor. 'I do know what you need Madam. There is a new suit of clothes for every life of a woman. You are just having a little bit of trouble with your wardrobe.'

'I don't know what you're talking about but my feet do feel good,' Eleanor said.

'Maybe I can ask you to do one favour for me.' She ran into the school bus and came back carrying something heavy hidden in the feathers of her arms.

'What? If you're selling –'

'No, no I think we're friends now. I want you to bring to the States this most special birthday present I send to my aunt.'

La Muchacha brought out a small package, a lumpy item, with layers of paper and twine around it. La Muchacha put it casually down next to the bucket where it sank into the grass.

'No, I don't think so,' Eleanor said. 'I've got too much luggage already.'

'It's not so big.'

'But it's heavy, I can see that from here.'

La Muchacha shrugged as she touched Eleanor lightly on the shoulder. 'And now I must make for my next appointment,' she said. She reached out and shook Eleanor's hand and disappeared into the bus.

Eleanor put on her shoes and walked back over the circus grounds, her purse bumping against her arm. The tents became smaller and the happy voices of the circus patrons faded into the distance. Eleanor saw a bench and sat down. She picked up each of her feet and rubbed the soles. Her feet felt great. There was no doubt about it. Some feeling, some white noise of ache that had been there for a long time was gone. Or was it just the vino tinto and the elixir of Mexico which was becoming addictive and made all of her feel alive and renewed – all over! – not just her feet? She looked back up at La Muchacha's bus.

A light went on. It swung back and forth for a while, a bulb rigged up on a string. Then it went off. Eleanor picked up her purse. It seemed heavy. Too heavy.

What was La Muchacha doing in the bus? Eleanor remembered those other old school buses. The hippy days, merry pranksters before some of the pranks turned into true crime stories. What *was* in there? In the purse?

Jesus, Eleanor thought, looking inside. It was that package. The present for La Muchacha's aunt in Fresno. Eleanor looked at the misshapen object, covered with hairy twine, an address scrawled in childish handwriting.

Well, she would just return it. Either it fell into her purse – not likely! – or the girl was drawing Eleanor into some plot of hers. The footbath had been paid for, Eleanor thought with irritation as she made her way back to the school bus.

'I hope you didn't do anything stupid,' she heard La Muchacha say from inside the vehicle. The young woman was not alone! Eleanor crouched down under the window. She should make her way around to the front of the bus, put the item by the stairs leading up to it, but something familiar in the voice made her stay, puzzling who it was.

'Of course not, I'm very careful,' the voice was derogatory. And familiar. 'There's three more days of the excavation left before the inspector comes. Now, where is he – '

'Hmmmm,' Eleanor heard the girl mutter.

'I think this piece looks very good, these are actually much more easy to get rid of,' the girl said. Eleanor heard sheafs of metal scraping against each other, she found herself crouching, frozen by the big mudcaked tires of the school bus.

'Be careful!' the man said.

'*You* must be careful,' La Muchacha was saying. 'The pharaohs killed the servants who buried them, my dear.'

'They were sealed up with pharaohs who were *already* dead,' the voice protested, just on the edge of recognition. 'Now where is the little man, my dear – '

'I like this one,' La Muchacha said. 'With the little Virgin and all the people of the village praying. Looks like a miracle about a corn crop or something.'

Retablo, Eleanor thought. The personal altar pieces now prized by collectors. And decorators who cashed in on the Mexican/Southwest fad they created.

'You'll never have trouble getting these things through to Texas, anything bigger, it will cost you a lot more. Hey, what're you doing?'

'Where is he?'

'Hey, not to worry, he's – ' Shuffling, a door squeaking on a hinge, the hollow sound of a wooden lid falling closing on an empty box. 'Oh my God.'

'What?'

'He's gone!'

'WHAT?'

'Stolen!'

'By who – '

'I don't know! What you want! This is a circus, not a bank!'

'You're going to pay for this!'

'I tell you, I don't know – '

'Then I want you,' the voice said

There was a long silence.

'I am not interested in doing fuck business like that with you.'

'Why not? I mean you do it for – '

'Listen, it's for me to say. It's my business – '

'How much are you getting from José, there?'

'You fuck, you – ' the girl hissed.

'Sorry, but I think you're ready for some overtime – ' A crashing and then the sounds of a struggle.

'No! Stop that you shit, you – '

There was a bigger crash and Eleanor fought to keep from peeking in the window in the ensuing silence.

'Well put away the gun, you know how to handle that thing?'

'Deal's off. No more business with you, gringo shit.'

'OK, OK!'

'Don't come any closer – hey, hey, what are you doing?'

'Do you hear something outside?'

'Don't try this shit on me – get out of there! Stay out of there!'

There was another scuffle, but no gunshot. Eleanor bent down and heard the man cursing as he left the school bus mixed with the uneasy laughter of La Muchacha. Eleanor got the package out and started to tiptoe around the front of the bus when she saw another pair of shoes arrive. The school bus leaned as the new person entered. Would it be safe now, to go around to the front? She heard more voices inside.

Maybe La Muchacha was entertaining a more comely guest. They were speaking Spanish and she made out a few words as she extended her legs, lifting herself slowly up to where a scrap of cloth flapped out a window. She held her breath until her eyes reached the level where the glass, had there been any, would have started.

In the darkness she could make out two figures.

'I like it very, very much,' La Muchacha was saying, the moonfaced young man Eleanor had seen by the tent was next to her. He was kneeling beside her, blowing the feathers on her breast. La Muchacha pulled him down on to a big bag of popcorn.

I shouldn't be watching this! Eleanor thought, but she found herself unable to stop. To the sound of the young man's heavy breathing, La Muchacha peeled her feathers off one by one. A muscled arm. The lower slope of her breast. An inner brown circle that seemed to spiral into a nipple center, hypnotizing Eleanor and the young moonfaced man himself.

His eyes almost too shy to meet her body, the Elastic Girl laughed in a way that was almost patronizing, but then she lifted up his round chin into her hands and he met her smile with a laugh of his own. Was this what love was like for La Muchacha? Eleanor tried to take her eyes away, but she couldn't. The shared smiles, the aura of complicit desire held her as she watched the figures sink further in the billows of soft kernels.

There was the removing of feathers, the stroking of long limbs as she took him inside of her. Eleanor watched the thrusts and parries of La Muchacha and the young man whose shell necklace lay beside them on the floor. A hole had opened in the bag of popcorn and white puffy flowers escaped, migrating on to the floor of the school bus, catching in hair and feathers, contrasting with beautiful brown limbs.

Yes, she was indeed La Muchacha Flexible and Eleanor wondered at the strength of her legs, hips and buttocks as she ground into her willing servant. It was a sight as heady as any drink she'd had. Jesus, she thought, realizing that she was peeping on their love making, she must be crazy! She must be drunk! The clock was striking – what was that, one, two three – up to eleven! She had to get back to the hotel!

Eleanor descended below the window again. The bus was rocking back and forth, the tires making squishy sounds in the grass and shock absorbers squeaking. Then it stopped. Eleanor Shoulder, newly fleet of foot, ran to the front of the bus, put the package down by the stool and hurried into the night.

Her feet continued to feel great, as if the cobblestones were now closely clipped grass, leading her back to the hotel. Not that she didn't need the help of a stop sign from time to time. It was the altitude and the alcohol. She'd forgotten that it was a stronger combination than she was used to. Maybe it wasn't such a great footbath after all. Maybe it was just that she couldn't feel her feet at all!

La Parroquia loomed before her, behind a heap of rubble. The jagged chunks of concrete challenged her to climb over towards the portal where a Madonna of pink stone rode on a crescent moon. Suddenly she wanted to go in there to visit Saint Anthony, to see the empty niche.

Crawling over the floes of concrete, bits of broken tiles and Fresca cans Eleanor eventually arrived at the entrance with scratched legs.

She hesitated by a plaster Christ figure, eternally dragging his cross over an offertory box. She wasn't in the mood for bleeding Christ figures, thorny hairdos dripping with blood. Nevertheless she went into the silence and darkness, pleasant to her alcohol addled senses.

Eleanor's eyes adjusted to the dimness which shimmered with pastel colors.

Then she saw the empty niche. A tiny place, a good sixteen feet off the ground. And then she found him. Right at eye level.

Eight feet high, a fresh robe of plaster, a blank face white enough to be porcelain. The new replacement Saint Anthony! A little pig strode next to him, the plaster combed like real hair over its round body. Its snout was still clean. A shiny perfect plaster object, fresh from some factory, devoid of the investment of millions of prayers and supplications. The snout of the pig, the feet of the Saint were barely rubbed with the callused palms of laborers, the sweaty palms of distraught mothers.

Eleanor looked up at them. They both had glass eyes, brown ones. They looked life-like. And sly.

'You're both understudies, you're not the real thing. And you don't have a real bone in you.' Eleanor realized her words were slurring as she put her arm around the body of the pig for support.

'Do you know who I visited today?' she asked. 'Someone better than you, a real circus girl ... somebody's brother paid his life for knowing about a footbath, and –' she stroked the feet of the Saint.

'Now you, dear, are not yet a relic.' She put her nose right up against the plaster pig's. It was cold. 'A relic! But not a real one. The real one is stolen.'

'And what about you?' She looked up at the placid porcelain face of the Saint. Then she remembered.

San Antonio. The man whom shingles had been named after. La Fuega del San Antonio. The fire of Saint Anthony. She threw a few coins in the box at Anthony's feet.

Eleanor wished for a prayer for Harold. An incantation, *Ignat Amara. Gem: Popoli. Axumg. Opium.* A way to ask for something for Harold that could be as good as that footbath. Pointless, she thought, suddenly frustrated.

She shook her finger right in Saint Anthony's face. 'Tlaloc and his rain dwarfs could have done a better job with la farmacéutica.' Eleanor invoked the names of the Aztec god and his henchmen who inflicted gout, rheumatism, tendon contractions, palsy, and most likely La Fuega del San Antonio. 'I have a mind to take my money back, you two-bit quack –'

She squinted her eyes at Saint Anthony remembering something else.

Young women took statues of Saint Anthony and turned them upside down, believing this to be a way to get a husband.

'I wish to hell you'd take your fire and go home,' she hissed up at the plaster face. The frozen rosebud lips curled benignly. The brown eyes looked milky. Blind. He seemed to be supported by a pole through his body. Frida Kahlo. Eleanor shuddered.

Tiny metal arms and legs were stuck to photos of people and laid at his feet next to the offertory box. Milagros. Miracles. Turn Harold into a young man!

'It's not quite as nice as the old one, is it?' a voice said quietly, a voice like velvet. Eleanor turned, surprised to see the source of the voice. It was the piñata woman.

Eleanor nodded and reached for another coin from her purse and listened to it fall dully on to a heap of coins inside the offertory box. 'Yes, I suppose the old ones are much better,' Eleanor said, but when she looked behind her the piñata woman was gone. These big churches were full of side chapels and little doorways, she thought. It looked like some of the floor was being pried up as part of the renovation. Several big stones with names chiseled into them, dates of birth, dates of death, had been etched across their surfaces. Removing remains. Eleanor shuddered and rushed out of the church.

She tried not to feel guilty about Harold as she wobbled down the streets, her feet nearly pirouetting on broken tiles and old potato chip wrappers.

Little twinkly lights had been strung in the jacaranda trees at the entrance between the walls. Even a hairbrush cactus had blue, green and red points of light turning off and on. The light was on in the reception area, and Larry's penthouse above it. She saw dark figures moving back and forth across the window. Dancing. Larry was dancing in his penthouse. And then she realized whose voice it was in the school bus of La Muchacha.

Eleanor looked under the veranda at the window next to their door. The light was out in their apartment. No, it just went on. Then she heard a noise. Harold? Falling out of bed? No. A shadow lurking on the edge of the garden.

Who was that, just entering the garden, behind that bush, the red skirt, the yellow petticoats of the piñata woman? The flash of colour disappeared between two buildings.

Well, she could get to sleep easily after this day. Her foot caught on another rock and she looked down. Under the toe of her leather slipper, something gleamed and Eleanor saw it was one of the little fetishes, one of the little silver symbols which clustered around the feet of Saints. A milagro! A miracle!

She held it up to the light. A little silver foot.

'I get it,' she cried out to the sky. 'Watch your step!'

She thought this was very funny and laughed all the way up to the stairs of their apartment where Harold lay awake, waiting for her.

'I'm much better, darling,' he assured her, and he looked better. Eleanor felt a huge surge of relief, and regret. She crawled into his arms and let him enfold her. 'Bit much to drink tonight, darling?' she heard him say and she thought about what a warm familiar voice Harold had as she drifted off. It was wonderful to be in Mexico together. Just for a moment. Somewhere a clock started striking twelve.

With every tone of the bell she fell deeper into sleep, so deep she didn't hear the wail of the siren at the crack of dawn.

The next morning Harold awoke in so much pain that Dr Alacá was summoned immediately and gave Harold a quick injection of morphine.

Eleanor looked into Harold's eyes and silently said goodbye to him as his gaze seemed to disperse and his eyes became windows into a head full of fantasies. And no pain. Harold was going on a second vacation.

Fantasy. Eleanor jiggled from foot to foot, anxious to

get outside as Dr Alacá explained the frequency of the medication. She tried to concentrate. Harold would be so out of it he would never be able to keep track of his dosage. The doctor was suggesting that they leave Mexico, that Harold could best be recuperating while at home. Eleanor thought about their tickets, the phone calls she would have to make.

Then she heard the noises outside. Screaming, fighting. Outside the curtain, on the lawn that surrounded the garden, La Muchacha! What was she doing there? Christ, the Elastic Girl was biting a policeman! Eleanor ran outside on to the bright green lawn, straight towards them.

'Señora,' La Muchacha cried out when she saw Eleanor and let go of the cuff of the officer's uniform which she had been holding between her teeth.

'¡Señora!' The Elastic Girl's eyes searched Eleanor's face. '¡Señora!' Was it an overly dramatic cry? Eleanor looked at the girl's face, remembering Iris. The girl was scared. And then she looked up into the policeman's. This was bad.

The policeman quickly whipped out a pair of handcuffs and had them sparkling around the girl's wrists in a second. La Muchacha let out a wail.

Several local police cars stood by, doors open, radio squawking police code. A number of uniformed men were marching in and out of the reception area, down from the stairway that led to Larry's apartment. A crowd was gathering.

'Murder!' breathed the balding red-haired tango dancer to the man with muscular dystrophy. 'Asesinato!' whispered the three gardeners to the linen ladies and, in another bright dress, the piñata woman was holding her sketchpad, starting at the hacienda of – '

'Señor Welsh!'

Mumble, mumble.

Larry Welsh, the hotelier, had been too hot to handle

for someone, Eleanor thought. She looked at the crowd. They all shook their heads, pointing to the penthouse, gasping, hands to mouths, and looking back at the Elastic Girl struggling with her captor.

'She was caught running away – back where the garbage is behind the kitchen,' one of the cooks said in rapid Spanish.

'Eleven o'clock – they say that his watch was smashed – '

'Who heard anything at eleven o'clock?'

'I believe I saw something last night,' a tremulous but clear voice cut through the crowd. It was the piñata woman. 'I believe I saw something in the evening,' she repeated but no one was listening to English, Eleanor noted. The woman was wearing a kelly green dress today, with bright red papier-mâché cherries attached to the shoulders, someone the officers were not prepared to take seriously. The woman ruffled the edges of her sketchpad. 'I saw a woman walking – '

'Officer, I believe I can make this matter clear,' Eleanor cut in quickly arranging each Spanish sentence before she said it. Make the matter clear. *Claro.* The officer stopped and looked at her.

Eleanor shoved her hand in her sarape bag and pulled out her sworn Deputy's Identification Card. It had been good for one week; they used to call it Deputy for a Day. Neighborhood Crime Awareness specialist. How Iris had laughed.

But they wouldn't scrutinize it closely here in Mexico. She knew their eyes would land instead on the hologrammed seal of the County of Alameda and the attached laminated photo of her. She flipped it shut.

'Officer, I think I might have some information pertaining to this case.'

'Madam, we are taking this girl to jail.' He started hustling her away. 'On a homicide charge,' he said in Spanish.

The crowd started rustling as a group of officers emerged

slowly down the stairs, just visible through the reception area. It was hard to maneuver down the steep narrow opening with a stretcher. Whatever was on it didn't move. The thing was heavy and the Mexican police officers swore quietly under their breaths.

Eleanor felt a fleeting remorse. Larry Welsh had gotten involved in some kind of criminal activity. He took a risk and lost. Eleanor looked at the Elastic Girl. How long would it be before she lost? The stretcher with the body passed in front of the crowd. Bad business.

Everyone was crossing themselves now, except the police officers. Eleanor took a quick look at La Muchacha's face whose eyes twitched in fear, but she no longer struggled in the handcuffs.

'I was at this girl's trailer last night. At exactly eleven o'clock last night. I heard the church bells.'

The officer's eyes squinted and Eleanor easily held his gaze.

'I am prepared to swear to it in court.'

'What were you doing there?'

'I was at the circus. Afterwards I poked around the grounds. I saw this girl going into her bus at exactly eleven o'clock. I counted the church bells. I had to get home and see to my husband. The circus had lasted longer than I'd thought.' Eleanor smiled. 'So you see, the girl couldn't possibly have done it.'

The officer seemed to be thinking this over. He didn't want to think it over. Life would be considerably easier if he could pin the murder of the Norte Americano hotelier on the circus girl. Nevertheless, she now had an alibi.

With a tentative nod from the captain, the officer who held the girl selected the handcuff key from a chain attached to his pocket. He fit it into the cuffs and released La Muchacha's hands. The officers stood solemnly behind her with their guns drawn aimed at her back. The policeman was taking down her name and address, but it was clear that she was no longer a suspect.

'Perhaps this lady could tell you what she saw –' Eleanor indicated the piñata woman. 'I will be glad to translate.'

The officer hesitated, looked around at his deputy. 'Si, Si.'

Eleanor nodded at the piñata woman who closed her eyes for a moment, then opened them, looking straight at the officer. 'I was going to the church – where we'd met later –' she nodded at Eleanor, 'to visit the new Saint Anthony. I used to visit him in the evenings, but now in his plaster reincarnation I'm not so enthused. In any event, I was convinced that the last one did something for my arthritis, the ankle bone, you know, so at eleven o'clock, I heard the bells, thinking that I wanted to get there before midnight mass –'

'What did you see as you left the grounds?' Eleanor prodded gently.

'A figure.' The woman closed her eyes and leaned back, the cherries jiggled on her shoulders. 'A shadow – walking along –' Eleanor translated quickly to the captain.

'Could you identify?' The Spanish words returned.

'No, no, it was too dark, but –' The piñata woman hesitated, and Eleanor, looking at her sketchpad, hoped that the woman had a strong visual memory. 'There was something – yes, the shadow was *limping*, that's it. I'm positive, limping!'

The effect of these words on the police was obvious. The stolen glances. They knew. The junkie.

Suddenly La Muchacha was of no interest. The officers retreated quickly back to their cars, picked up radio microphones and turned on a few sirens for good measure as they sped out of the driveway, leaving the inhabitants of Hotel Dolores, and all the villagers who worked there, staring at the dust.

*

'Madam, you have saved my life.' La Muchacha came up to Eleanor, her hands were still trembling.

'It probably would have come out in court.' But Eleanor was wondering, in fact, if that was likely as she saw how the sweat had run down the girl's forehead and stained her cotton T-shirt.

'The circus will not provide lawyers, Madam, I am deeply in your debt,' La Muchacha said formally. Eleanor wondered what she had been doing at the hotelier's house in the morning. Perhaps she *was* lucky. A young man nearby called to La Muchacha and the girl drifted into the crowd, but not without a backward glance at Eleanor.

'Mrs Shoulder, I must say how pleased I am to meet you,' the piñata woman broke in, introducing herself a trembling smile on her withered lips. 'Let me introduce myself, Edna May Trellis.' The two women shook hands. Edna May threaded her arm through Eleanor's and peered at her from under the brim of the hat.

'I like your drawings,' Eleanor smiled and strolled with the elderly woman over to a bench, helping her to sit down. Edna May spread her skirts and petticoats around her until she sat at the center of a big colorful circle.

'May I look at your sketches?'

'Of course. They're gorgeous, aren't they?' Edna May said.

'Yes, you're very good.'

'No, not the drawings. The cops of course.' She lifted her face to the sun and let the intense light warm her skin and waved a hand over to where several officers were barking orders at the crowd.

'Not my taste,' Eleanor said. 'Now if you'll excuse me – '

The Elastic Girl was approaching, more relaxed after her meeting with the young man. She had regained her freedom, that Elastic Girl, and her face showed that she really understood that.

'Madam, I owe you my life,' she said almost happily.

'I must find a way to pay you back! Please!'

'Just stay with the circus,' Eleanor said. 'It's a better job than the bank.'

Eleanor Shoulder was packing up. She and Harold would leave San Miguel. There was a flight in Leon that they could just make, if she could get his dopey body on the American Express bus.

She'd promised to make a last visit to the circus to say goodbye to the Elastic Girl.

'There wouldn't be enough time,' she'd told the young performer as they parted on the lawn under the wary eyes of the police officers. But La Muchacha was eager, anxious to say goodbye.

'Just come with your luggage, on the way to the airport,' she insisted.

'Sure, with my husband in the cab waiting.'

'What time you leave San Miguel?'

'Four-thirty.'

'Come at three-fifteen. It's enough time,' the girl pleaded. 'I surprise you, Madam.'

'I'll see.' Eleanor turned and walked back to the room where Harold lay on the bed, waiting for her. But she knew she would return. There was nothing she liked more than a pleasant surprise. She watched the Elastic Girl make her way out of the hotel complex the way she'd tried to escape, behind the kitchen, along the dumpsters.

Yes, she wouldn't mind a surprise, and the answer to a few more questions.

Three hours later Eleanor stood back in the circus field ready to say a quick goodbye to the Elastic Girl. Her flight bag hanging off her shoulder was filled with last-minute gifts she wanted to buy, mostly stuffed dolls in native dress, with the slash of yarn smiles.

'Over here!' The little pony stood by La Muchacha's

side, munching out of her hand. The Elastic girl viewed Eleanor's big flight bag with interest.

Eleanor looked at the girl and felt a tug of war inside herself. The girl was a con, more experienced than any Saint Anthony. 'I've got a lot of questions to ask you young lady,' Eleanor began but one look at the smiling girl told her that it was an impossible situation.

'Come on, come, come!' La Muchacha laughed and led the pony away. 'I have to pay you back for saving my life!'

'Let's go over here, this is better.' She led Eleanor into a little empty Winnebago camper.

'This is where I meditate,' La Muchacha said, ducking deeply to squeeze through the tiny doorway. 'First I have to know your name.'

'Eleanor. Eleanor Shoulder.'

'And you are from – '

'Walnut Creek, California.'

'You are,' she squinted her eyes, 'listed in the phone book?'

'Yes, of course, but what does that have to do with – '

And then the Elastic Girl pulled her arm and Eleanor was popped into the interior of the tiny Winnebago.

The little space was completely padded, quilted, in synthetic fur and water-stained satin. Handles and stirrups were placed at odd intervals on the ceiling and the rounded walls. Two windows provided air and Eleanor could just hear the circus noises humming about the little shiny wagon.

'Sit down,' La Muchacha demanded, suddenly all business. Eleanor was glad, in fact, to be off her feet. She sat down cross-legged on the floor, following La Muchacha's lead.

'This is where I come to relax,' she said and her eyes rolled back into her head. Eleanor saw her perfect young foot rise up and place itself in a stirrup. La Muchacha was so young, so beautiful. Before she knew it, La Muchacha was hanging upside down, like a butterfly in a cocoon. She twirled around, her long hair brushing Eleanor's face; Eleanor closed her eyes and felt a strong breeze bathing her body, enveloping her in some kind of metallic air, alive with electricity.

'There.'

Eleanor opened her eyes. La Muchacha was on the floor again. 'We can begin now.' Eleanor looked into the face of the young woman. 'Madam, don't take it so *seriously.*' She laughed. 'Now, when I saw you walking down the field that day and I knew that you and I were going to be special friends, I didn't know you were going to save my life.'

'Apparently I'm not always good at saving people.'

'Nobody's perfect, Madam. But too bad you walk like a muñeco –

'A puppet.'

'Eleanor, you got a big pain in your back! But I show you what to do. You will remember me always for this!'

But will my health insurance cover the damage, Eleanor thought, looking up at the stirrups on the ceiling. Well, chiropractors had stranger office equipment.

'Don't worry, this is strictly amateur stuff,' and then the young woman turned Eleanor around so that she was facing away from her. La Muchacha spread her legs out and put her arms at Eleanor's side. A sliding motion and Eleanor was circled at the waist, clenched between the steely thighs of the Elastic Girl. She closed her eyes.

'Now, we just do very slowly this way.' Eleanor felt the girl's strong arms wrapping around her rib cage and then she pulled Eleanor tight, squeezing Eleanor's backbone into her rib cage. Flickering white bones danced before Eleanor's eyes, like a Day of the Dead puzzle, she saw skeletons assemble on the backs of her eyelids, take new form and emerge, the bones of two women, young and old, knitting and fusing into a confluence – an X-ray of some new kind of animal, some new kind of life which was offered to Eleanor. The beast swayed –

'Ha! Ha! I think you are ready now!'

Eleanor awoke – she must have been asleep! But still relaxed, she sank back into the firm hold of the young girl, trusting now, where the Elastic Girl would take her.

'Don't fight it now. I promise it to be OK, OK?'

Eleanor took a deep breath. She was scared by that vision of the beast of bones, it was her bones! It felt wonderful. She didn't want to impede that feeling. She never wanted to impede that feeling again. She willed herself to relax.

'Yes, that was good. It begins, now.' La Muchacha twisted their torsos more quickly in the other direction, and Eleanor relaxed even more fully now, letting her eyes rove down the impossibly long legs of La Muchacha and down to the purple feathers at her feet.

'Ahhhhhhhh,' the Elastic Girl's breath was warm on her neck, her breath was sweet, like roses. 'I think you are almost ready now. Yes, are you ready?'

Eleanor nodded. She realized she was limp, almost paralyzed in the arms of La Muchacha. The brown hands came before her face, and then two fingers reached out and closed her eyelids. Like a corpse. But if death is like this – La Muchacha was bending Eleanor's head now, her hand firmly on the back of Eleanor's head, her hand confidently instructing, folding, the branch that was Eleanor's spine which seemed to melt, the pain easing out even as Eleanor felt her chin touch chest. And yes, the pushing continued, a clear force, a will, that was La Muchacha's hand pushing Eleanor's skull, elongating her very bones, extruding her neck until Eleanor's head hit what was the carpet and she dared not open her eyes to find out that she was nearly folded, folded in half!

A rushing sound began and Eleanor, sensing the indomitable will of the fingers behind her head, gave in to the noise, and she willed her eyes to open a crack. Yes, her head was going down, her neck was melting and she could see the carpet, no the threads of the carpet, the carpet padding underneath, her head was –

A piece of sheet metal curled away before her eyes, there were struts there, and then the outside air met her lips – she wasn't breathing! Grass! And dirt! The force above continued sending her down and down. Worms! Eleanor closed her eyes.

Her spine seemed to have melted and mingling with the earth, her very bones gone, she was only a muscle, a bunch of jellied tissue, she was being sent into the ground under-neath the Elastic Girl's Winnebago. She tasted the damp dark soil, it thickened, became diagonal stripes of clay clinging to her teeth, mixing with her blood until the acid taste of limestone found the marrow of her bones and the crystallized layer of glimmering quartz spears entered her heart. Circling towards some rhythmic center of darkness and flames, where flesh and blood were suspended, Eleanor sped along into the light.

A cord fused and became her self, something com-pressed, like diamonds, fused in light and strung on a long string, like a long piece of elastic it stretched and contrac-ted, marrow and water, earth, worms, iron, salt and clay collected around the strand of crystals, creating flesh. A scream, a bearing in on all sides of her, sounded, shrill, insistent, angry. Eleanor was pushed back out of the earth, head hitting stone, roots of trees combing her hair, the twinkle of grass and a breath of air before the sheet metal curled and she was back in the Winnebago again.

'Ahhhhhh, ha-ha,' said La Muchacha looking at the woman who was back in her arms again. Wilting on the young woman's chest Eleanor struggled to move but found herself unable to awaken her body. Her eyes must have registered panic because the girl stroked her face.

'Shh, not to worry,' La Muchacha muttered, her voice an easy tonic. Like a mother with a baby, holding Eleanor's head with one hand, La Muchacha reached over to the side of her belt and felt for a flask. Eleanor smelled something sweet, like honey, and a dangerous hypnotic fume. Ether. *Ignat Amara. Gem: Popoli. Axumg. Opium.*

'It's my spirits. Actually, this isn't alcohol. Last time I put a banana in for a week. Works wonders.' She turned Eleanor's head towards her and inspected her eyes. 'But you are very much better now, I think. You don't need any more. I thought maybe you were going to pass out for a second there! You went kind of deep. But that's usually a good thing.' Then she tapped Eleanor on the head with her fingers, and slowly Eleanor watched each of her limbs come to life. A finger, a leg, her eyelids. She could move them all now. There were no creaks or squeaks in limbs. No tension. No cartilage. No memory of years of strolling in front of the classroom. She sat up and scooted slightly away from the young girl so she could face her. 'Thank you.'

La Muchacha only smiled. Suddenly Eleanor was through the little door of the Winnebago and was standing out on the ground, alone on the field.

'Transaction complete,' La Muchacha called from behind the page fence. She waved and threw Eleanor a big kiss and disappeared into the blue bus.

Eleanor walked to the perimeter of the field and sat on a stone bench. She listened to her body, to her head and her spine which seemed to be in some new order. It was an order without pain.

Eleanor stood up and touched her toes. Easily. She bent to the side. And touched her toes. She sat on the grass. And did the splits!

Laughing, she picked up her flight bag, her body had become lighter, the flight bag heavier, the bones in her body felt just born, just beginning. She felt so good she forgot to ask the Elastic Girl the questions that had been forming in her mind.

The closest airport to San Miguel is listed as Leon. But the airport is really in Silau. It costs you 70,000 pesos to get to Leon from Silau. Maybe you can catch a bus there to San Miguel. Maybe not.

The airport building is beautiful. Like a cathedral open to the sky, the clear ceiling lets in light. It's like a big atrium, and even some birds fly in and out.

Eleanor and Harry Shoulder sit at the airport bar and look at the television. Harry is still full of painkillers and he's drinking a coke. He hasn't shit in three days and the boiling points of shingles are starting to act up inside of him as he becomes more used to the narcotic effects of the painkillers. He cannot wait to get home.

Eleanor Shoulder carries a flight bag heavy with a lot of stuffed yarn dolls in it. She sits up straighter than she ever has in her life. But then a certain flickering image on the television set makes her stand up and lean over the bar.

Closer, she sees a newsman standing in front of Hotel Dolores. People are crowding behind him, trying to wave at the camera. He flicks them away like a horse with flies at its tail.

Then he realizes he's on the air and begins to tell his story. A hotelier by the name of Larry Welsh has been discovered, dead, shot in his hotel penthouse apartment.

The man had long been known as a collector of early religious Mexican art and it was suspected that he was illegally transporting retablos, and other items now coming under strict exportation restrictions, across the border into the United States. And now there is some question about his being involved in narcotic trafficking as well. One suspect has already been identified by a witness.

'Please attend to your baggage. All unattended baggage will be immediately removed,' squawked the loudspeaker.

'I'm sorry to be such a drag,' Harold apologized, his tongue still thick with painkillers.

'I'd hardly call you a drag, darling. I've done exactly what I've wanted,' Eleanor said, remembering the stretching exercises she'd done that morning. She'd practically done the splits! Again! Her body felt remarkably good, relaxed and energetic at the same time.

'Flight 362 for Guadalajara,' intoned the speaker. Eleanor collected her baggage and Harold's as well. Hoisting the bag heavy with yarn dolls she suddenly realized it was much too heavy for the simple cloth toys.

Before she signaled Harold to get up she put the flight bag on the ground and quickly unzipped it. Brown paper. Raggedy, hairy twine. The same package that the Elastic Girl had wanted her to post for her to her aunt in Fresno. The supposed present was now stashed in her flight bag. Questions answered.

'Please attend to your baggage. For security reasons all unattended baggage will be immediately removed,' squawked the loudspeaker.

So that's why the Elastic Girl had wanted to know if she was listed in the telephone book. Eleanor joined the row of passengers lining up to board the flight, Eleanor slipped the heavy little package on the floor next to her. When the line advanced the package was revealed, sitting alone on the linoleum floor. Ticking away like a time bomb, waiting for someone's attention.

Eleanor was just going through the security check-in, throwing her flight bag on the conveyor belt when she heard someone cry out, pointing at the little object wrapped in brown paper. Another quick glance behind her showed her that a security guard had been summoned.

The rest would be easy, Eleanor thought. They would isolate it, put it in a lead box. X-ray it. Prod it. Poke it. It would reveal itself simply and clearly. Saint Anthony and his pig with the much stroked snout. Someone would find out where the beloved item had come from, and the people of San Miguel would have their Saint back to help them heal their aches and pains. Well, Eleanor thought, whatever works. More than being relieved of her pain, Eleanor had a spine of glittering diamonds that seemed to fill her with energy.

'I'm sorry about the trip, honey,' Harold said, but Eleanor only smiled as the scene grew behind them, the security men, the forklift with the lead box, beeping as it made its way over the marble floor.

'It's all right, dear. I've seen enough of Mexico.'

'What'd you say, dear?'

'I think I'd like to go home and take tennis lessons, for a while. Always wanted to play tennis.' Eleanor helped Harold on to the tarmac. And then, she thought, although she knew she wouldn't tell him for a while, not until he was a little better, she would start planning their next trip. Perhaps, to Bali . . .

ACKNOWLEDGEMENT

Thanks to Margarita Natali of San Miguel de Allende. Her stories and presence helped to shape the characters and plot.

Contributors' Notes

Paula Gunn Allen is professor of English at the University of California, Los Angeles and an American Indian of Laguna Pueblo and Sioux heritage. She is one of the foremost Native American scholars and literary critics. In addition to *Grandmothers of the Light: A Medicine Woman's Source Book* (The Women's Press, 1992), her many books include a novel, *The Woman Who Owned the Shadows*; a collection of essays, *The Sacred Hoop: Recovering the Feminine in American Indian Traditions*; and several books of poetry, *Spider Woman's Granddaughters: Traditional Tales and Contemporary Writing by Native American Women* (The Women's Press, 1990), of which Allen was editor, won an American Book Award in 1990.

Jean Buffong is a Grenadian and has lived in England since 1962. Her novella, *Jump-Up-And-Kiss-Me*, was published together with Nellie Payne's *A Grenadian Childhood* in the popular *Jump-Up-And-Kiss-Me: Two Stories From Grenada* (The Women's Press, 1990). *Under the Silk Cotton Tree* (The Women's Press, 1992) was her long-awaited first full-length novel; she is currently working on her second.

Fiona Cooper was born in Bristol in 1955 and after many years working in London she was defeated by parking meters and emigrated to Tyneside in 1989. She has worked as a writer-in-residence, on a women's writing project and run many workshops on every aspect of writing. She has published five novels, *Rotary Spokes, Heartbreak on the High Sierra, Not The Swiss Family Robinson, Jay Loves Lucy* and *The Empress of the Seven Oceans*, as well as a collection of stories *I Believe in Angels*. She has written many articles and features for the gay press and is a regular columnist for *Second Shift* magazine.

Margaret Elphinstone is the author of two novels, *The Incomer* (The Women's Press, 1987) and *A Sparrow's Flight*, and a book of short stories, *An Apple From A Tree* (The Women's Press, 1991). She teaches English Studies at Strathclyde University, lives in Edinburgh, and has two grown-up daughters.

Katherine V Forrest was born in Canada in 1939 and now lives in San Francisco. She worked successfully as a business manager for several years, and became a full-time writer in 1979. She is well known as the bestselling author of the Kate Delafield lesbian mystery series and she is also fiction editor at The Naiad Press.

Elyse Guttenberg lives with her husband and two children in Fairbanks, Alaska. She is the author of *Sunder, Eclipse and Seed*, the first of a trilogy, which received an honorary mention from the International Association for the Fantastic in the Arts for best US first fantasy of the year. She is currently at work on *Summer Light*, an Alaskan 'prehistory' about a young woman who becomes a shaman and her lover, a hunter exiled from his own people.

Leigh Kennedy was born in Denver, USA, but is now a British citizen. Her previous publications include *Faces*, a short story collection, and two novels, *Journal of Nicho-*

las the American and *Saint Hiroshima*. Married to author Christopher Priest with two children, she spends a lot of thinking time on the shingle of the home beach at Hastings. She is presently working on a new novel.

Ellen Kushner is the author of the novels *Swordspoint, a Melodrama of Manners*, and *Thomas the Rhymer*, winner of the World Fantasy Award and the Mythopoeic Award. She now lives in Boston, Massachusetts, where she hosts and produces programmes of classical and worldbeat music for WGBH, a public radio station. She is at work on a new novel.

Rosaleen Love is an Australian writer who loves exploring new myths, even creating a few of her own. (Every word in *Evolution Annie* is the truth.) She teaches at Swinburne University, Melbourne, both fiction writing and the history of science, and sometimes gets the two hopelessly confused. Tired of reading histories of science in which women are rarely mentioned she decided to set the situation right. Her mother, Lucille Bishop, wrote *Love in the Doghouse*, a comedy of life with a vet; her daughter Penelope Love has just published a novel of dark fantasy, *Castle of Eyes*, in the USA. Writing, like evolution, is in her family's genes.

Sara Maitland was born in London in 1950, and brought up there and in south west Scotland. In 1978 she won the Somerset Maugham Award for *Daughter of Jerusalem* and has been writing full time since then. She has published four more novels – most recently *Home Truths* – several volumes of non-fiction, and a steady stream of short stories, including a collection, *Women Fly When Men Aren't Watching*. Her main concerns are around women, myth and religion.

Patricia A McKillip was born in Salem, Oregon, and grew

up in various places, since her father was in the Air Force, including a village in Northamptonshire, England, where she began to write. She has written for both adults and young adults, mainly science fiction and fantasy, with occasional (and brief) forays into contemporary novel writing. Among more recent works are *Fool's Run*, *The Changeling Sea*, and *The Sorceress and the Cygnet*. Her best known work is probably the *Riddle-Master Trilogy*. She has also written a number of short stories.

Jennifer McLean was born in 1933. She gained a degree in English from Canterbury University College, then spent thirty years raising nine children. She now lives with her lesbian partner in Dunedin, New Zealand.

Charlotte Watson Sherman is a graduate of Seattle University and has worked as a sexual abuse counsellor, outreach co-ordinator for Seattle Rape Relief, and as a mental health specialist. She is the author of the novel *One Dark Body*, and *Killing Color*, a collection of short stories. Her poetry and prose have been printed in *Obsidian*, *The Black Scholar*, *Calyx Journal*, *Painted Bride Quarterly*, and *Ikon*, as well as in anthologies such as *When I am An Old Woman I Shall Wear Purple*, *Memories and Visions*, and *Gathering Ground*. She is currently editing a collection of short fiction and poetry entitled *Sisterfire: A Black Womanist Anthology*, to be published in 1994. She lives in Seattle with her husband and two daughters.

Mary Wings has written three novels to date, *She Came Too Late* (1986), *She Came in a Flash* (1988), and *Divine Victim* (1992), all published by The Women's Press. 'Murder in San Miguel' is one of a series of stories intended for a collection of mystery stories. Mary Wings lives in San Francisco and her work has been translated into Dutch, German, Japanese and Spanish.

Jane Yolen was born in New York, and now lives in Hatfield, Massachusetts. She has written more than 130 books, for children, young adults, and adults. She has won the World Fantasy Award as well as the Kerlan Award for Children's Literature, the Regina Medal, and has had four novels as finalists for The Nebula Award. She is editor-in-chief of Jane Yolen Books, an imprint of Harcourt Brace Company, specialising in fantasy and science fiction for young readers. Jane Yolen is also a folksinger and story-teller.

Also of interest:

Charlotte Watson Sherman
One Dark Body

'Sherman's prose exhibits the varied textures of a true poet . . . her words conjure up images imbued with magic and mystery.' *Booklist*

One Dark Body is the story of Raisin, almost aborted in the womb, abandoned at birth and nursed by Miss Marius, with other rejected children . . . The story of her mother, Nola, as she returns to reclaim her daughter and to put to rest the ghosts of the past . . . Of Sin-Sin, the fatherless fourteen-year-old son of the local school teacher . . . and of Blue the wanga-man and healer living in the forest out of town.

'A tapestry interwoven with stories about ancestry and blood and underknit with mysticism and magic . . . Sherman's prose is pithy, her dialect lilting, and her themes universal.' *Publishers Weekly*

Fiction £6.99
ISBN 0 7043 4384 3

Paula Gunn Allen
Spider Woman's Granddaughters

According to Cherokee legend, Grandmother Spider brought the
light of intelligence and experience to the people. *Spider Woman's
Granddaughters* is a marvellous collection of traditional tales,
biographical writings and contemporary stories by her spiritual
and literary granddaughters.

'Covers nearly a century of tradition . . . despite its richness, the
book may be read right through without surfeit. But one will
want also to dwell on individual pieces, as one's gaze returns to
the bluest turquoises in a fine bracelet.' Ursula K Le Guin, *New
York Times Book Review*.

Mythology/Spirituality/Fiction £6.95
ISBN 0 7043 4238 3

Grandmothers of the Light: A Medicine Woman's Source Book

Imagine a world where personal freedom and communal
harmony work in tandem, where conversations with animals
reveal absolute truths, where people change into bears and birds,
where supernaturals exercise special powers and wisdom. Here
that world is revealed, through traditional, mythological tales
from the Cherokee, Navajo, Aztec, Maya and other North
American cultures.

Mythology/Spirituality/Fiction £7.99
ISBN 0 7043 4318 5

Anne Cameron
Daughters of Copper Woman

Anne Cameron's bestselling retelling of the legends carefully
guarded and shared with her by the Nootka women of
Vancouver Island, Canada. They speak of the first woman and
how she gave birth to the first man; and of the time when people
lived 'almost as they were intended'.

'This book spellbinds me with its blend of image and rhythm as
Anne Cameron resonates her own word power with the inner
magic, ritual sequences and elemental forces of Copper Woman's
arrival, journeys and blessings.' Caeia March, author of *Three Ply
Yarn*, *The Hide and Seek Files* and *Fire! Fire!*

Mythology/Fiction £4.99
ISBN 0 7043 3946 3